eyes

Like Mine

OTHER BOOKS AND AUDIO BOOKS
BY JULIE WRIGHT:

My Not-So-Fairy-Tale Life

eyes
Like Mine

a novel

Julie Wright

Covenant Communications, Inc.

Cover image *Cultura* by Chev Wilkinson © Jupiter Images

Cover design copyrighted 2009 by Covenant Communications, Inc.

Published by Covenant Communications, Inc.
American Fork, Utah

Printed in Canada
First Printing: July 2009

16 15 14 13 12 11 10 09   10 9 8 7 6 5 4 3 2 1

ISBN-13: 978-1-59811-625-0
ISBN-10: 1-59811-625-8

To Julia Romania Brown Peterson

I cannot believe it's been twenty years since I last saw you. Not a day goes by when I don't hear your advice in my mind and feel your love in my heart. So often I see glimpses of you in my daughter— and on my extra good days, in myself.

Acknowledgments

When I was fifteen, my grandmother had a stroke. It was a close call. We thought we'd lost her. A few weeks later she told me how, in that moment of nearly dying, her regret was not doing her genealogy. She knew she'd left a huge task undone and felt as though she'd been given "one more day" to complete that task. I remember sitting there with her in her living room and hearing the stories of my ancestry. She breathed life into these people to whom I owed my hair color, eye color, and stubborn personality. I'm glad to have met them through her. My heart turned that day to my fathers—to the generations long gone whose existence gave me existence. Thanks, Grandma.

The actual book came while driving down the road listening to a Jenny Philips CD: *Journey to Zion.* Jenny's music rocks. The complete story came in nearly full detail all at one moment, and I rushed home to write it. I appreciate all my first-draft readers who helped to make the book better and who helped to keep me from embarrassing myself: Josi Kilpack, Annette Lyon, Heather Moore, Polly Troseth, IvaLou Zeigler, and Jenny Philips. A big thanks to J. Scott Savage for believing in me enough to put his own reputation on the line for silly little me.

The day Kirk Shaw joined me for lunch to discuss Covenant and my place in it, I walked away feeling like I could move mountains. Kirk Shaw is a fabulous editor, and I am lucky enough to get to call him friend—a rare combination (*editor* and *friend*) in the publishing world. I appreciate Kathy Jenkins and her support, as well as all those within Covenant who agreed to let me into the family. Thanks, guys! May you never put me up for adoption.

Someone once told me that the acknowledgments page is to thank all those who made the book possible. It stands to reason you would thank the people at your publishing company and the people who edited the book. But I could never do any of this without my husband, Scott. Behind any successful writer is an incredibly supportive spouse. I read every novel to him during the various stages of drafting, and he offers advice, humor, and tells me when my characters are lame. I have to be honest—any humor in my writing is not for the sake of the reader, but just because I like to see my husband laugh when I'm reading to him. I also have to thank my kids for putting up with a writer mom. I know it's not easy, guys, but remember . . . your friends all think I'm cool. I love you all.

And I'd like to thank my Heavenly Father. I don't think I'd be able to get through the day without the secure knowledge that I am His daughter, and He loves me, and is aware of me.

Finally, thank you, reader. Thank you for taking this journey with me. And if you have a minute, or can make a minute, I invite you to search out and meet one of your own ancestors.

CHAPTER 1

1852

CONSTANCE BOLTED UPRIGHT. "What was that?"

Another crack of thunder pealed through the night as lightning flickered brief illumination into the darkness of the wagon.

"Just a storm, love." In the snatch of light, she saw William pull a suspender strap over his shoulder.

"Where are you going?"

"I heard the horses. They must've broken their tethers."

Constance leaned back on her elbows. "Do you need help finding them?"

"No. You sleep. I'll be back soon." His kiss missed its mark on her forehead and caught part of her eyebrow. She smiled out at the darkness and laid her head back down, grateful for more sleep.

The wagon shuddered as more thunder cracked through the sky, and the baby whimpered. William stretched his hand into the basket beside their bedding and whispered soothingly to the infant. He hummed a lullaby until she stopped fussing. Constance liked to hear him sing and was disappointed he only hummed the tune. His English brogue charmed her, far more than the clipped, perfect English she'd been raised to speak. Her father would have called William's speech "the peasant's language." If he hadn't already exiled her for her choice in religion, her father would have exiled her for her choice of husband.

Constance caught his strong shape silhouetted against the flash of lightning as he opened the flap of the wagon. "Keep my place warm for me, love."

She smiled again, thinking the words, *I will*, before drifting back to sleep.

* * *

Constance awoke with a start in the dim, early-morning light; her heart raced. While she struggled to understand why she woke with such fear, Eliza cried from her basket. Constance picked up the wailing child and settled in to nurse the infant.

And then she realized how cold it felt beside her. Her hand probed the blankets. The quilts were empty. "Where's your father?" she said to Eliza.

Memories rushed her mind. She had been exhausted. There had been lightning, thundering . . . horses . . .

The horses. William has not returned from searching after the horses!

She rubbed at her temple. He could have been struck by lightning or thrown off one of the horses. Or perhaps Indians attacked him.

She was on her knees and settling Eliza back into her basket so she could go searching. The infant let out a cry of protest. Constance paused. "I'm behaving irrationally again," she said to Eliza. "Your father is likely out gathering wood or stoking the fire for the morning meal." Constance took a deep breath. She'd never given way to panic before when she'd lived in England.

William consistently teased her when she acted hysterical without provocation. There would be no end to his teasing if he knew how she'd reacted to his absence.

Forcing herself to push aside her alarm, Constance cuddled Eliza back to her to finish nursing. Once done, she slipped her feet into her shoes, threw a blanket over her shoulder to shield the baby from the cold air, and crawled out of the wagon. Her eyes picked through the morning shadows of wagons and others in the wagon company as they busied themselves with morning chores.

He wasn't there.

One of their horses, a paint mare, grazed in the field just beyond her own wagon. She walked quickly to the horse and picked up the frayed leather reins. The horse switched her tail, continuing to graze, unconcerned with Constance's presence.

Constance gripped the thin leather straps. "William!" she shrieked to the morning as it closed in around her.

* * *

Constance drew a deep chilling breath. Two days. He'd been missing for two days.

The night smelled clean with the fresh rain. "William!" The cold air burned her throat—now raw from yelling—and made her teeth ache. "William!" she called again. The wind whispering over the field grass was the only answer. Her chest constricted against the sob she'd been holding.

Searching alongside others from their company, they'd removed themselves far from the camp. But the hills and riverbeds revealed no clues as to where her husband could be.

The captain of the wagon company, Brother Smoot, appeared more nervous with every passing hour. He kept frowning and looking upward as though he expected the sky to fall on them for continuing the delay.

Constance knew what he wanted to say when he came near enough to speak—though they felt her pain, though they loved her husband like a brother, they had to give up the search for him and continue their trek across the plains to meet the Saints in Zion.

But each time he made his approach, he faltered. His shoulders would slump as if he had battled against the fear in her eyes and lost. Instead, he would offer words of encouragement and hope. And the search continued. The rest of the company had been sympathetic and had given her their full support in looking for William. Some of the older girls in the Hatch family and the Nielson family had taken turns watching Eliza while Constance joined the men to scour the hills and riverbeds for any sign of William.

Brother Hatch approached her and shook his head, his leathered face pinched in layers of worry. "Sister Brown, you need to get some rest. You need to strengthen your reserves for your daughter's sake. It's getting too dark to search farther today. We'll resume at first light, but no more tonight."

Constance nodded, her chest tightening further. She didn't trust her voice to respond. The walk back to the camp felt empty. Her eyes continued to scan the plains for William's tall shadow.

When she got back, Sister Nielson held a shawl out to her. "You look frozen, Sister Brown! I've got some stew waiting for you."

"Thank you," Constance said. "How is Eliza?"

"Oh, she's been no trouble at all. She's certainly the most pleasant baby I've had the privilege of caring for. With seven of my own, I should know. She's sleeping in my wagon. Do you want me to fetch her?"

"No, let her sleep." Constance sank to the quilt-covered ground, her breath coming out in a steamy sigh that rose up in the cold. The horses near Sister Nielson's wagon whickered as they settled into the night. Constance glared at them.

"Cursed animals!" Constance felt her chest tighten enough that she couldn't breathe. She covered her mouth as the sob that had been building up finally escaped her. "If they'd been tied more securely . . . If he hadn't gone searching for that foolish horse, we'd be together! We'd be *whole!*" Constance was glad Sister Nielson hadn't handed her the stew yet. She knew that if she were holding onto anything, she'd have cast it into the fire.

"Don't say such things." Sister Nielson patted Constance's shoulder and stood. "Any man would have gone looking. Horses are valuable property."

Constance drew a cold, ragged breath. Of course they were valuable. Of course he would try to find the stray animal, but to not return? Where could he have gone? What ill fate could have befallen him? She thought again of the lightning. If he'd been struck . . .

"No. I will not think on it." She bit into her lips and closed her eyes against the images in her mind.

Brother Smoot interrupted her mutterings with a soft clearing of his throat. "We cannot wait any longer," he said, not meeting her gaze. She jumped to her feet and tried to stand in front of him, tried to make him look into her eyes, hoping that if he could see her pain one more time, he would change his mind.

His chapped lips pressed into a thin, firm line before he went on. "We've delayed so much already. Food rations are low; I fear there won't be enough to last us to the end of our journey. I am so sorry . . . so sorry." His voice cracked at the last. "I wish I could do more for you, Sister." He briefly put his hand on her shoulder, still not looking her in the eyes. He turned and walked away, his image shadowed instantly as he left the firelight.

Constance dropped to her knees and allowed herself to be overcome with tears. "We can't leave him," she cried. "What if he's injured and waiting for rescue? If we leave, the wolves will drag off his body, or the

Indians will surely cause him harm." She feared those things had already occurred.

Sister Nielson stopped her oldest daughter from trying to offer comfort. "Let her cry, Lynnette," Constance heard Sister Nielson say to her daughter. "Her soul needs to let it out."

Lynnette was seventeen, only three years younger than Constance, and the two had become good friends, closer than friends. The two were "thick as thieves," as William always said.

After Constance calmed herself, Lynnette ventured closer with the stew in one hand. She clutched at her skirts with the other hand and offered a timid smile. Lynnette finally knelt and pulled Constance into an embrace.

"I'm sorry, Lynnette. I just . . . I just want to die when I think of that last moment when he touched my face and sang the baby to sleep . . . will that really be all I have left of him? A memory? Will that really be my last moment? I don't even think I told him how much I loved him! I was so tired."

"He knows," Lynnette said, and pulled away to try to offer her stew. The stew was cold and had a scorched smell to it from the time it spent waiting for Constance to return.

The very thought of eating made Constance feel queasy. "No, thank you. I'll just go to bed. Please ask your mother to wake me when Eliza wakes."

"But you need to eat something," Lynnette implored. "How can you nurse a child when you have no nourishment of your own?"

"She's nearly weaned. I'll be fine. I'll eat in the morning." Constance left for her own empty wagon. She almost went back to ask Sister Nielson to fetch her baby for her after all but couldn't bear waking little Eliza. She knelt on her blankets and poured out her heart in prayer. "Lord? What would you have me do?" Her mind felt numb. She had never felt so alone in her life. Even when she had been cast off from her family in England and all of her letters were returned unopened from her mother, she had not felt this alone. Had God abandoned her?

"What direction should I go? What, Lord, do you want of me? I have done everything you've asked. Everything. I've left everything I loved, yet found new love, then *he* is torn from me as well. Still you want more of me!" She shouted the last and knew the other families in their wagons would hear, but she didn't care. Many nights, others in the company cried over the loss of a child or an elderly parent due to sickness or other misfortune. Would they judge her for giving in to the weakness of her own despair?

Thoughts of her infant daughter filled Constance with grief. Eliza would never know her grandmother or aunt . . . and now, was she to grow up not knowing her own father?

"It isn't worth it, Lord." She allowed her thoughts to drift to her own mother and to all the trials she'd overcome to get to this very point. "I don't care what Zion is anymore. It could be more beautiful than Eden and it would not be worth it. I cannot leave him. To go on without him would be wretched enough to blind me to any beauty Zion might hold. I'll not go another step!" The blasphemy tasted bitter on her tongue.

Constance buried her face in her pillow to muffle the sounds of her crying. And though she never finished her prayer vocally, in her heart she continued pleading for a miracle. With no way of knowing what time it was, she slipped out of her wagon, bundled a blanket around herself, and walked. She was not leaving with the company . . . not without her husband.

CHAPTER 2

2009

"Liz! Sister Peterson's on the phone!"

Liz rounded the corner and glared at her mom through the banister at the top of the stairs. She shook her head violently, trying to get it through her mom's head that there was *no way* she was talking to Sister Peterson or anyone else from the Young Women presidency.

Her mother held the phone to her chest to muffle her words. "*Now,* Liz."

Liz shook her head again and mouthed the word, "No."

With a deep breath, Clair King put the phone back to her ear. "I'm sorry, Sister Peterson. Liz refuses to come to the phone right now. You know how teenagers are . . ."

"Mom!" Liz hissed in disbelief.

When her mom hung up, she folded her arms across her chest. "What?"

"Why would you tell her that?"

"What did you think I was going to do? Lie to her for you?"

Liz's green eyes flashed. "It would have been more tactful."

"Tactful would be coming to the phone when you get a call."

"She was going to ask me to sing. I'm not singing in the sacrament program."

"Why?" Her mother met her glare, but Liz saw that the green eyes were tired, and her heart wasn't in the fight Liz insisted on battling.

"They're singing the song 'Families Can Be Together Forever.'"

"So?"

"So, it's not true. *You* said I should never lie."

Clair rolled her eyes and jerked a hand through her short hair. "You're just being difficult. It is too true."

"It isn't for *me*. Not anymore. So forget it. I'm not singing."

Her mother pressed her palm to her forehead. With her other hand, she clutched the emerald necklace hanging at her throat as though it could offer some magic to quell Liz's growing resentment. Liz snorted at that. No necklace could fix their family no matter where it came from. The emerald stone was part of the family inheritance that would be passed to Liz when her mom died. Liz's mom said it was fitting since Liz had already inherited her grandmother's green eyes and dark hair. "Do you want to talk about it?"

"Talk about what?"

"Your father."

"No. He's a lousy, stupid, cheating son of a—"

"Eliza Josephine King!"

"*Gun,* Mom. Son of a gun. I'm still not singing."

"Then you can explain that to Sister Peterson when you get to church today."

* * *

Liz showered and dressed for church slowly. After the phone call, she wanted to stay home and pretend to be sick. She wouldn't really have to fake much either. The idea of facing Sister Peterson after her mom said Liz wouldn't come to the phone made her want to throw up.

When she went downstairs to fix some toast, her mom interrupted any idea of breakfast. "Come here. I want to show you something." Clair turned and went down the hall, leaving Liz with no choice but to follow. Liz sighed. She was likely going to get chewed out for not respecting her Young Women leaders or something like that.

They finally stopped at her dad's study . . . well, what *used* to be her dad's study, anyway. On the wall behind the door was a huge chart of their family tree on her mother's side. Clair pointed to the chart.

"I want you to sing in the program. It's two weeks away, and I don't expect you to decide whether or not you want to right now. But I wanted to show you why the song is true."

"Mom, really—don't. It's not important."

"Yes, it is. It's very important." Her mom's hand went to the emerald pendant at her throat. Liz stared at it, and the way her mom touched the gemstone like a lucky rabbit's foot, and sighed in frustration. One more lecture on how her ancestors rocked the foundation of the world was enough to make her scream. Just because her mom was a genealogy zealot didn't mean Liz deserved constant lecturing.

"It's important because you have an eternal family. Generations and generations of ancestors are watching and waiting to see what you'll do with the genetics and history they've handed to you." Her mom waved a hand over the chart. "You have Grandpa Brown who built the Alpine Stake Tabernacle. You have—"

"I know!" Liz interrupted. "And great-way-back-there somewhere, some grandma died on the plains, and another one crossed the whole way on foot, and we need to be strong like they were."

"This isn't a lecture, Liz."

"Really? 'Cause it sounds like one." Liz looked at her mom's crestfallen face and took a deep breath. "I'm sorry, Mom. I know what you're trying to say, and I get it . . . I do. I just don't see what any of this has to do with *my* life." She walked away, hearing her mother sigh behind her.

* * *

Sister Peterson moved aside, revealing the words *Your Personal Plan* on the whiteboard.

"When was the last time any of you *really* prayed?" she asked. "When was the last time you knelt and asked Heavenly Father what direction He wanted you to go? When was the last time you took a few minutes to listen after you put a question to Him? When did you last ask Him what He wanted from you, rather than tell Him what you wanted?"

Liz shifted uncomfortably in her seat. She couldn't remember *ever* praying like that. She looked over to the other girls who were nodding. She rolled her eyes. *So different . . .* Liz was glad for the empty chair next to her. She'd sat on the end, away from the others on purpose. Since gossip of her father's scandalous affair, excommunication, and the following divorce had raged through the ward, she'd felt like an outsider. It wasn't so much that anyone treated her different as it was that she *felt* different. They had their perfect families. Her family was the object of criticism and hushed discussions on sin. What good was a temple marriage for all eternity when eternity couldn't make it past two decades?

Before class was over, Sister Peterson challenged them to all kneel down and really pray sometime over the next week. "You owe God a real prayer. Go out and find your own personal Sacred Grove. See if, in the next week, you can discover His plan for you."

A closing prayer marked the end of class. The Laurels gathered their scriptures and hurried to leave the room so the Beehives could come in and put the chairs away. Sister Peterson had looked at Liz several times during the lesson as though she were trying to talk to her personally, but now that class was over, Sister Peterson busied herself with cleaning up her stuff and getting the board erased.

Liz lingered. She usually stayed a little behind the other Laurels so she could walk home without anyone trying to talk to her about her family. She stared at her teacher's back a moment before speaking. "Hi."

"Hey. You ready to talk?"

Liz cringed. "Sorry about earlier."

Sister Peterson turned to face Liz. "It's okay."

"You were calling to ask me to sing." Liz looked at the birthday calendar on the board behind Sister Peterson.

"I was. You have a beautiful voice. And I'd like you to be part of the Young Women program for sacrament."

"I can't sing that song," Liz whispered.

"Why not?"

"'Cause I'd feel like a liar."

"The song isn't a lie, regardless of what's going on in your family right now."

Liz sucked in a deep breath. Bitterness over the choice her father had made washed over her. "I just would rather not sing."

Sister Peterson shrugged. "That's your choice. But I'd like to see you take the opportunity to ask Heavenly Father what He has planned for you. Maybe He wants you to sing."

Liz nodded as Sister Peterson reached out and gave her a hug. Then Liz mumbled something about having to get home and fled the room as fast as reverently possible.

She walked home alone, the view of Salt Lake City from South Mountain sparkling up at her in the summer sun. She liked walking home when the weather was good. Becky Dunford's red BMW streaked by, and Liz sighed. Not too long ago, she'd been with Becky in that car. The thought made her stomach twist. How she and Becky had ever been best friends still mystified Liz. But back then, they both rode horses. They'd been through jump camps and riding lessons together. Everything changed when Becky decided to try out for cheerleading.

And if itty-bitty skirts, cheer practice, and the time-consuming responsibility of attending every high school game weren't enough, Becky was made cheerleading captain. Becky became too good to be friends with anyone who didn't know how to conform to the cheerleader pyramid. Now the two were more like bitter enemies than just estranged friends.

The cheerleaders thought Liz's horse was boring. She thought the cheerleaders were drones. So the feelings wedged her apart from her one-time friend and kept them apart. Things escalated when news of her father's excommunication filtered through the gossip chain. Liz was the daughter of a cheater. Everyone knew. And everyone knew how much the divorce had hurt the family financially. But it would be over soon. Liz graduated this year.

She would start her senior year in two days, finish in June, and move out of Utah altogether. She'd go east or west, north or south. It didn't matter as long as it *wasn't* Utah. A lot depended on which colleges accepted her. She'd applied to seventeen different universities, giving her a fair amount to choose from.

She walked slower than needed, pondering high school politics, when a voice behind her said, "Hey, Liz."

"Garrett." She turned to face him. "Hi."

He smiled, his tall frame shadowing the sun's glare so she could see him clearly. "Hi."

"Car broke down?" she asked.

"Nope. Decided to walk. It's a nice day."

She'd never seen him walk before. Since he'd gotten his license, he'd driven the family car everywhere. She sighed inwardly. Since her dad had moved out, her driving options had become seriously limited. So many things in her life were ruined with her father's announcement.

"So how's your family doing?"

Liz wanted to throw something at him for asking the question she hated more than anything in the world, but all she had were her scriptures. "Fine. We're fine." The words were so well rehearsed she could've uttered them in her sleep. She spoke them through gritted teeth, wondering if he'd only bothered to talk to her to inquire after more gossip on her dad.

"Good. Speaking of family, I better hurry before mine freaks over how long I took."

"Oh. I . . . me too. I gotta go." She turned her back on him before she gave in to her own self-pity and started crying. She rushed into her own house.

Her two brothers and sister were already there. Five-year-old Matt attached himself to her legs as she strained against his weight to walk to the kitchen. "Lizzie! I learned a new Primary song today!" His high pitched voice started singing, "Whenever I touch a velvet rose . . ." as he rode her feet to the kitchen. She untangled him from her legs and set him on a chair where he sang the verses out of order twice more before she finally stopped him with a tickle.

Matt giggled. "I sing good, huh?"

Liz nodded. "Yep, Matty, you're a regular pop star."

Matt frowned. "How am I s'posed to sing if I'm drinking pop?"

Liz laughed and tickled him again. He jumped from the chair and fled the room to escape her tickling. Liz knew he wanted her to chase him, but she made her way up the stairs to her room instead.

She changed out of her dress into a pair of jeans and a T-shirt then pulled the hair she had tried to curl that morning into a ponytail. The curls hadn't turned out anyway.

Her mom had pitched a fit a few days before about organization and grounded Liz from the stables until her bedroom was spotless. For the first time in a month, there were no dirty clothes on the floor, and her dresser was cleared off. She'd even emptied the overflowing wastebasket.

The organization made her feel a little of the peace she'd been missing over the last few months. She thought about what her teacher said. Could she ask Heavenly Father what He wanted her to do in her life? Would He answer if she asked? He wasn't very responsive when she'd begged Him to make her parents stay together. He'd ignored her. Sometimes Liz wondered if He'd ignored her because of what her dad had done and because He felt she was guilty by association. "That's stupid," she said to herself. She knew thinking things like that was totally wrong, but sometimes the thoughts surfaced whether she asked them to or not.

In direct defiance of her own feelings of inadequacy, she was on her knees. She clasped her hands together and began. "Heavenly Father, I am really thankful for all of my blessings . . ." She wasn't exactly thankful, but she tried to be and figured that had to be good enough for right now. "I just don't understand. Why is my family so lame?" She wondered if it was a sin to call your family lame in a prayer. But they *were* lame, and it would probably be a bigger sin to lie in a prayer and say they weren't. "Sister Peterson said I should ask what you want me to do in my life. So I thought I'd give it a tr—"

Thump, thump! "Liz!" It was her mom. Liz ignored the noise.

"So anyway, I—"

"Liz! I need you to come downstairs now."

"I'm busy!" Liz called back, unable to hide the frustration in her voice.

"Now, Liz. No arguments." Her mom's footsteps faded away down the hall.

Liz glared at her still-folded hands and with a huge breath of frustration muttered, "See, I told you they were lame!" She pushed herself up and stalked downstairs.

Liz stomped into the living room. "What do you need?"

"Don't take that tone. It's time for family home evening." Her mother's voice trembled.

"Family home evening is on Monday."

Her mother's shoulders slumped. "We have to do it today. My new job goes until 7:30."

Liz stiffened. "What new job?"

"I'll start working as a receptionist at the optical shop in the mall. They're open until nine, but the other girl closes. I'm really lucky to get to go home earlier."

"And you waited until now to tell us?" Liz was entirely baffled and totally ticked to be slammed with such news.

"They called me yesterday to ask me to start tomorrow. I didn't really think I'd get the job."

"Why would you even apply?"

"If we want to keep the house, I need to work. There isn't enough in child support to pay the house payment and keep eating too."

"Then we should move!" Liz shouted. She was sick and tired of the ward and neighborhood anyway. This was the last straw. For her mom to work to keep the house seemed insane.

"Liz, be reasonable. This isn't forev—"

"What about staying home and being a mom?" Liz was so mad she could've walked straight into her dad's new apartment where he was likely kissing his new home-wrecking fiancée and kick them both. She'd kick the fiancée twice!

Her sister, Alison, glared at Liz and gave a small shake of the head to show her disapproval. Alison was four years younger than Liz, but since she'd turned thirteen, she had taken on a bossy, know-it-all tone. Her mom said Ali was just growing into herself and needed time to get the hormones balanced.

Nathan and Alison were twins, though he seemed pretty normal in comparison as he sat reading his new science fiction book and lounging on the couch, oblivious to the family drama erupting around him. For a few years, her mom and dad had thought they would only be able to have one child until they found out her mom was pregnant.

Even more glorious was the day they found out they were having twins. Liz had gone from the adored only child to all but ignored in the wake of trying to keep up with twins. By the time Matt had come along, Liz was glad to see another child usurping the authority the twins had usurped from her.

But now Matt's little five-year-old face pinched in worry as he stared from his mom to his sister. Liz focused on her siblings as if seeing them all for the first time. That was when it occurred to her to ask, "Who's going to watch the kids?"

Clair's eyes closed briefly, as though she'd reached the end of her patience. "I'm really going to need your help in this."

"What? *I* have to take care of them? I have riding lessons at the stables twice a week! Then there's school . . . I have a life!" She didn't really have a life outside the stables, but such points were never good to bring up in arguments like this.

"Lizzie—"

"Don't Lizzie me. Are you kidding me? You call me down here for family home evening and then tell me you're getting a job, and *I* have to take over as mom. That's insane!"

"Go to your room, Liz." Her mother didn't yell, but the whisper felt like a sonic boom.

Liz opened her mouth to reply, but she was too angry. She wanted to scream and shout and stomp her feet. Another part of her wanted comfort. She wanted to run to her dad and have him smooth her hair and say, "You're my little Snow White." Hating him and needing him at the same time only served to fuel her anger.

She turned on her heel and stomped away. She glanced back when she got to the stairs. Alison was still shaking her head and tossing dirty looks in Liz's direction. Her mother held tightly to Matt; her eyes were shut tight as though she were very tired. And it was all Liz's fault.

Back in her room, even the tidiness didn't feel comforting. She kicked at her beanbag chair. It wasn't fair! How could life have gotten this crummy?

She thought about praying again but decided it was a waste of time. With her luck, her mom would come in or something, and that would be weird. Plus, He wasn't listening anyway. If He were, her dad would've stuck around, and her mom wouldn't be getting a job. She was being abandoned on both sides.

Her mother had never worked, not once in Liz's entire life. Liz never had to be the babysitter for her mom except on special occasions, which Liz had never minded simply because they were temporary. The permanence of this new situation was infuriating. One more thing to blame on her dad. She sat on her bed, thinking she'd just take a quick nap. By the time she woke up, the sky had darkened.

The house wound down in activity. She heard brushing teeth along with the other nighttime rituals of stories and prayers. At some point in the bustle, her mom stood outside her door. Liz could tell it was her by the heavier footstep and the way the floor squeaked under pressure. She waited for the knock, but it never came. Her mom moved away after Matt called from his bedroom for a story. All the kids loved reading, and Matt was no exception. He always wanted a story.

When the house went quiet, Liz avoided the squeaky floorboard by her door and made her way down the stairs. She slipped out the back and got on her brother's motor scooter. It was an expensive toy, and they weren't all that popular anymore, but her dad had gotten it for him anyway for his birthday. Alison was given a pricey new sewing machine.

Her mom was mad about the purchases, ranting about gifts replacing the time he should have been spending with his children. Nathan had been thrilled by the scooter. Matt had already put in his request for a scooter on his birthday. Liz silently agreed with her mom, but she wasn't sure if it was due to her mom actually being right, or because she was mad at her dad for leaving the family to spend all of his time with Patty.

Liz hated Patty. Patty was the reason for the divorce. Patty was young and what her dad called "carefree."

What he meant by *carefree* was that she hadn't been to church since she'd blossomed into womanhood. She was the type of girl who hung out with sleazy guys, and it made Liz sad to think her father had become like one of those types of guys—checking out the exterior when the interior was rotten. Patty swore a lot and said things that Liz's mom called inappropriate, but Liz's dad laughed at those things. He was entirely alien from the man who used to torture them with two-hour sermons for family home evening.

As she rode the scooter down the sleeping streets of Draper, she pushed Patty out of her thoughts. Even if he wasn't the dad she wanted, Liz wanted to see him, and if she had to see Patty in order to make it happen, she'd deal with it.

He still lived in Draper, and it didn't take Liz long before she was parked by his car in the carport of the apartment building.

After she took several deep breaths, her finger pushed the doorbell. She almost turned and headed back down the stairs to the carport, but footsteps sounded from behind the door only seconds before her dad whipped it open and stared at Liz. His sandy brown hair had a suspicious rumpled look to it. The thought of why it might look rumpled made Liz want to vomit.

"What are you doing here?" He looked more annoyed than glad to see her, making her heart sink into her stomach.

"I . . . just wanted to see you." She tucked herself deeper into her jacket, hunching her shoulders and lowering her chin.

He didn't want her there.

She wanted to explain herself better than just telling him she wanted to see him, but Patty's high-pitched, childlike voice rang from deeper inside the apartment.

"Who is it, babe?" She opened the door wider to see for herself. Her mouth fell open at first, but she recovered quickly. "Liz! Come on in!" She ushered Liz into the apartment while chastising Tom for keeping his daughter out on the porch.

The apartment was furnished as though they were expecting royal company. Everything plush and more expensive than Liz knew her father could afford. How many credit cards had Patti managed to max out?

"How'd you get here?" Tom asked. "Did your mom let you use the car?"

Liz shrugged. "I took Nathan's scooter."

"Is something wrong?" Her dad moved some vacation magazines off the couch. "Here, sit down and tell me what's up."

So she sat. He sat across from her on the loveseat next to Patty.

He took Patty's hand and Liz cringed. She focused on the floor, her gaze falling on the vacation and travel magazines. "Planning a trip?"

"Oh! We're trying to decide on what to do when we're on our honeymoon!" Patty lit up, her voice rising to a soprano lilt.

When Liz's dad saw her flinch at the word, he jumped in. "So, you never said what's up."

"Nothing's up really. I just . . . I don't know, just wanted to get out of the house I guess."

"Having troubles with your mom?" he asked.

Liz stiffened, instantly defensive. "No. Not at all. Mom's great. She's doing really well; you know she got a new job and starts tomorrow."

"Really?"

Liz forced a smile. "Yeah. I'm really proud of her for doing whatever it takes to keep things running in our family. Her commitment is unshakeable. And she's so smart and talented; she'll be great with her new job."

"What about you? How are you doing?" Patty asked, clearly steering the conversation away from any praise of her fiancé's ex.

"Great. Really. I start new jump training at the stables next week. I'm really excited about that. School starts Tuesday, so I'll get some more college credits before I graduate."

Patty's high tinkling laugh made Liz shudder. "Oh, come on! You're starting your senior year, and all you can think of is smelly horses and college?" She cast a glance to Liz's father. "When I was a senior, all I could think about was the next dance and the next boyfriend!"

The two of them laughed together. Liz sat with her back rigid. "Yeah, well sometimes it's smarter to focus your energies on things that are really worthwhile instead of *fluff.*"

They stopped laughing. Her dad looked at her pleadingly and then said, "Oh, Liz, you're sounding like your mother now. There's no reason not to loosen up a lit—"

"What's wrong with sounding like Mom?" She stood.

Her father rose too, his face a wrinkled mass of confusion. "There's nothing wrong with that. C'mon, Snow White. What's bugging you?"

She wanted to slap him for throwing out his pet name for her with such manipulative intent. "Nothing, Dad. I need to go home now. Mom'll get worried if I'm gone too long."

"Right. You don't want to worry her. You come by anytime you want."

Liz looked at her father. The offer almost sounded sincere, but she couldn't help but feel depressed by it. Not like he was ever really available before the divorce, but at least he'd been in the same house. Now he was too distant—not just physically, but also mentally out of reach. He was planning a wedding and a honeymoon. Patty was still young enough that she would probably want her own children. He would be consumed by a new life, and it wouldn't include Liz. She didn't belong in his life, but she couldn't stop herself from really wanting to belong.

"Yeah, Dad . . . later."

As she headed down the stairwell back to the scooter, she heard her dad admonish her to call him when she got home to make sure she arrived safely. He grumbled to Patty about how irresponsible her mother must be to let her dash around on a scooter in the middle of the night.

"It's not the middle of the night," she said to herself as she jerked the chin strap of her brother's helmet a little too tight. She was so upset she didn't bother to loosen it up. What had she been thinking going there? What did she expect to have happened? She didn't know, but the naked truth of her father's new life angered her. Her mom was getting a new job. She was going to have to take over as babysitter and caregiver for her younger siblings while her dad was off suntanning on a beach with a girl dumber and more absurd than a Chihuahua dressed in a pink tutu. She ground her teeth and sped from the apartment complex.

When the scooter came to a stop, she took a deep breath, inhaling the familiar scents of the stables where her horse, Sassy, was housed.

She clipped the helmet to the front handlebar and made her way to Sassy's stall. She unlocked the gate and went in, rubbing her hand along the horse's nose. Sassy whickered and swished her long tail, blinking her big, dark eyes. "At least *you're* glad to see me." Sassy's soft chestnut coloring was the reason Liz fell in love with the Arabian mare three years earlier. Her dad was good friends with the breeder; one thing led to another and then Sassy belonged to Liz.

Liz ran her hand along Sassy's neck for a long time, finally brushing the horse down before settling herself on the hay at the back of the stall. Sassy turned her head to stare at Liz.

"I don't know what I'm doing here," Liz said as though the horse had asked a question. "I don't know what I'm doing anywhere." She muttered the last, flicking a handful of straw at the wood-slatted walls in frustration.

She thought about Sister Peterson asking her to pray and find out what Heavenly Father wanted her to be and where He wanted her to go. *Find your own personal Sacred Grove.*

Making the decision to actually pray took some time. She didn't feel like praying yet felt like she needed to. At least this time no one would tell her to come down to family home evening. She was on her knees before making the conscious decision to talk to Heavenly Father. She had her arms folded while still chiding herself for thinking Heavenly Father would really tell her what direction to take. Then she was praying.

Liz poured her heart out to the Lord like never before. She cried and whined, thanking Him for blessings she felt truly thankful for while yelling at Him for not helping her when she needed it most. Then she asked the question, "What do you want me to do with my life? What is it you really want me to become?" Her heart pounded, and her stomach felt all those tingling feelings everyone said happened when people got real answers to prayer. Then she listened for those real answers she just knew would come.

She felt exhausted, unaware of the time that passed, only knowing that a lot of time *had* passed because her knees ached and her legs were asleep. Her back popped as she stretched and laid herself back into the straw. She had listened so long waiting for an answer, but the heavens remained silent.

Liz felt betrayed by the silence. Especially when she'd known that He *would* answer. So why didn't He? She hadn't just believed He would, she'd *known* He would. Did she not kneel long enough? Did she not wait long enough?

She was so disappointed and yet so tired that she was asleep as the first tears slid out from her closed eyes.

CHAPTER 3

1852

CONSTANCE HAD NO WAY OF knowing how far or how long she'd walked. When the light from the stars and moon disappeared behind the dark cover of clouds, she knew another storm was coming. The wind whipped at the stray strands of hair across her face as she continued moving.

"William!" She'd waited a good distance from the wagons before she started calling. She had to find him—to bring him back so they could continue to Zion together. So they could live their lives as they planned.

"William!" The first drops of rain pelted her face, lightning flashing in the distance followed by thunder shortly after. The wind picked up, and the thunder rolled along the hillside, indicating that this storm would be big. She looked back in the direction she'd come. She'd never beat the brunt of the storm to the wagons. In the next flash of lightning, she saw a small slope with a rock overhang. She ran to the shelter it would provide.

Constance watched the storm from her new vantage point. The wind whipped through the soaked layers of her dress as she huddled into herself for warmth.

"Lord. Please help me!" she cried out over the thunder.

But the storm only worsened at her plea.

"I will not leave him! This whole journey was a fool's errand, and it was not worth it!"

The thunder shook the ground under her as though trying to bait her into a fight.

"Do you hear me?" she screamed. "I'll not go any farther! It's not worth it! You cannot let Eliza and me be abandoned like this!"

She battled back and forth with the thunder until her voice was entirely spent. She shook her head and whispered, "We'll never survive without him. There's no point to any of this. My daughter needs her father. And I need my husband."

Exhaustion consumed her as a fine white mist swirled around her knees where she knelt. The mist rose to her waist and then her shoulders until she felt as though she'd been bundled into an embrace. As the warm mist touched her cold cheeks, Constance felt herself falling through the mist as though she'd been flung from a tall mountain. Yet she felt no fear. The embrace held her tight—kept her warm . . . kept her safe. She furrowed her brow. "A strange dream . . ." she murmured, as she succumbed to the warmth of the mist and the exhaustion in the very marrow of her bones. She slept.

* * *

Constance awoke with a moan. Her muscles, stiff and sore from sleeping on the ground, burned as she tried to stretch. She blinked her eyes against the morning light shining down on her through thick wood slats . . .

She sat upright. Wood slats? There should be no wood slats. There should be rock—stone. She'd gone to sleep under the rocky overhang. Her body trembled as she took in her surroundings. The endless fields and rolling hills were gone. The rocky protection from the night previous had vanished.

In their place stood buildings. Many buildings. She scrambled to her feet and stood under a small lean-to at the edge of a green field. Structures crowded in on all sides of the field. Constance squeezed her eyes shut and snapped them open again, but everything remained the same—unfamiliar . . . terrifying.

Constance wrung her hands, unable to stamp down the panic rising up inside her, not caring that William would mock her hysteria. "This is wrong. This is all terribly wrong!" Her chest constricted in fear as she turned in a quick circle, trying to get her bearing—to latch on to anything that would be familiar to her.

"Oh!" she gasped and covered her mouth with her hand. "I've been abducted. Carried away in the night." She uttered an oath that would have made her mother blush and instantly regretted being so loose with her tongue. She'd likely been carried off by savages. Obscenities would not help such a situation. She had to get away—to get back to the wagons. To get back to her daughter.

The thought of her daughter moved her to action. Her shaking legs carried her forward, though she did not know what direction she should go. She broke into a run.

* * *

Liz awoke with a start. The pale morning light shone through the cracks of the wooden slats in the gate of Sassy's stall. "Oh, no!" she groaned, running a hand through her dark hair to clear out the straw. "Mom is going to kill me!" She jumped up and locked the stable then dashed for the scooter.

As she turned the corner of the Little Barn, she ran smack into someone. A jolt of pain traveled through her spine as they both landed on the ground from the force of Liz's momentum. She rolled a bit to her side with a whimper. "I am so sorry! I—" Liz looked at the girl and blinked.

The girl looked to be her same age and could have been Liz's sister. They had the same dark brown hair and a similar sprinkle of freckles lightly over their noses. But it was the eyes—green like emeralds—that surprised Liz the most. The only other person she knew with eyes like hers was her mom. Those eyes were so startling that it took Liz a few moments to realize the girl wore a dirty pioneer dress and looked positively terrified.

Liz stood and reached a hand out to help her up. "I'm sorry," she began again. "I didn't know you were there. Are you okay?" Maybe they were filming a movie. Liz couldn't think of any other reason the girl would be dressed like she was.

The deep English accent trembled. "Something has gone wrong!" Constance brushed at her skirts in agitation and smoothed her dark unkempt hair back away from her face. "Where am I? There were no structures where I slept. It was a cove in the rock . . ." She stared at Liz, her eyes wide with fear. "Am I your prisoner? Did you bring me to this place while I slept?"

Liz backed up a few steps, holding her hands up in protest. "Whoa there. I didn't bring anyone anywhere. And though this little conversation is . . . well, weird, I gotta go. My mom's gonna kill me for taking off last night. And so, you know, good luck with your movie." Liz hurried past the girl.

"Wait!" the girl called. "You cannot leave me here alone! What if whoever did take me returns? Please!"

Liz couldn't say why she stopped and turned around. It seemed insane. Did this girl really think she was kidnapped? And yet, who knew? Maybe some predator was lurking in one of the stables. The thought quickened Liz's pulse.

"You were kidnapped?"

"I've no idea what happened, I assure you. The storm commenced not too long after I left the camp. I sheltered under a rock overhang. But when I awoke, I was in that bit of field . . ." The girl frantically cast her eyes around as though trying to get a grip on her location. "Over there?" She seemed uncertain. Her voice cracked and her eyes shone with tears. "And these buildings and structures were here, and nothing at all looks familiar to me. Please, help me."

After a moment's consideration, Liz decided she should at least call the police. Liz's mom had likely already done that very thing to search for *her*. If there was a kidnapper running around . . .

Naturally the scooter was big enough to hold a passenger, since her dad had spared no expense to buy her brother off. Thinking of the scooter brought back all the bitterness of the previous night.

Liz took a deep breath. "Come with me." She sounded a little more secure than she felt. She really just wanted to leave this person here, but every time she considered that, she felt dread.

No, she had to take the girl with her. Her mom would know what to do.

When she got to the scooter, the girl stopped short and goggled at it. Liz didn't have the patience to wait around any longer and jumped on, strapping the helmet to her head. She felt a little guilty about taking the only helmet, but there were rules at her house. No one was allowed to ride the scooter without the helmet unless they wanted to be grounded for a month. Her mom couldn't ground the stranger.

"Get on," Liz said.

The girl's face registered confusion. "Why?"

"So we can leave."

"And *this* will help us leave?" She looked doubtful, as though she'd never seen a scooter in her life.

Judging from her accent and archaic dress, Liz thought it possible the girl *hadn't* seen a scooter in her life. *Maybe she's Amish.*

"Just get on." Liz made the decision that if the girl didn't get on, she would just leave and tell her mom about it when she got home.

But the girl listened this time, trying to sidesaddle the small seat. Liz grumbled impatiently. There would be no riding sidesaddle in a dress long enough to be a bedspread. The dress could get caught in the tires and kill them both when they got onto the main roads. "No." Liz let her panic and irritation seep into her voice. "Sit like I'm sitting, or we'll both get killed." The words carried the desired outcome as the girl lifted her skirts and sat on the scooter correctly.

Liz turned the key and pressed the starter button on the left handle. The little engine sparked into life. The girl gasped behind her, but Liz wasn't paying much attention to that as she pulled back on the throttle so it didn't quit as she shifted out of neutral. A terrible scream erupted from behind her. Liz spun around, knocking herself off balance and sending the scooter to its side. The girl had leapt from the back and was standing there screeching like her dress had caught fire.

Liz managed to remove herself from the fallen scooter. "What's wrong? You gotta stop screaming, or your kidnappers will hear you and come back." Liz eyed the Little Barn, wondering if the predator lurked around the corner.

"What is it?" the girl wailed. "What have you done?"

Liz looked around trying to understand the reason for the psychotic episode unfolding in front of her. "What?"

"The noise! How?"

"The scooter?" Liz looked at it. The engine had killed when she knocked it over, and it sat on its side rather benignly.

"Who are you?" the girl demanded. Her eyes were wide with fear.

"Liz King, no relation to Stephen, though you're creeping me out enough that I feel like I'm in one of his books. Who are *you*?" Liz had worked over her fear enough to decide it was time to bolt. Girl or no girl, kidnapper or no, she was leaving.

"Constance Miles Brown."

Liz had already stood the scooter up when the girl answered. She said it without preamble or any trumpets, but Liz felt the hairs on the back of her neck rise. The name was familiar. "And you got here how?" Maybe she recognized the name from the back of a milk jug or from a face on the corkboards in the grocery store with the big word MISSING emblazoned across the front.

"I hardly know. My husband is lost. The wagon company was leaving today. My daughter is with the wagon company. She needs me. And I must return to her. Even if I cannot find my William, I must return to Eliza!" Tears rolled down her cheeks, leaving smudgy trails of dirt behind them. Her green eyes glowed as she cried and begged for help.

The names were familiar . . . far more familiar than something seen in passing at the grocery store. She *knew* the story. Her mother had told it dozens of times when she was trying to point out how Liz needed to be stronger like her ancestors, the pioneers who blazed the trails to Utah and made her own easy life in Utah possible. Liz stared at Constance Miles Brown.

No. *No!* There was no way this was really *the* Constance Miles Brown. It was a joke. Her mom was playing a sick joke on her for taking off in the middle of the night. Fine. She could play along. Liz looked at Constance again, with a grin.

"I'm not dumb, you know."

Constance wrinkled her forehead, which, Liz noticed for the first time, was red and weathered as though she'd been outside for far too long without sunscreen. "I never questioned your intelligence."

"Did my mom send you after me?"

"I am quite sure I do not know your mother. Unless . . . unless she is amongst the Saints in my wagon company."

Liz's heart pounded against her rib cage. *Listen to her,* a voice whispered in her mind. "Okay. Fine. Let's pretend you really are Constance Miles Brown. Let's pretend my mom's not messing with me, and you are who you say you are. What's the date today, *Constance?*" She felt empowered saying her name like that, as though she were catching the young woman in a lie.

"It is the tenth of July."

The Constance girl was totally off on the month. What was this girl playing at?

"Oh, yeah, what year?"

The girl's features crumpled in confusion. "1852, of course."

Liz stiffened but tried to keep her face smooth. "What happened to your husband?"

"I told you—he went after the horses and never returned."

"No. I mean after that. What happened to him? How did you find him? My mom surely must have told you what happens next in our little family saga."

"I *have not* found him!" She was crying again. Only this time her shoulders shook, and she fell to her knees. "Please, if you can help, then do so. If not, why torment me? He's gone, and I am lost myself! My child has no mother until I return. Why ask how I found a man I have only just told you I am searching for?"

Liz could only gape. "How?" Liz fell to her knees too and stared at the girl. "How is this possible?" Constance didn't answer but sat on the dusty ground, her body shaking with sobs.

She speaks the truth.

"Let's go." Liz didn't know if she believed Constance or not. She wasn't sure if she believed the whispering in her own mind, but she knew she couldn't leave the girl here all alone. Liz helped Constance up and had her settled on the scooter again while trying to soothe her about the scooter's engine. "It isn't a big deal. I'm going to push this button, and the motor will start. It's loud, but it's totally safe. No matter what, don't let go of my waist and don't be scared."

Liz felt stupid. This was crazy; she was talking to someone her own age as though she were a small child instead of nearly an adult. The sane part of her mind kept saying it was all a joke, some object lesson trick from her mom. But she couldn't stop treating the situation as though it were real, as though Constance had stepped out of her family genealogy and into Liz's life.

Crazy, she told herself again as she felt Constance tense behind her when the scooter started. This whole thing was crazy.

"You should keep your eyes closed and your head down, no matter what you hear. Just keep your eyes closed!" Liz said over the whine of the engine. She pulled back the throttle and eased the scooter forward. Constance held on tighter but had her head tucked into Liz's shoulders as instructed. At least she knew how to do what she was told.

It wasn't long before they were parking the scooter on the cement RV pad next to the garage. Once Liz turned the scooter off, Constance loosened her grip but didn't let go.

She twisted her head back and forth staring from one thing to another, then looking up to view the top of the house. "You live here?"

"Yeah. It's home till we stop paying the mortgage. With the divorce, that could be any time now."

"It's lovely," Constance exclaimed.

Liz shrugged. "It's . . ." She couldn't think of what it was. It *was* a nice house. Nicer than most people lived in, but knowing her mom had to work to keep it seemed insane to her. Knowing all the gossip that surrounded the house and knowing that the memories in the house weren't all that good to begin with made her mom's job to keep the house that much more ridiculous. They should just move. It would be better to live where no one knew them and no one bothered them in church asking if they needed anything.

It wasn't like her dad was dead. For Pete's sake, he only lived a mile down the road. If they needed anything, they could call him. But that wasn't right either. Why would he care if they needed anything? The neighbors understanding that he *wouldn't* care hurt as much as the fact that he didn't.

"We should go in." Liz pulled Constance's arm. She almost had to drag her inside through the side garage door.

The only sound in the house came from the hum of the refrigerator. Only then did she take a breath of relief. *Mom's not up yet.* Liz checked the clock on the microwave. The aqua digital numbers declared the time to be 6:09 in the morning. "Safe," Liz murmured, settling onto a barstool at the island. She rested her forehead against the cool granite tile and twisted a little so she could peek at her guest.

Constance did a slow circle as she took everything in. She touched the digital numbers on the microwave. Constance spun suddenly, making Liz sit up straight. "Have I died?"

"I don't think so."

"Then what?"

"What do you mean, *what?*"

"What has happened to me? Where am I? What is all *this?*" Constance raised her hands to the air.

Liz spoke slowly, still hoping this was a joke, but her heart pounded with the knowledge that, though something weird was happening, it was a *real* something weird. "You're in the—future. 1852 was like a gazillion years ago . . . okay, not a gazillion, but long enough ago that it may as well be a gazillion."

Constance's green eyes widened. "You're lying!"

She said it so loud that Liz jumped to her feet making shushing sounds and doing everything but sticking her hand over Constance's mouth. "You're going to wake everybody!"

CHAPTER 4

CONSTANCE PACED WITH ENERGY. "I'M dreaming. This is all a nightmare. I am dreaming . . . dreaming . . . DREAMING!"

She shouted the last word, making Liz wave her arms while hissing, "SSSSSHHHHHHH!"

Constance squeezed her eyes shut and, using both hands, pinched both of her own cheeks so hard that Liz winced just watching. When she opened her eyes again, she glared at Liz. "Disappear! You're like some wretched phantom!"

Liz had to get control over the situation or the whole family would be awake. She didn't want to tell her mom she spent the night in Sassy's stable.

"Sit down," Liz whispered and pulled out a barstool for Constance. Constance sat.

"Look, I don't know how you got here any more than you do. I admit I'm freaked too, but waking up my entire family *isn't* going to help." Liz felt good about her ability to take charge. As the oldest, she'd had years of practice bossing her brothers and sister around.

"What country am I in?" Constance asked after a moment.

"The United States. Utah."

Constance shook her head. "Utah?"

"It's a state. We're part of the United States of America, you know like Connecticut or Ohio."

"I do not understand."

Liz didn't understand either. She almost wanted to believe she had a visitor from the past. But logic and skepticism kept coming back every time she felt she had successfully pushed them away. "What year were you born?"

"In the year 1832."

Liz tried to keep her features neutral. She had no idea when her great-great-way-back-there grandmother had been born. Her mom was into all that stuff, and Liz never paid much attention.

"This is a nightmare! You're not real!"

"I'm real," Liz said, wondering if duct tape would work to keep her from shouting like that.

"This is not real!" Constance said.

"It's real enough. Look, I'll prove it to you." Liz grabbed Constance's arm and led her to the TV. She flipped it on with the remote and then flipped it off again, remembering that her mom had gotten rid of the satellite last month to save money. No CNN.

In the flash when the TV was on, Constance jumped. "What was that?"

"TV."

"Make it happen again."

Exasperated, Liz handed her the remote. "You make it happen. Push this button here."

Constance closed one eye and held the remote out like she was aiming a gun and, with a whole lot more fanfare than Liz thought the situation was worth, she pressed the button.

When it came on and stayed on, Liz realized it was too loud and swiped the remote from Constance's hand to turn the volume down.

Constance approached the TV, her fingers almost but not quite touching the screen. "It's like a bewitched painting," she breathed.

Liz looked at the cartoon, silently moving across the screen, and shrugged. "It's a cartoon."

"This proves nothing to me." Constance straightened and folded her arms across her chest.

"Okay, fine." Liz grabbed Constance by the arm again and dragged her to the entry hall at the front door. "Stay here."

Liz quietly exited the house and stared at her empty porch. She tsked. Her mom had stopped taking the paper to save money as well. She took a deep breath and did something she'd never do under normal circumstances. She crossed the lawn to the Mitchells' house and stole the paper from their front porch. She hurried back in case anyone was awake and watching her crime, silently vowing in her heart that she'd replace the paper in a minute.

Ripping the elastic off and letting the paper unfurl, Liz held it out and pointed directly at the date. "There! See! That should be proof that I'm not lying."

Constance took the paper from Liz's hands, her own shaking. "But . . . no. No!" She tried to force the paper back on Liz as she started yelling again. "No, I tell you!"

"Lizzie?" Her mother's voice came from upstairs.

"Brilliant." Liz really wanted to throttle Constance. Even though she had wanted her mom to sort this out when she'd been back at the stables, she felt very reluctant to bring anything up now. "You woke up my mom!" Liz grabbed Constance again and half dragged her up the stairs. She felt the tight muscles in Constance's arm and knew that if Constance hadn't been so confused, she could probably have beaten Liz up.

Grateful Constance was in a bit of a daze, Liz pushed open her bedroom door, pushed Constance through, and shoved it closed with her foot. She circled the room, thinking of what to do next.

She heard her mom's door open and click shut again, followed by her mother's slippered feet whispering as she shuffled down the hall. Liz was out of time. "Closet!" she said and shoved Constance that direction. She chided herself for the entire situation. Why she brought this girl home, she couldn't say. Why she didn't run and tell her mom what was going on defied all common sense, and yet there she was—stuffing a girl dressed for a 24th of July parade in her closet.

Liz had time to hiss, "Stay quiet," before shutting the door as her mom knocked. Liz crossed the room and opened the door, attempting a smile. "What's up?"

"You're the one that's up." Her mom wrinkled her brow as she tried to peer around Liz's shoulder. "What's going on?"

"Nothing." Liz shrugged.

"When did you finally come home?"

"What?" The blood drained from Liz's face in a way that made her feel the numbing shock of being caught doing something wrong.

"You think I didn't know you were out? I'm not dumb. I called Alton last night. When he said the scooter was parked by Sassy's stall, I stopped worrying."

"You aren't mad?"

"Of course I'm mad! You sneaked out in the middle of the night, and you told your dad about me getting a job!"

Liz froze. "How did you know?"

"I called him first when I realized you were gone. Liz, what I do is my business and not his. The last thing I need right now is a lecture on the importance of staying home by a man who couldn't." Her mom wasn't shouting or even talking very loud, but Liz felt as though she'd been screamed at.

"I'm sorry, Mom," Liz whispered.

Clair's shoulders sagged. "Me too. I'm sorry for all of this. I know you needed time to cool off and figured you were safe at the stables. Are you cooled off?"

Liz nodded.

"Can I depend on you to help me with this?"

Liz nodded again. Her mom reached over and hugged her. "I am sorry, baby." Her mom's voice was strained. "This isn't easy for any of us." When her mom pulled away, she ran her fingers through her hair and moved to rest her hand on her necklace. "But we'll survive it. We come from a long line of survivors who would probably laugh at the things we find difficult."

Her mom took a deep breath. "Can you keep it down for another half hour so the kids don't wake up? You know what a bear Nathan is when he gets up too early."

Liz nodded again, casting a glance toward her closet where, luckily, Constance stayed quiet. Clair shuffled back to her room and closed the door behind her.

Liz breathed a sigh of relief and closed her own door again, taking care to lock it. She'd begged her mom to get her the lock to keep Matt out. There were rules about the lock. She could only keep it locked when getting ready or when leaving for an overnight trip. It was never allowed to be locked when friends were over, though those occasions never came up anymore. Whatever the rules were, Liz was grateful for the lock at that exact moment.

When she opened the closet, a tear-streaked face met hers.

"I remained silent as you requested. Now please help me. I must return to the wagons."

Liz led her to the bed and sat Constance down. She sat next to her. "What's the last thing you remember doing when you were wherever you're trying to get back to?"

Constance gulped. "I . . . I was praying, and then I fell asleep."

"Me too," Liz whispered. A chill shivered up her spine. "Before I ran into you. Prayed and fell asleep." She had no idea what the coincidence meant, but it felt significant. It was all just so surreal. "What's your mom's name?"

"Julia Miles."

"Your father?"

"Henry Miles."

She felt no familiarity in those names. "Do you know who I am?" Liz asked. Fear edged her own voice. Fear of whatever Constance might tell her about herself.

"I cannot remember your name. Did you say were Stephen King's daughter?"

Liz smiled. "Nope. Not even a distant cousin. My name is Eliza."

Liz watched Constance to see if that meant anything to her.

CHAPTER 5

CONSTANCE FELT HER HEART TIGHTEN. Eliza. *My daughter is named Eliza*. What was happening to her small daughter now? Did the company move on without her? Would Lynnette take over the care of her daughter? She hoped so. Of all the women she had known and befriended since leaving England, Lynnette was the only one she trusted enough to raise her daughter well. And William. *Dearest William . . .* she thought. *I am farther from you today than I have ever been*. She felt the tears falling down her cheeks again but tried not to give in to the racking sobs. She had never cried so much in her life as she had these past few days. It shamed her to show such weakness. She could not truly trust this girl named Eliza. In the first place, the girl dressed like a boy. In the second . . . well, there were too many seconds to count.

But the girl *looked* like her. The eyes and the hair. And then there was her name . . . Eliza . . . "My daughter is named Eliza." Constance heard her voice crack.

"I was named after my fourth great-grandmother," Eliza said. "But nobody calls me that. People call me Liz."

Constance didn't want to form this new acquaintance. She wanted to be with her family. "I am afraid, Liz." Constance felt sick to appear so weak.

"I know. I'm sorry."

"How did this happen?"

Liz bit her lip and shrugged. Constance straightened her own shoulders as she watched the girl slouch. "I have no idea how to help you . . . you know . . . return."

"Did you bring me here?"

Liz blew out a long breath. "I don't think so. I didn't do anything. I was just praying too. I swear that's all."

"Are you a witch?"

The girl, Liz, rolled her eyes, going from empathy to impudence in the space of an eye blink. "Do you really think witches pray? And you believe in witches?"

"My mother did. My sensibilities have always swayed toward logic. However, I have found myself in a situation so wholly dissatisfying and void of all logic that I cannot help but ponder what I believed prior to this moment."

"O-kay," Liz said slowly, drawing out the O.

What could the girl mean by "okay"?

Logic. Where was logic to be found in this house so full of foreign *things*? "So you say I have come forward in time. Why?"

"Why?"

"For what purpose would I be involved in such a—journey?"

Liz shrugged. "Maybe you're an answer to a prayer."

The comment gave Constance a jolt. *Maybe the answer to a prayer . . . but whose prayer was getting answered?* "What will become of my family?"

"I don't know—" A knock sounded at the door. "What?" Liz called out.

"Lizzie, can I come in?" a young voice called out; whether male or female, Constance couldn't say.

"No!" Liz yelled loud enough to make Constance jump. "Just my brother," Liz said as if that explained everything. "Look, I gotta help the kids get ready for school."

Liz wasn't going to help her? She seemed to be shrugging off any responsibility to find a solution. "I need to get back to my daughter!" Constance stood and crossed her arms over her chest.

Liz's eyebrows climbed her forehead. "How old are you anyway? You look like you're my age, and it's creeping me out to hear you talk about having kids. That's just not normal."

"I am twenty on my next birthday. I married later than some but am perfectly normal aside from that." If anything, Constance believed herself to be the only normal thing in her current circumstance.

"So you're nineteen?"

"Yes."

"Then why not just say that?" Liz shook her head.

Constance stared. "I did just say that!" Of all the impertinent, wildly disrespectful—

More thumping at the door. "Who you talking to? Let me in! Lizzie? Let me in!"

"Go away, Matt!"

"Mom said you had to come downstairs," the voice from behind the door whined.

"I'm coming." Liz looked at Constance as she said it. Constance understood the look.

"I will not leave nor will I make any noise. But you must return immediately."

"Of course I'm coming right back," Liz said and let herself out of the door without opening it wide enough for anyone to peek in.

Constance covered her face with her hands. How did she get here? She took deep, calming breaths, anything to keep herself from screaming. She paced the room, trying hard to remember her manners and not touch anything. But there were so many things that looked foreign enough to merit the desire to touch, and she found herself running her fingers along many different objects. There was a box like the one downstairs, only much smaller, but there were no moving pictures on this one. There were unframed pictures of horses, of all things, pinned to the walls. Cloth animals, made with a finer workmanship than any of the toys she had played with as a child, sat on shelves. There were trinkets and baubles and a quilt made of fabric so fine that Constance almost felt envious.

But with every *thing* there was to touch, it was the window that commanded her attention. She crept forward almost fearing what she might see outside. She'd been out there only moments before, but she had gathered her wits a bit since then, and she now had the proper frame of mind to know she *should* fear whatever she saw.

She parted the curtain carefully and looked onto the street below. Carriages with no horses transported people up and down a road that looked smoother and more perfect than any she had ever seen. Green court-yards and colorful flower beds adorned every home. None of the endless fields and dusty trails to be found anywhere. The world seemed absurdly false without the scenery she was accustomed to seeing. Each home looked incredibly large compared to any she'd seen since her arrival to America, and she felt a pang of regret at the loss of her home in England . . .

"No," she said aloud, "I will think on that no more." But it did not stop a new supply of tears. She fell to her knees and started praying. If this outrageous occurrence had started with a prayer, she could end it with a prayer. She begged to return to her own time, to her child, to her life, but the heavens remained quiet. She remembered feeling a surge of peace the night before as she had ended her prayer and drifted off to sleep. Peace in the embrace of a warm mist. And she remembered feeling that the peace was misplaced since every utterance from her mouth smacked of contempt and borderline blasphemy. This was certainly not what she had anticipated awakening to.

And now there was no peace to be had. "Was the feeling before little more than a cruel trick?" she asked aloud, feeling betrayed to find herself in her present condition.

What could she do? What *should* she do? She should go back to the stable where the horses were. Go back to the very place she awoke, and somehow the nightmare would end. She'd make it end. All she had to do was convince this insolent Liz girl to return her to that place.

There was the chance that Liz would refuse, however unlikely. It would be best to have a full plan for all circumstances. She stood and peeked out the window again, trying to get a bearing on her direction. She had no idea where they'd been that morning. She had closed her eyes as Liz instructed while riding the . . . whatever *that* was.

The voices from downstairs were noisy, sounding like unloosed chaos. She wondered about that. How was it Liz felt so bold as to speak to her mother with such abruptness? There had only been one time in her life where she had spoken to her mother that way, and the consequences had been . . . unpleasant.

"No," she chided herself. "I will think on it no more." But she did think on it, and the questions from her prayer the night before repeated in her mind: *What more can you expect from me, Lord? After all I've given and lost, what more do you want?* She knew it was wrong, and likely an outright sin, to think such thoughts, and yet she still harbored those thoughts when Liz finally returned.

CHAPTER 6

LIZ FELT SADDER THAN SHE'D ever felt. Watching her mom pull out of the driveway to enter the workforce was something she didn't feel prepared for. They had family prayer, her mom said she had to leave a few hours early to run errands, and then she was just . . . gone. Liz was so distracted by the displacement she felt toward her family she'd almost forgotten that Constance still hid in her room. When Liz finally made it back to her room, Constance looked horribly depressed. Liz sat on her bed and hugged a pillow to her chest. She felt depressed too.

"So now what do we do?" Constance ventured after a moment.

"The other kids have gone to school. My school doesn't start 'til tomorrow. It's totally stupid to start the first day of school on a Tuesday, but the administration isn't filled with the sharpest tools in the shed."

When Constance blinked at her, Liz sighed. "You know what that is, right? I mean, you'd have to know what school is."

"I know what school is."

Did Liz imagine that stuck-up tone? Before she could think of a retort, Constance walked out the door.

"Hey! Hey, where you going?" Liz jumped off the bed and darted after her. She was almost halfway down the stairs before Liz caught up to her.

"I need to return to your stables to find my way back home."

"What? You think that hanging out with my horse is going to get you home?" Not that Liz was against the idea . . . any chance she had to be with Sassy was a good thing. It just seemed a little weird, but no weirder than an ancestral visitation.

"I think that we should both return to the place of action and both pray as we did before. Then maybe the effects of this . . . situation will be reversed. You'll be rid of me, and I'll—" She straightened her shoulders in a way that reminded Liz of corsets. "I'll be home."

"Fine. Let's go, then." Liz opened the front door and walked smack into Garrett Mitchell from next door. "Garrett!" she said, pushing her hair out of her eyes while looking away.

Garrett didn't seem to notice that she wasn't willing to meet his eyes. He smiled. "Hey, Liz." He grinned outright at Constance. "This your cousin?"

"Yes," Liz said at the same time Constance said no.

His smile quirked to the side. "So . . . which is it?"

"Neither—look, we gotta go." She tried to pass him, but he didn't move out of her way. Liz glared at him. "Seriously."

"Where you going? Pioneer trek?"

"Right. Pioneer trek. Now we need to get going."

He still didn't move. "I need a favor first."

Liz rolled her eyes. "What?"

"I need our newspaper back."

Liz felt her stomach drop into her toes. Her face warmed to the temperature of the sun's surface. "Your paper?"

"Yeah, the one you took off our porch this morning."

"How did you . . . I . . ."

"Don't sweat it. It's no big deal. I saw you sneaking back to your house with it, and while I never picked you for a thief, it made for some good entertainment. But the entertainment's over. Dad'll freak if he doesn't read the paper with his breakfast. You can have it back when he's done."

Liz wanted to disappear. "I was going to give it back; I just needed to borrow it for a minute."

"You *stole* his property?" Constance's tone carried a definite sense of scandal.

Garrett stopped leaning on the doorframe and looked at Constance. "You from England?"

"Yes," she said.

"Cool. Foreign exchange student?"

"She's just staying here for a while," Liz interjected before Constance said anything crazy about being warped here from the past.

Garrett shrugged. "So, about that paper . . ."

"Right. I'll go get it." She winced when she realized that both Constance and Garrett had followed her back into the house.

"Where'd the piano go?" Garrett asked.

Liz looked away to mask her surprise that he remembered there had ever been a piano. He hadn't been in the King home for years. "Mom sold it." She didn't explain why, and he didn't ask, though she felt pretty sure he knew why. Her mom had sold it because a Steinway baby grand in that great of shape and quality fetched a good price.

"So things not going so well?"

"Things are fine. We're fine." Liz felt indignant that she had to parrot the phrase yet again. What business of his was it how things were going?

His smile softened. He was trying to be nice, but it bugged Liz a lot that he knew the truth about their lives. He knew everything—from the scandal to the divorce and right down to their finances. The only way Liz could find to react to her irritation was to react badly. She grabbed the paper and pushed it into his chest. "There. I'm sorry, and it won't happen again."

"Hey, whoa! Lizzie, I didn't mean—"

"Don't call me Lizzie. Just leave. Please."

His face flashed a momentary look of hurt. Liz wondered if that had been her imagination then figured it must have been, because she knew there was no way Garrett Mitchell would ever care how she felt about anything. He certainly wouldn't be worried about her kicking him out of her house. He hadn't cared the last time she'd done it a few years back.

Liz had been through a lot of best friends in this neighborhood. But they all left her, not the other way around. It started with the tension in her family. Friends would come over and stay for dinner. When her dad started griping about things and the tension at the dinner table mounted, they all found things they had to do. Liz couldn't blame them. Why would anyone want to hang out at a house where so much contention dwelled? Garrett and Becky had lasted the longest of her friends. Garrett was the cool basketball player who'd sold out—he'd traded his brain for sneakers and cheerleaders. And Becky was the cheerleader Liz got traded for.

She turned on her heel and stomped to the front door. She didn't bother waiting for him. He knew how to shut a door.

When she went out to where the scooter was supposed to be, she found the spot empty. There was a note duct-taped on the garage wall: "You said you'd stay home, Lizzie." A smiley face and a heart and the word *Mom* ended it.

"Great." Liz tore the note off the wall, leaving a chunk of duct tape.

"What's the matter?" Constance asked.

"The scooter's gone. We aren't going anywhere."

"Need a ride?" Garrett hadn't gone home as Liz had hoped he would but had followed them to the side of the garage.

"No." Liz stiffened.

"You look like you need a ride," he said.

"Well, I don't."

"Don't be proud," Constance murmured. She turned to Garrett, all smiles and cordiality. "We would very much appreciate your help."

"Okay. Just let me get the paper to my dad and borrow the keys. I'll be back in a minute." And then he was off, trotting across the joining lawns to his own house.

"Why would you want him along?" Liz asked as soon as he was out of earshot.

Constance seemed bewildered by the question. "He has offered us an escort. I hardly think that arguing with him as you do is the best way to recommend yourself to a prospective suitor."

"A prospective suitor? Are you kidding? He's hardly a prospective anything except a *witness*. If he sees you disappear into the past, he'll think *I'm* crazy!"

"But if he can help us—"

"What's he going to say when I leave you at the stables and come home alone?"

"Tell him I have my own home. That way, you speak the truth without revealing irrelevant information."

Liz blew out a long breath. "I just don't like Garrett." She knew it was pointless to keep arguing about it. They *did* need a ride and he *was* willing to give them one.

"Why would you not like him? His temper seems perfectly amiable."

"He's a . . . jock."

"Then you should approve, as you seem fond of horses."

Liz couldn't believe how everything she said was turned to mean something else. "No, not a *jockey*, a *jock*—a guy into sports and cheerleaders."

"I do not understand."

"Never mind, forget it. Let's just get this over with." Liz watched as Garrett backed out of his garage. She hurried to his driveway so he wouldn't have to be obligated to pick them up.

She got in front after settling Constance in the backseat with a seat belt. "Don't say anything at all. If you get nervous, close your eyes." She whispered the instructions, but her way-back-there grandmother didn't seem to be listening since she was gawking at every new thing she saw.

"And what do you call this we're riding in?"

"It's a car," Liz said, covering her eyes with her hands.

"Look how they're everywhere!" Constance pointed out the window.

Garrett seemed amused by his passenger. "What part of England are you from that they don't have cars?"

"They ride bikes where she lives," Liz interrupted as Constance was about to respond.

"I am from Stratford-upon-Avon, Warwickshire, England."

"Really? Isn't that the birthplace of William Shakespeare?" Garrett asked.

"Yes, it is!" Constance seemed delighted to have someone know this. Liz certainly didn't know. "Have you been there?"

"Nah. I haven't really been anywhere."

"England is beautiful. My father owned many estates there, and though we lived quite well, it is nothing compared to what I have seen here."

"Yeah, Americans are spoiled, I guess. Not that I mind." He turned and winked.

Liz glared at the sight of him winking and speaking so casually to her. Well . . . maybe not to *her* exactly, but in her presence. He acted like she and Constance were part of those cheerleaders who were always hanging on him. Liz certainly didn't want to be treated like one of them.

Constance interrupted Liz's thoughts. "See how smooth your roads are, not the bumps and jostles one gets from a carriage on cobblestone. And certainly not the ruts and mud of the trails."

Garrett laughed. "You must come from one of those older villages."

Liz rolled her eyes. "You have no idea."

"What's up with the dress? You doing a play or something? Pioneer trek's over." He smirked at Liz. "But it was a nice try to get rid of me."

"How would you know about pioneer trek?" Liz asked.

"I went last month. I was the pa. It was really cool. I got to catch a turkey!"

Liz raised an eyebrow at that.

He ignored her look of disbelief. "The handcart was a lot harder to pull than I thought. I felt like my arms were going to fall off."

"Handcart?" Constance tried to scoot forward on her seat and frowned at the seat belt for holding her in place.

"Yeah. It was a great experience. I'd suggest everyone go on it. Why didn't you go, Liz?"

"I had a competition."

"Right, your horse. I almost forgot about that." He pulled out of the neighborhood and onto the main roads where he picked up speed. "Mind if we listen to some music?" he asked as he flipped the radio on.

The music certainly wasn't anything Liz would think twice about. It was even tame by her mother's standards, and her mom was a first-rate prude, but Constance seemed horrified by it. She clapped her hands over her ears, her eyes wide enough to be airplane hangars.

When Garrett shifted to take a look at what Constance was melting down about, Liz turned the radio off. "Inner ear disease," she whispered in case Constance decided to refute the lie. "She can't take certain levels of sounds. Radios are tough on her."

"Weird." Garrett shrugged his shoulders and sped up to keep up with traffic.

With the increase of speed, Constance flattened herself as much as she could into the backseat. "I fear I am feeling a bit unwell."

When Liz turned to look at her, she could see that Constance did indeed look ill. "Do we need to pull over?"

"I feel as though I were again on the boat coming to America." She finally took Liz's advice and closed her eyes.

"You took a cruise to America?" Garrett whistled low as he glanced at her in his rearview mirror. "I would so love to take a cruise! I heard they feed you all day long, even all night if you want to. I could so totally handle that."

Constance didn't respond, just pressed herself further into the seat.

"So tell me more about your horse." Garrett glanced at Liz. "Did you win the race?"

"I took second." Liz couldn't keep the bitterness out of her voice. She hated that she took second.

When they pulled up to the stables, Liz wanted a way to apologize for her earlier behavior without sounding like a chump.

"Thanks for the ride," she said.

"No problem. Will you be very long?" Garrett asked.

"Yes. Probably. We'll be a long time," Liz replied.

"Man, I can't really stay. I told my dad I'd only be a minute. Will you be okay to get home?"

"I can call my mom. Thanks again. Sorry about earlier. I guess I'm just a little hypersensitive about things right now."

"Don't you worry about it. *I'm* not going to."

Liz tried to smile at him, but the smile felt goofy, and she finally just shut the car door.

CHAPTER 7

"THAT WAS THE WEIRDEST THING in the world." Liz grimaced at Constance. "Even weirder than you."

"I found him very pleasant."

"Yeah . . . he used to be. We were friends in elementary school and even a little in junior high, but then . . . you know. Life happens."

"Yes . . . it certainly does." Constance's eyes shimmered with a sheen of tears, but she shook herself and straightened. "Where do we go from here?"

"Where were you when you woke up?"

Constance scanned the stables and the exercise ring. "I was a bit disoriented, so it's difficult to say . . ."

"Let's go back to where I ran into you. You might be able to better guess from there."

They rounded the first set of stables to the back where Sassy's stall was. "This is where I knocked you over." Liz pointed to the ground.

Constance pivoted as if trying to get her bearings before she brightened and started off at a quick pace. She passed Sassy's stable and the large silver maple that shivered slightly in the summer breeze. She stopped when she reached a little lean-to with hay under it. "I was there." She looked back at Liz, her eyes fearful. "What must I do?"

"How would I know? I've never time-traveled before. Try sitting down."

Constance hurried to comply, arranging her skirts around her legs, her back erect, looking like the queen of the farm people.

Nothing happened.

"Maybe we should say a prayer again." Liz folded her arms, and Constance quickly followed the example.

They both closed their eyes. Liz waited for Constance to say the prayer. After a moment of silence, Liz peeked out from under her eyelashes to see that Constance was staring out at her. Exasperated, Liz rolled her eyes. "Well?"

"I assumed you would offer the prayer." Constance's folded arms looked more like a mother about to give a scolding than they did a token of reverence.

"You're the one who wants to go back; you say it." Liz had no idea what kind of prayer to offer and was terrified to say the wrong thing.

Constance frowned but nodded and closed her eyes again. Liz did too. The prayer was sweet, yet pleading. Liz felt to her very bones that Constance had a far greater strength in testimony than she did. The faith that God would return her to her daughter and continue to bless her husband struck Liz so deeply that she almost fell to her knees.

The prayer lasted a long time, but it wasn't like those prayers where you wanted the guy at the podium to stop thanking and blessing and just get on with it so you could get home, kick off your shoes, and eat your dinner. When Liz echoed, "Amen," she really meant it. Liz only ever had that feeling with prayer when she was really paying attention to the sacrament prayer. And it had been a long time since Liz had paid any attention to the sacrament.

Liz kept her eyes closed for a moment, nervous about opening them to find Constance gone. Everything had happened so fast from the moment she knocked Constance over that Liz hadn't really taken the time to comprehend the magnitude of what it meant to have Constance here. Liz was struck with a sudden worry that Constance might go away before she had time to talk to her and ask her questions. Liz could've kicked herself for letting the precious moments slip by without asking Constance about the life she lived.

Finally curiosity won out over the fear, and she peeked through one eyelid. Constance was still sitting, erect and regal, aside from her face scrunched up and her eyes clenched tightly. Her face finally relaxed into the smooth lines of calm serenity. And with a deep breath and a small smile playing over her lips, she opened both her eyes. And then she immediately frowned. "I'm still here!"

Liz shrugged apologetically. "Sorry." She felt insensitive for feeling relief that Constance *was* still there.

Constance lifted her skirts to get on her feet again. "But how could that be? How is it possible that I'm here in the first place?"

Constance's glare intimated that she somehow felt like this was Liz's fault.

"I felt such peace when I prayed. It was as though someone whispered on the wind that I was where I needed to be." She raised her hands and shook her fists to the sky. "And yet I am still *here*!"

Liz shuffled her feet and stood there, shrugging her shoulders. Constance continued her tirade, her English accent thicker with the anger. Liz continued shuffling and shrugging and taking steps back in case Constance decided to start throwing punches.

"Maybe I need to be where I was too," Liz finally interrupted. "I'll go back to Sassy's stall, and you stay here. We can try our prayers separately." She jogged over to the second stable where Sassy could be heard whickering from inside. She ran a hand over the horse's nose and gave her a quick hug before kneeling in the hay.

* * *

Once Liz entered the stable where her horse was housed, Constance knelt again. She took a deep breath and began to pray. Warmth exploded in her chest immediately. She felt aware of her own heart beating, aware of the wind on her face, aware of every sound and movement around her. In that moment, she knew her prayer would be answered. The intensity of the warmth and chills colliding up and down her spine was exactly like the time she had prayed about the Book of Mormon.

Giving up her life as a gentleman's daughter—indeed, as the daughter of Henry Miles—would not have been possible had it not been for her very real answer to the truthfulness of the gospel. She pondered the moment of her first real prayer. She remembered the warmth and the voice that came so clearly to her mind, that all else in the world mattered not, so long as she followed the precepts of the gospel of Jesus Christ.

Now as Constance prayed, the same power fell upon her, and she did not doubt whence the power came. She felt, were she to open her eyes, the heavens would be opened to her, but she kept her eyes closed, listening for the instruction that would get her back to her child and husband.

Constance frowned when the instructions came.

She knew as powerfully as she knew the gospel was true that she was not to return . . . not yet. Her lip trembled. "Please, Lord. No," she begged. Tears spilled from her eyes as she argued her answer. But the answer did not change.

Fear overwhelmed her. Fear that she might never return. There had been no promise of a return, only the promise of necessity for her presence here in a world so foreign to anything she'd known.

Feeling very ill-used and a bit sullen, if not angry, she stood and brushed the loose strands of hair from her eyes. She looked heavenward and shook her head. She was to stay in this future time and help the family of this Liz girl. She was to help them . . . to do what, she did not know; for how long, she could not say. Constance sighed. Of all the predicaments she'd been in, this was by far the most jarring. She would stay, not that she had a choice, but she'd try to mend this girl and this girl's family and accomplish the task quickly in the hopes of returning home.

* * *

Liz stayed dutifully on her knees until she heard the sound of a throat clearing itself. She looked up to see Constance standing forlornly in front of Sassy.

Constance scratched the horse behind the ears as she kept her gaze down and said, "I'll not be leaving. It seems I must be here for some duration. A day, perhaps . . . or longer."

Liz was intrigued. Did Constance have a vision? If she had, Liz was sorry she'd missed it. "Did someone tell you that?"

"Not in words—not exactly. But yes." Constance slumped against the stall door. "What if the company moves on without my husband? Who will care for Eliza?"

"She'll be taken care of," Liz said.

"You cannot know that." Constance's voice quivered with the sob she held back.

"I do know that, because if she doesn't get taken care of, she won't survive and have kids, who have kids, who have kids, and I wouldn't even be here."

Constance shook her head. "You cannot know such a thing. You cannot promise such a thing."

"Yes I can. She's my fourth great-grandmother. The one I was named after."

"That's ridiculous."

Liz shrugged, feeling like she'd done a lot of shrugging since meeting Constance. "Not really. My mom's a genealogy zealot. I know my pioneer ancestry . . . well, sort of."

"That makes *me* your fifth great-grandmother."

"Exactly."

"Absurdity."

"It isn't absurd. Look how much we look alike." It offended Liz that Constance looked so chafed by having to claim a bloodline with her.

Sassy twitched her tail and blinked at the pair of them debating and then let out a whinny that sounded like a chuckle.

"I agree with your horse. It's impossible," Constance pressed. She slumped down onto the ground as though her legs had been cut from under her. "This entire situation is impossible . . . but . . ." She straightened. "Why else to come here if not to help my own posterity?" She eyed Liz suspiciously now. "What's the matter with you?"

"What do you mean, what's the matter with me? What's the matter with *you?*"

"Don't get saucy, girl. You summoned me here because you are in trouble of sorts and need help. As soon as we solve your problem, I can leave and find my husband and take care of my child." She stood again.

"Nothing's wrong with me! I don't need your help, and don't go calling me girl. You aren't any older than I am. Well . . . not technically."

"Hey there, Lizzie!" Alton Henderson, the stable owner called out. He was an older guy who looked like the last real cowboy. He always wore chaps and boots and a cowboy hat. Liz used to think he did it for show to make his business seem more real, but after getting to know him, she realized he did it because he really believed he was the last cowboy in the world.

"Alton." She sketched a glance at Constance, who straightened her shoulders and glared at Liz.

"Your mom says I'm to tell you I won't allow you to take up room and board with Sassy." He grinned, his leather skin folding into itself with the motion.

Liz tried to smile back. "I'll try to remember that."

"I didn't know you had a twin sister." He nodded to Constance, who bowed her head in form of greeting. *Did she curtsy?*

"She's not my sister, just a distant relative."

"Funny, you could pass for sisters . . . I got some new sprays in the Big Barn for you to take a look at. UltraShield has a guarantee that seems hard to beat. The flies are worse this season than I've ever seen 'em. You wouldn't always have to keep the blankets on her."

"The spray we're using seems okay, but I'll check on it." Liz had been using the blankets more and the sprays less to try to cut back on costs. Foregoing the use of the sprays felt neglectful, but she kept the stall cleaner than ever to try to make up for it.

"Good. Well, you girls behave. And don't go worrying your mother."

"I won't."

When he left, the silence settled between the two girls like a chasm.

"I'm sorry," Liz said finally. "I really am. We'll get you back. I promise." Liz wondered how big of a lie she was telling. She had no idea how to get Constance back.

"We should return to your home," Constance said.

"Let me exercise Sassy first. I don't want her to feel like I'm neglecting her. Plus, we'll need to call a ride. It's a long walk home."

"How far?"

"Two miles . . . maybe three."

"That's an easy enough distance to walk in such fine weather."

Liz raised a brow at that comment as she ran an eye over Constance. Liz didn't doubt for a minute Constance would enjoy walking three miles.

"Yeah . . . easy. Whatever."

Liz adjusted the girth and bridled Sassy, making a few minor adjustments while Constance watched. "She's a lovely animal," Constance said finally.

"She definitely is. Her pedigree is more impressive than the Queen of England's. She's not only beautiful, but nice too. She's my best friend in the world." Liz said it before realizing how lame it sounded and instantly wished she hadn't.

"Aren't there many girls around? With all those houses, there should be someone—"

"Well, there isn't anyone. At least, not anyone worth knowing. They all worry about boys and clothes and cheerleading. I can't stand any of them."

"Then what about suitors? Surely you have suitors. There's that Mr. Mitchell who brought us here. He seems kind."

"Sure, he's kind. But he also prefers to hang out with the cheer-leaders, who only care about boys and clothes. Kind isn't everything, you know."

Constance fell silent, and Liz was glad. She mounted up. "I'll be back in a few minutes. Just stay here. Or maybe stay in Sassy's stall so no one bugs you." Once Liz had Constance's assurance that she'd stay put, Liz clucked her tongue and gave a barely perceptible dig of her heels into the animal's flank. She was off, leaving Constance alone.

CHAPTER 8

CONSTANCE STARED AFTER LIZ AND finally backed up again under the shade of the stable. How was it possible she'd come forward in time to see her own posterity? Liz was a determined girl, certainly a bit like Constance herself had been before joining the Church and coming to America. But Liz was old enough to have settled a little or to at least be looking toward settling. She seemed decidedly displeased with her life and situation.

After pondering Liz and the situation, and the eyes—those eyes so much like her own—she concluded that Liz was definitely her fifth great-granddaughter, or however many generations may have passed, though it galled Constance to find a member of her posterity with a wildness and independence that was altogether shocking. *Could any of my posterity be truly so arrogant? So wholly without decorum when addressing a male?* Perhaps that was Constance's mission in coming here . . . perhaps she was to find Liz a proper suitor.

That would be a terrible task indeed, considering how roughly Liz acted around the opposite sex. Dressing like one of them would have to be put to a stop. There was simply nothing feminine about the girl. Constance wondered if that was something that could be changed as she inspected the tack closet Liz had left open. It was organized, and the equipment looked well cared for. It seemed a pity her fifth great-granddaughter didn't spend so much care on her own person as she did on her animal.

After Liz returned and curried down the horse, neatly stowing her tack in the closet, she hunted Alton down to borrow something Liz called a phone. Constance watched with mild interest as he handed Liz a small metallic object that fit neatly in her palm. Liz pushed her fingertips to the device and then began speaking into it. Baffled, Constance edged closer. A tinny voice came from the device. She quickly backed away.

When Liz handed the item back to Alton, she turned to Constance. "Looks like you get your wish. Dad won't come get me, and I can't call my mom, or she'll pitch a fit for me leaving the house. We're walking. And we'd better hurry so we're home before the kids are. They'll tell on me if they come home to an empty house."

Constance turned back to look toward the stables. "If it's so much trouble for you to walk, why don't we take the horse?"

Alton chuckled as though Constance had made a joke. Liz grimaced and said, "It's no trouble to walk. We'll be fine."

Liz thanked Alton for his phone and started walking. Constance fell into step beside her.

Liz stepped down over the curb onto the black road. A blaring more deafening than anything Constance had ever heard shrilled through the air. She grabbed at Liz's arm.

Both girls jumped back as a truck driver glared at them for getting in his way.

"Stupid driver," Liz muttered as she glared right back. "Watch where you're going!" she shouted after he'd made his turn.

"What was that noise?"

"He just honked his horn at us to be a creep. He could've waited 'til we were past."

Constance felt utterly astonished that something so terrifying could be treated as if it were nothing at all. Her heart still pounded so violently she felt as though she'd been running. Constance worried this future would be far more than she could handle.

* * *

Liz stole a peek at Constance every few moments as they walked. It had to be hot under that huge dress, but Constance didn't show any signs of discomfort.

Liz tried to keep her own breathing even and tried not to swipe at the trickle of sweat at the back of her neck under her hair. "Was it cold where you were?"

"No, the weather was excessively hot except at night when the summer storms came."

Liz felt an immense amount of respect for someone who could tolerate such weather. She was bundling up and whining to her mom to turn the heater on when the temperature outside dipped under seventy degrees. And whining just as loud when the air conditioner didn't work during the summer.

"So what was it like? I mean, really. We hear all about how the pioneers crossed the plains, but what was it like?" Liz rubbed her hand over the back of her neck.

"Wretched, if you must know. To be a part of the wagon companies was a mistake. I should have stayed in England." The bitterness in her voice chilled Liz, in spite of the hot sun drenching over her skin.

"But—"

Constance's eyes flashed. "Do not judge me. You've no idea what it's like to watch people you've grown close to bury a child or a parent. You've no idea what it's like to lose something you cannot replace. It was altogether too much. I never should have come to America."

"But you said you wanted to go back to the wagons."

"Of course I want to go back!" she snapped. "Do you think me devoid of all feeling? My husband is lost, my child unattended. The very things I fear to lose are *there,* and I am here to be a governess to a grand-daughter of my posterity who's old enough to have come out and made herself a suitable match already."

"You're not here as my governess." Liz felt scandalized to her toenails. If she didn't think she'd get slapped right back, she'd have taken a swing at her pioneer ancestor.

"Forgive me. I meant no unkindness." Constance didn't really sound like she was sorry, but Liz let it go. After a few moments of silence, Constance asked, "What is your life like?"

After hearing Constance gripe about crossing the plains, Liz didn't feel much like talking about herself. "My life's fine . . . in comparison. And wait a minute. How can you say it was a mistake to come to America? How can you act like that? Don't you know we sing songs and make movies about the heroic pioneers? Everyone reveres you guys. You're not being a very good example, you know."

"And to whom have I come to be a good example? You're a pampered girl with no inkling of sacrifice or suffering."

"It isn't a sacrifice if you're whining about it." Liz repeated the words of her mom when Liz complained about fasting.

Constance frowned, her lips tightly pressed together. She kicked a worn boot at a small rock, sending it skittering across the road they'd come to.

"I am sorry," she said again, though this time she did sound like she might actually *be* sorry.

"So, what was England like?"

Constance sighed and looked far away as her eyes misted over, making them greener. "Like honey. I was the daughter of a respected gentleman. We didn't have a governess. My mother took joy in spending time with us and teaching us to read and write. She was very intent on all of her children being well educated. She had hair so dark it looked like polished ebony. She was a very proficient musician."

"Did she play the piano?"

"Oh, yes. She went to no party or gathering without being asked to play."

"My mom plays too. So does my sister. They love it."

"Music is a blessing to every home. My father loved to hear her play, though he was gone quite often, overseeing his other estates to be sure they were managed properly. He was a good, strong Christian and much sterner than our mother. We weren't terribly sorry to have him absent as often as he was."

Constance pursed her lips out and shuddered involuntarily. "The only time it seemed I had ever made him happy was when my betrothal was announced to a young man with excellent prospects. Of course, all of that unraveled rather rapidly when I was baptized. Daniel immediately determined not to marry me when he heard. He told me he would pray for my lost soul. Father locked me in my room for several days. Julia, my sister, pinched some food from the kitchen and secreted it up to me so I didn't go hungry. Mother never spoke to me. She never visited me while I was in my room. She placed the family Bible on my dressing table before Father locked the door. That was the last time I saw her."

Liz tried to imagine her own mother acting like that. Even if Liz were to commit the worst sin in the world, she had no doubt her mother would still treat her with love.

"After several days, Father came to release me from my room; he asked if I would go to the priest and confess my sin. He wanted me to publicly denounce the decision I'd made. I refused. He put me out of the house."

"He kicked you out?"

"Yes. He was ashamed of me in every way."

"My dad is a total meathead, but he'd never kick me out." Even as she said the words, Liz wondered if that were true. With Patty in his life, everything was different. He might kick her out if Patty told him to.

Constance merely sighed. "Julia cried and begged him not to. But Mother was nowhere to be seen. Julia was the only one with any compassion—the only one who ever thought to worry over me. My one and only champion. She found me the next day sheltered in the stables where they kept the plow horses. She brought me some money so I could get a new start. It was quite the scandal for the daughter of a gentleman to be deserving of such treatment by her own family. I couldn't find work and had to travel some distance before I found employment as a teacher to a small boy. Edward was his name."

Liz felt herself growing more horrified by the second. Even though she'd slept in Sassy's stable the previous night, she had done so just to be stubborn, not because anyone was making her. "What did you do then?"

"I found others who had converted and were saving their money to go to America to join the Saints. That was when I met William. We married shortly after meeting." Her eyes grew misty. "He was stable and strong but had a gentleness I'd never seen in a man, and I could not help but love him. We saved our money together, and though we didn't have the luxuries I had grown accustomed to as a child, we managed tolerably well."

Liz stared at this girl, barely older than her, who had lived lifetimes in comparison. She couldn't imagine a life like that, and even though her dad was a snake who didn't care about anyone other than himself, he'd never locked her up for days on end. "Did you ever see your family again? Did you ever get to say good-bye?"

Constance let out a derisive laugh. "Hardly. Julia came to see me off just before the ship set sail to America. She gave me a most precious gift."

"What?"

Constance reached into the neck of her blouse. Her eyes went wide as she clawed at her own neck. "It's gone! My necklace is gone!"

"What necklace?"

Constance searched on the ground as though she'd lost it in that exact instant.

"It's on a silver chain with an emerald stone."

Liz stopped. "An *emerald* necklace? Are you serious?" Could this be the same necklace her mother flashed at her on an almost daily basis?

Constance looked up from the ground, her face a mask of hope. "Do you know where it is? Have you seen it? The filigree work is very ornate around the stone."

The description convinced Liz the necklaces were the same. "Oh, I've seen it. It's our most valued family heirloom. My mom uses it against us all the time as a symbol of the things our family suffered to bring us to America and the gospel. She drives us nuts with that thing, always telling us if our great-great-grandparents could manage all that, then we shouldn't whine about having to do family home evening every week."

Liz snapped her fingers in understanding. "I'll bet it's missing because you're here!"

Constance looked panicked. "Why would my being here make any difference?"

"This morning my mom had her necklace, but don't you see? There is only *one* necklace, and it can't be in two places at once, so when you came forward in time, the necklace didn't have to come. It was already here."

"Are you mad? You're saying the necklace dissolved from my throat to grace the throat of your mother?"

"It didn't dissolve. Her grandma gave it to her." Liz really didn't know if her theory was right or not, but her explanation at least sounded plausible. Her brother, Nathan, always talked about time travel from his science fiction books. He was a first rate nerd. The only real knowledge Liz had about time travel came from watching *Back to the Future*. She very much doubted Doc Brown and the space-time continuum were even close to the truth. "There was supposed to be a matching set of earrings that were lost when you crossed the plains. Gotta be honest— that story's really the only one I've ever paid attention to. Seems kinda cool . . . you know, a lost treasure and everything."

Constance reached her hand up to touch her ear. She then pulled away her hand so Liz could see.

On Constance's earlobe sparkled an oval green stone set into filigreed white gold.

CHAPTER 9

THEY STARED AT EACH OTHER for quite a few minutes before Constance frowned. "I wonder what happens to Mother's earrings. I'd be most unhappy to have them lost. You don't think they were stolen, do you?"

Liz shrugged, trying to think back to anything she'd heard about the earrings. "I don't know. The stories don't say."

Constance nodded and looked away. "William was very supportive when I asked him not to sell them. We needed the money to make the journey, but those jewels were the only link I had to my family. I couldn't do it. You do not blame me, do you?"

"No. I don't think I could've, either."

"Do you think the necklace will be mine again when I return?" Her eyes widened at the black truck that rumbled by with its loud diesel engine.

"It'd have to. How else would my mom end up with it?"

Constance seemed to accept this explanation, though she wasn't happy about it. "Well . . . now you know all about me, or certainly more than you cared to. Tell me about you."

"There's not much to tell. I haven't done anything as exciting as getting kicked out of my house or moving to a different country."

"Why were you praying last night? For what reason did you need to hide and pray?"

Liz twitched her shoulders and put her arm out to stop Constance from walking into the street against the light. "No reason."

"That doesn't sound entirely honest."

Liz allowed herself to smile. "I was being a pampered brat."

Constance smirked. "So I was right, then?"

"Not right . . . just not exactly wrong. My mom got a new job, and that means I get to be the one to stay home with the kids after school.

And I've got to be the one to do all the cooking and cleaning and taking care of the house. Just seems so unfair."

Constance swiveled her head so much to stare at the city of Draper that Liz wondered if Constance was even paying attention. But she turned to Liz and responded in a way that proved she was listening to every word.

"Many of the families of the Saints have needed both the husband and wife working side by side to support them through hard times. And their children shoulder the responsibility of the household. Your situation is not uncommon."

"Yeah, well my parents aren't exactly working together on this one." There was more to it than just her having to do more work around the house, but that was the part she couldn't put into words. How could she say her parents abandoned her when she knew exactly where both of them were on a day-to-day basis? How could she explain the shame she felt when people stopped talking when she came near enough to listen, which only meant they were gossiping about her and her family? How could she explain that her parents' "eternal temple marriage" shattered her every hope of eternity for herself? *Families are forever . . . Yeah, right.*

"I don't understand."

Liz shook her head and herded Constance into the road before the light changed again. The heat from the asphalt rose up and made Liz feel like the soles of her shoes were melting. The heat mingled with the need to hurry faster across the road made her impatient. "It's too lame to understand. Don't worry about it. I don't feel like talking about it anyway."

Once they were on the other side, Constance stared up at the crosswalk sign. "So is this Zion?"

"The crosswalk?"

"All of this!" She spread her arms out and turned in a circle, making her skirt flutter gently.

"I guess it is. Are you disappointed?"

"No! Of course not! Does everything in your world cast such a brilliant light?"

Liz stared at the red hand on the crosswalk sign. "Brilliant, huh?" She smiled. "Yeah, everything glows, but I wouldn't go calling any of it brilliant. It's just the way it is."

"Are you saying that it's not impressive? Look at everything. The very path on which we walk is firm and smooth. A woman could walk on these paths and never muddy her skirts! And the roads! All firm like the walkways. No ruts or holes or uneven cobbles . . . It's perfect . . . absolutely perfect!"

"I guess it's okay. I don't ever think about it."

"How can you not think about it? To *be* in Zion! The dream and hope of so many . . . and here you are not thinking about it . . ."

Liz could only shrug at Constance's bewildered face. They spent the rest of the walk with Liz being a tour guide, defining cars, motorcycles, and backhoes from the construction site they passed. Constance was thrilled by all of it. Well, not exactly *all* of it. She almost had a heart attack over the woman jogger who ran by wearing only jogging shorts and a tank top.

Constance's widened eyes and loud expressions of disgust over the jogger's lack of covering made Liz intensely grateful the jogger wore headphones.

Constance beamed when they arrived at Liz's house, bounding up the stairs to the front entryway and leaning against the sidelight window as Liz twisted her house key in the door. "What a marvelous day. To think that not so many hours ago, I was cold and wet, and now here I am with the sun and warmth of a world I only dreamed of. If the others could see me now . . . If they could see what I see, it would give them the strength to forge on toward Zion with nothing but praises and songs in their hearts. If only William could see! It's all so beautiful! Zion is so much more than any of us dared hope."

"Uh-huh. It's really something, isn't it? It's polluted, noisy, and the crime rates are up. I get chills just thinking about it."

Constance followed Liz into the house. "You're mocking me."

"Of course I am." Liz kicked off her shoes and sank onto the sofa. "I hate walking."

"That was hardly a walk."

"Now *you're* mocking *me*. Sorry, but not all of us were raised to be Amazon women. Sit down, would you? You're making me feel guilty for needing to rest."

Constance sat, back erect. Liz rolled her eyes at that. She also noticed that though Constance was exuberant just moments before, now she seemed unhappy. The girl changed moods faster than a runway model changed outfits. "Do you think I'm dreaming?" Constance asked, folding and unfolding her hands in her lap.

"Not likely."

"I am quite sincere. Could this be like Nephi's vision or where other prophets were given the chance to see things and then awaken in their beds? Am I dreaming or am I here?"

"You're here. Because *I* am definitely not dreaming. My muscles hurt too much to be dreaming." Liz rubbed at her offended feet as if to prove the point.

Liz felt her gaze slip from her feet to the side window toward Garrett's house, making Constance turn her head to see what had attracted Liz's attention. Constance smiled. "He is a very nice young man."

"Huh?"

"Your neighbor friend. He's charming, really."

"I already told you there's nothing there. He's a mindless chump. Besides, he's dating Becky. She's got the frizzy blond hair that bounces when she does her cheerleading to the Alta fight song. He is totally not interested in me. And I am totally not interested in someone who prefers girls like that."

"Cheerleading?"

"At games, where the boys play sports—you know . . . football and basketball and things like that—the girls jump around and excite the crowd into a frenzy to show we support our team."

"And this is a desirable skill?"

"It is to guys." Liz tilted her head to view Constance better. "We should get you some decent clothes."

"I was thinking I should offer you such a courtesy."

"Whatever! *I'm* not the one dressed for a pioneer parade. You look ridiculous."

Constance straightened her back even more, if such a thing were possible. "Well, you look like a ten-year-old boy."

"Yeah, but what I'm wearing fits in with what everyone else is wearing. You stand out like a pimple at the prom." Liz shook her head. "You're the one changing clothes, not me. If I go back into time, I promise to change into whatever dress you want. But until then, you need some jeans."

Constance followed Liz to her bedroom, where Liz picked out a pair of jeans and a long-sleeved, button-up shirt her mom had bought her but that Liz had refused to wear. Constance seemed unabashed at dressing in front of others and undid the eyehooks under the worn lace at her bodice. She was out of her skirt and blouse quickly, leaving her standing in what looked like thin loose shorts and a camisole. Liz figured she could keep her own underwear on since they weren't too thick to wear under the jeans.

Constance fumbled at the buttons on the shirt Liz handed her. "Could you help me? I never really became accustomed to buttons. My mother's maid always dressed us. Of course, that was back when I had dresses fine enough to have buttons." Her face went red upon this declaration.

"You had a lady's maid?"

"My mother did. But her duties were extended to include Julia and me. She would plait our hair and make certain we were well groomed. She was a lovely woman and knew to hold her tongue in front of the other servants. She was kind to me even after my baptism." Constance held up the jeans. "What am I to do with these?"

"Put them on."

"Britches? You want me to put on boys' britches?"

"Unless you want to be put into an insane asylum by running around in your clothes and telling everyone you came from the past."

Constance frowned, making small lines in her weathered skin. She slipped in one leg and then the other. By the time she had pulled them up, her eyes looked like they were going to pop out of her head, and she started pulling them down again. "I can't! It's positively indecent!"

"You have to. Put them back on. The kids'll be home soon, and I can't let them see you dressed the way you were."

The pants were a little long in the leg and slightly baggy on Constance's slender frame, but they worked. She refused to tuck in the shirt, preferring to leave the baggy shirttail to help cover her backside. Her hands kept smoothing over the denim at her thighs. "They're so tight!"

"They fit fine," Liz tried to assure her. If anything, the pants were too loose, and Constance had the baggy gangster look in them, but Liz was smart enough not to be critical . . . not out loud anyway.

"If my mother ever saw me dressed in such attire, I promise you, I'd be unable to sit for a month."

"Well, if my mother saw you the other way, she'd likely have a heart attack."

Constance didn't stop complaining about the clothes, at least not until Liz handed her a pair of thick socks and tennis shoes. She put the socks on and then gasped in amazement. "One wouldn't even need shoes with such stockings!" She bounced on her stockinged feet for a moment, looking quite pleased, when Liz heard the front door slam closed.

"Lizzie! Lizzie, I'm home!" Matt bounded up the stairs and burst into her bedroom before she could think to hide Constance. He stopped short when he saw her. "Who's that?" His eyes narrowed.

"My friend. Be nice to her, Matty, okay?"

He shrugged and handed her his backpack. "Kindergarten is so cool! I've got a note for you—well, for Mom, but you're Mom today!" He turned around to reveal a note from his teacher pinned to the back of his shirt. He scrubbed a hand under his nose. "Teacher says she wanted to make sure you got it. She was 'fraid it would get lost in my backpack."

"But that's what backpacks are for, Matty—for putting things in so we don't lose them."

"I told her that, but I don't think she liked me telling her."

The note detailed the homework requirements and welcomed them to a new school year. On the back was a list of important dates to remember. Next week was picture day. Liz made a mental note to write that one down on the family calendar in the kitchen. Once, the twins forgot to tell their mom about picture day, and they both came home with the ugliest kindergarten pictures known to the history of mankind. Alison had refused to have her hair combed that morning, and Nathan had insisted he wear his shirt inside out since he just knew it was backwards day. They looked like war refugees.

"Something smells dirty," Matt declared, sniffing the air with his mouth twisted as though he'd bit into mold. "It smells like your horse."

"Sassy does not smell! If you say mean things about her, I won't let you help me exercise her when Mom's working." With the time she spent sleeping in Sassy's stable and then walking in the heat, she knew she had to smell pretty bad, but she also knew that Constance didn't smell any better.

"I wasn't being mean. Sassy's my pal! Just something smells is all I was saying." He twitched his shoulders. "Can I get a drink?"

"Sure."

"Sprite?" Matt looked hopeful.

"Nope, that's for Alison's Beehive stuff."

"Why does she get to go to Beehives? I never get to."

"You're a boy. You don't want to be doing all that icky girl stuff anyway. Go get a drink."

When he had thumped down the stairs, Constance looked away, a red blush forming in her sunburned cheeks. "I haven't bathed properly for quite some time. The boy is likely smelling me."

Though Liz felt embarrassed by the whole situation, she determined not to show it. She was in charge, after all, and that meant all baths were her responsibility, even Constance's.

She led Constance to the bathroom and showed her where the towels were. Constance ran a hand over the brass-plated faucets hanging over the tub. "They're very beautiful."

"They came with the house." *The house my mom has to go get a job to keep*, she thought with more than a little bitterness. "This side controls the hot water, this side controls the cold."

"Hot?"

"Yeah, that's this one." Liz pointed to the left handle again. "Be careful not to do too much hot, or you'll get burned. Turn the cold on first." Liz felt dumb explaining bathroom safety to a twenty-year-old, but she didn't want Constance having to go to the ER with third-degree burns.

Constance didn't ask anything else but instead stared at the left handle with curiosity. Liz straightened. "Take as long as you need. I gotta go check on Matt. He isn't allowed to play on his Xbox until he finishes his chores. Soap and shampoo and everything are in the bottles right there." She pointed to the corner.

She checked on Matt and gave him a half-hearted lecture on getting his chores done to which he grumbled but complied. Once he'd settled, she left to take a shower in her mom's bathroom. She kept her shower quick, just enough to soap down and rinse off. Not only did she not want to use all the hot water, but she didn't want Constance finishing before she did and talking to Matt.

Liz pulled her wet hair into a ponytail holder and changed into clean clothes. When she was ready, she took a few tentative steps toward the upstairs bathroom and put her ear against the door. Constance was humming, and the noise of water dripping indicated she wasn't done yet.

Downstairs she inspected the kitchen to see what there was to make for dinner. But what did one make for a time-traveling ancestor? She looked in the freezer. Tacos? Meatloaf? Spaghetti? Liz rolled her eyes at the quick-and-easy meals she produced when she had to cook dinner for the family. Constance was a time traveler, for pity's sake—she deserved better than that.

Liz opened the pantry and pulled out the recipe box. There on the front was a recipe for bacon-wrapped sirloin. It sounded great. At least great if they had all the ingredients. Liz was pretty sure that there was a pot roast in the fridge.

She hoped Constance would like this for dinner. They'd skipped two meals already, and Constance hadn't even murmured a complaint. Liz could've eaten the walls, she was so hungry. What did people from England eat anyway? What did pioneers eat, for that matter?

Constance took forever in the bathroom. Liz wondered if she should have explained the toilet. Did they have toilets in England? She assumed as much before, but now thinking on it . . . that was a long time ago. She remembered even her grandmother having spoken of outhouses and Sears catalogs. And here was Constance—her *fifth* great-grandmother.

Liz sighed. Maybe Constance would figure things out for herself. She opened the fridge to retrieve the pot roast. Her mom had likely meant to make it for dinner the night before. But meals were getting less extravagant as the stress of holding everything together consumed her mom. Liz frowned at the red hunk of beef as though it were at fault for everything going wrong in the King household. She was grateful to at least have a recipe. And though the pot roast wasn't exactly what the recipe called for, it was close enough.

She pulled out the beef along with some bacon. She'd done a bacon-wrapped sirloin for her Occupational Foods class the year before. It turned out well enough to earn her the high praise of her teacher. She hoped her mom didn't have other plans for the roast or the bacon.

"Since I'm in charge . . ." She didn't finish the sentence. Since she was in charge, a lot of things would be different. She would make the dinners. She would get the kids to school and activities. She would . . . She groaned. She would just be giving up any semblance of the typical American teenage life she felt entitled to. Not that she had much of a life to lose.

Liz gritted her teeth and slammed the roasting pan on the counter.

"Are you mad, Lizzie?"

Startled, Liz dropped the roast on the floor, making a loud, wet splat.

"Matt!" Liz stooped down to pick it up, scowling while inspecting it for damage. She put the meat in the sink and ran the tap.

"What are you doing?" Matt asked, pulling himself onto the counter so he could see into the sink.

"Washing it."

"But it's been on the floor!" he protested.

"Deal with it. We're broke, poor, busted, and people with no money can't be picky about where their food comes from."

"But it was on the *floor*!"

"And I'm washing it."

Matt jumped down from the counter and scowled at Liz. "I'm telling Mom!"

"Go ahead and tell her. She put me in charge, and we're having a roast." She shook the slab of meat over the sink after turning off the faucet to get rid of the excess water and showed it to Matt. "See. It's fine now. Nothing's wrong with it." She tried to sound convincing. In reality she felt a little sick at the idea of eating meat that had been on the floor. But the floors were clean, she tried to rationalize. And if she cooked it thoroughly, it would burn out any germs. At least she hoped it would. The fact remained that there wasn't anything else they could do for dinner except mac-and-cheese, and she wasn't about to feed her ancestral visitor *that*.

She seared the meat, which ended up searing more of her skin than it did the actual roast. Flecks of oil popped out and burned all over her arms. "Maybe I should have done mac-and-cheese," she grumbled.

Liz stared at the recipe card and mixed the mustard, brown sugar, and other ingredients together. Matt's eyes grew as she rubbed the pasty yellow sauce over the meat. "Why are you doing that?"

"It's what the recipe said to do."

"But you're ruining it!"

"Matt, go clean your room."

He backed up a step as though she had tried to swat at him. "My room is clean."

"Then go watch TV."

"We only have dumb channels now."

Liz glared at him. "You have exactly to the count of three to get out of the kitchen and let me make dinner in peace, or I swear I will make your little life miserable."

"But I'm not doing anything—"

"One!"

He turned around, grumbling, "You already make my life yucky." But he scooted out of the kitchen before she could chew him out for disrespect. It made her feel bad to hear him say that. Matt had been her buddy since the day he was born. She hated it when he acted like she was a grouchy grown-up. She hated how much she felt she had no other choice but to *be* the grouchy grown-up.

Liz tried wrapping the roast in bacon the way it looked in the picture. When she was done, she determined the thing looked close enough to the picture on the card. She shoved it into the oven and turned the timer on.

CHAPTER 10

CONSTANCE FELT LIKE SHE WAS floating in paradise. The water wrapped her in warmth that seemed to permeate her skin and soak into her bones. She felt as though she might never be cold again.

She loved the moment and despised the moment all at once. She worried over her baby. She worried over her husband. She worried over who would care for her child while she was in this new, comfortable world and felt guilty that she *was* comfortable.

The soap made the water froth and felt like silk at her fingertips. She never wanted to get out, but after a while the water grew tepid and lost much of the joy it had begun with.

The chamber pot had taken some time to figure out, but once Constance did, she made the water swirl in the bowl again and again. Ingenious! She'd heard of new homes being built with a water closet but never really took the time to ponder on the miracle of the idea.

She grudgingly put back on the clothes Eliza had given her. It simply was not decent for a woman to wear such attire.

When she got out of the washroom, she was met by the large, inquisitive eyes of Eliza's littlest brother. *My own posterity . . . my great-grandson,* she mused.

"Why do you have the appearance of a boy who's being sent to the corner?"

"Lizzie's mad at me."

"Whatever for?"

"I told her the dinner she's making is yucky, and then she got mad at me. I was just being honest!"

"I see. Well sometimes unsolicited honesty goes unappreciated."

"Huh?"

"Better not to say anything than to be unkind."

Matt scrunched up his face. "Why do you talk funny?"

"Pardon me?"

"You sound like the people on that movie . . . the one where the old ugly guy doesn't like Christmas and so ghosts haunt him."

"I'm from England. It must be my accent."

He blinked but didn't say anything until he had another question. "What are you doing here?"

Constance felt her lip tug at an involuntary smile. Her father would have had her locked in her room for a fortnight if she'd even considered such impertinence to an adult. The little boy was almost refreshing, if not a bit unsettling. "I'm here to help your sister."

"Can you cook?"

"I am capable."

"Then you should go help her right now 'cause she dropped our dinner on the floor and then put mustard on it. I'm not eating tonight. I think I'm going to be sick." He held his stomach and stuck out his tongue as he walked away.

* * *

Liz stared into the fridge, trying to figure out anything she could do for side dishes when Constance came in. Matt was behind her, but he was smart enough not to actually enter the kitchen.

"Do you need help?" Constance had already rolled her sleeves up.

"No, we have a few hours to think about the rest of dinner while the roast cooks. We should get something to tide us over, though. I don't know about you, but I'm starving!"

"I am a little hungry," Constance admitted.

"Let's just have a banana and some yogurt. It'll get us by until dinner." Liz opened the fridge and pulled out three yogurts. She handed a yogurt and a spoon off to Matt, who still hovered near, but not in, the kitchen. She ruffled his hair as she handed him the snack and gave him an encouraging smile. "Dinner will be good. I promise," she said, though he didn't look as though he believed her.

Constance made sour expressions while eating the yogurt, but she ate it. She seemed intrigued with the package and turned it over and over in her hands to read all the words. But it wasn't until the banana was introduced that she became positively charmed.

"A fruit, you say?"

"Yes. Fruit." Liz felt as though she had explained the whole thing at least five times already. She began peeling her own banana as Constance watched. When she took a bite, Constance opened her mouth, mimicking the gesture.

"Quit watching me eat. You have your own. Eat it."

"You haven't ever had a banana?" Matt asked, having edged his way farther into the kitchen. He put his spoon on the counter, prompting Liz to remind him that it belonged in the sink. "Are you from outer space?"

Constance looked to Liz, who got up from the table, snatching up peelings and empty yogurt containers to discard. "Mind your business, Matty. That wasn't polite."

Constance didn't respond to Matt but resolutely took a bite of her fruit. Her eyes widened as she chewed. "It's . . . well it certainly isn't quite what I had expected."

"Do you like it?"

"I think so."

Matt shook his head and took his banana. Liz heard him mumble, "Weird," as he left the kitchen. Liz smiled at that. If he only knew the half of it.

Left alone with Constance again, Liz felt more at ease. Constance's wet hair hung all around her shoulders, down to her waist. She looked more normal in Liz's clothes and without her hair frizzed out. It was easier to talk to her, and talk they did. Liz loved the fact that everything Constance had seen and done was new and interesting.

Nathan and Alison were home before Liz realized the hours had passed.

It was the first time Liz had talked to another girl in over a year, to anyone at all really. The bond of the new friendship was unsettling, since thinking about her last experiences with friendships made Liz angry.

Nathan sauntered into the kitchen, dropping his backpack to the floor with a thud. He opened the fridge, stopped, and turned slowly to look at Constance and Liz at the table. "What happened? You get twin envy?"

"What?"

He pointed at Constance. "Looks like you found your own twin." He shrugged and went back to the fridge.

Alison came in just behind Nathan. She didn't seem to notice Constance except to mutter something about the surprise of Liz having a friend, then she too went to the fridge.

It took Liz a few minutes to shoo them out after letting them know that dinner would be soon and that they had homework to be doing first anyway. Dinner had always been served at five PM in their house. Liz wondered if maybe she should do it later so her mom could eat with them but decided to wait and see what her mom thought about altering the schedule.

Dinner was a stressful affair. Matt refused to eat. His chubby arms folded over his puffed-out chest, his green eyes flaring. Once he announced that the food had been dropped on the floor, it was tough to get the twins to eat too.

Constance had no misgivings over eating the food, floor or no floor. She acted as though she had not had a decent meal in months. It seemed strange since she ate the yogurt and banana with such hesitation. But this meal she devoured. Liz smiled, glad to know the meal at least pleased the one person it was meant to please.

"So you go to school with Lizzie?" Alison asked.

"Yes," Liz called out to make certain she answered before Constance could say anything different.

"I've never seen you around before. Did you just move here?"

"I've only recently arrived." Constance ducked her head.

"That's why you're with Liz, then. You haven't had time to meet anyone else."

"Ali!" Liz felt her ears go red.

"I've had time enough here to know that your sister makes a very amiable companion. I'm pleased to know her."

Alison snorted and went to picking at parts of the meat as though she hoped she was choosing pieces that hadn't touched the floor. All in all, Liz wanted to kill her siblings and hide under a rug for how embarrassing she felt they were.

She took Constance upstairs once she had convinced Alison and Nathan that they needed to do dishes since she had made the dinner. Constance pummeled Liz with questions about her family and life. "If you could fix something in your family, any one thing, what would it be?" and, "What could happen that would give you the greatest happiness right now?"

Constance seemed annoyed when Liz told her she'd be happiest if her family got banished to a deserted isle. Liz evaded most discussions on her family by turning them into jokes, but after a while Liz was only able to escape the discomfort of admitting her family was a lost cause by going downstairs to settle the argument between Matt and Nathan over the TV.

Constance followed her downstairs, and Liz, to avoid any more weird Q&A sessions on her family profile, did a house tour of modern conveniences. By the time she'd shown off the ice maker, microwave, light switches, flashlights, and ballpoint pens, it was almost ten. She yelled at the kids to get ready for bed and took Constance upstairs.

"You can sleep here by my bed." Liz pointed to the small space between the bed and the wall where she would be shielded from the view of anyone at the door.

Liz had considered letting her sleep in the playhouse out back, but Matt still went in there every now and again, and she didn't want to take the chance of Constance wandering off on her own and getting hurt. The new century was a scary place. Besides, she was pretty sure spiders had taken up residence in the playhouse. She pulled out padding and a sleeping bag from the hall closet and made a little bed while Constance watched.

"So what are we to do?" Constance asked as Liz pulled a pillow from her own bed and dropped it onto the sleeping bag.

Liz shrugged. "I have to make certain that the kids get their teeth brushed, and then we can go to sleep. I guess we could watch a movie or something . . ." As Liz said this, she wondered what kind of movie would be appropriate for Constance to watch. Maybe one of her mom's sappy classic movies like *Tammy and the Bachelor* or *The Sound of Music* would work. She definitely had to stay G-rated.

"No, I mean what do we do to return me to my own life? I'm not trying to sound ungrateful; it's so lovely here . . . I just cannot walk away from my responsibilities there simply because I have found a place that is comfortable."

"We'll think of something, but tonight we need to get some sleep. I have school in the morning—" She blinked. "Oh! I have school in the morning." Liz rubbed at her forehead. "What am I supposed to do with you? I can't enroll you in high school! Alta is enough to strangle the life out of anyone." She heard a shout and a door slam from down the hall.

"You'll just have to hang out here while I'm in school. I'll be back in a sec. The bedtime bickers have already started." Liz stalked out of the room, muttering about what a good idea sending Alison to boarding school would be.

After yelling at the twins to turn out their lights and to stop pounding at each other through their walls, Liz read Matt a story. She skipped half the pages to hurry the whole moment along and get out of his room faster.

"Lizzie?" he said after she had flipped off the light so that he was nothing more than a small voice in the dark.

"Yeah, Matty?"

"I'm hungry."

"Then you should've eaten dinner."

"Lizzie?"

"What?"

"Don't drop dinner tomorrow, okay?"

Liz laughed in spite of herself. "Whatever, Matty. Go to sleep."

Outside Matt's room, Liz leaned against the wall and stared at the ceiling.

From downstairs she heard the door open and made her way to the sound. Her mother jumped at Liz's voice. "You're home late."

Her mother looked tired, and for the briefest of moments Liz actually felt bad, but she was tired too, and the twins had gotten water all over the bathroom floor because Nathan thought it would be funny to dunk Ali's toothbrush in the toilet. Ali had retaliated by cornering him in the bathroom and spraying him down with the showerhead that detached from the wall. Liz was tired too, and she wouldn't have been if her mom hadn't been late.

"I'm sorry, Lizzie. There was so much to learn today, and they were so busy! I never dreamed a doctor's office in the mall could attract that kind of attention. Are the kids in bed?"

"Yeah. I should be too, since my first day of school is tomorrow, but it was hard getting there when Matt insists on ten drinks of water and half the Dr. Seuss collection read to him. And since Ali and Nathan decided to fight and hose down the bathroom." Liz didn't believe there was any way her mom was really at work all that time. There were labor laws against working that many hours. But she didn't have the guts to call her mom on the lie.

"I'm sorry." Her mom passed a hand over her eyes.

But she didn't sound sorry. She only sounded tired. Tired and annoyed that Liz was complaining, which only served to annoy Liz. "Dinner's in the fridge if you want to heat it up. I'm going to bed, so you'll have to finish cleaning up the bathroom."

"I'll do it tomorrow."

Liz turned around. "What? I thought you worked tomorrow."

"I forgot to get Matty a sitter for when he gets off the bus, and one of the other ladies wanted me to work for her on Saturday, so we traded shifts. It'll give me time to work out a schedule for Matt."

"But I'm competing with Sassy on Saturday!"

Her mother reached her hand out. "Lizzie, I just need—"

"A babysitter!" Liz dodged her mom's hand. "Don't ask me to do this. You can't ask me to babysit on Saturday. I've trained all summer for this event. Can we try to be a normal family and allow me to be a normal teenager for like two minutes?"

"Lizzie—"

"Whatever!" Liz threw her hands up in the air. "I'm going to bed!" She stomped to her bedroom and slammed the door closed. "Change of plans, Grandma—looks like you're going to school with me."

"I am your fifth great-grandmother by your calculations."

Liz snorted. "What? And you think I'm going to call you that? It's a tongue twister. I bet you can't say it fast three times."

"Why would I want to do such a thing?"

Liz picked up a few things she'd left on the floor earlier and threw them in the hamper. "Exactly. You wouldn't want to. So we can drop the formalities and just say grandma. And anyway, you have more important things to worry about. You're going to school."

"I am quite certain I shall be capable of handling it. I've already been through all my schooling. Things can't have changed so much."

"Oh, yeah? This isn't finishing school. You'll be killed."

Constance gasped. "Is your school so violent?"

Liz rolled her eyes. "No . . . I mean . . . okay, some schools are, but Alta is safe physically. It's just full of cheerleaders and drill team drones with their tight leotard show-every-wrinkle outfits."

"These are the girls you mentioned previously. The ones Mr. Mitchell's fond of?"

"Yes. Exactly, the ones *Mr. Mitchell* is so fond of."

"I don't understand the problem."

"You will tomorrow. I can't leave you here with Mom. You're going to have to go to school with me." Liz flipped off the lights and cuddled down into her own bed, feeling a twinge of guilt that Constance was on the floor while she had the comfortable spot. But she knew if her mom came in unannounced and saw Constance there instead of Liz, there would be way more explaining to do than Liz felt capable of. Her mom would lock her in a funny farm for trying to explain what was going on.

"Liz?" Constance's voice whispered in the darkness.

"Hmm?"

"I appreciate your hospitality, and I'm sorry I said there was anything wrong with you. Aside from your clothing, you are perfectly normal."

Liz snorted. "You just don't know me very well, Grandma. My clothes are the only normal thing about me." She felt herself blush in the darkness. Whether Constance knew her or not, it was nice to have someone her age, sort of, tell her she wasn't a freak.

CHAPTER 11

"MATT! COME DOWNSTAIRS NOW! YOU'LL miss the bus, and I'm not driving you!" Liz tried not to yell so her mom wouldn't wake up, but if he didn't listen, she planned on scalping him. She heaved a sigh of gratitude that the twins were already gone. Matt's school started after Liz's, but he was the first picked up on his bus route, and Liz was the last on her route, so he had to be first out the door.

Matt stomped down the stairs, a scowl set deep on his face. "Lizzie, you're always mad."

"'Cause you're always slow!"

"You're mad all the time like Mommy."

"Don't be so dramatic. No one's mad like Mommy. I'd have to set a goal to reach that level."

"Huh?"

"Nothing."

"Where's my lunch?"

Liz wanted to tear her hair out. "You eat hot lunch."

"But I want a sandwich."

"Yeah, well they cost more to fix than hot lunch. Sorry, bud. Make do."

"I think a hot lunch sounds lovely, Matthew," Constance said from behind Liz, making her jump.

Matt looked to Constance and then shot back to Liz. "Did Mom say you could have a sleepover?"

Liz groaned. Why couldn't Constance have just stayed in her room like she was told? "Yes, Mom said it was okay. Now go, or you'll miss your bus and be stuck here alone."

"I won't be alone. Mom's still here."

"But she's sleeping."

Matt jutted out his chin, which still had a little baby fat to soften the square line. "Sometimes you sleep when you babysit me."

"If I have to count to three . . ."

Matt bolted. Liz felt guilty for forgetting to send him off with a prayer. They'd always had family prayer in the morning before they left for buses. She knew Matt depended on the prayers to feel good about the day in front of him. She silently vowed to do better tomorrow.

"We need to go too," Liz said after giving Constance a once-over to make sure she looked okay. She actually looked better than Liz usually did, which was annoying in every way. Her long hair was back in a single ponytail at the nape of her neck, and her body was far more shapely in Liz's clothes than Liz's body ever was. The fact that she wasn't wearing any makeup, and didn't need to, made Liz sigh.

"It's good of you to let your mother sleep," Constance said.

"Yeah, whatever."

"She didn't sleep last night."

Liz stopped midway as she did the zipper to her backpack. "What? How do you know?"

"I could hear her crying."

"She was crying?"

Constance nodded and took the backpack from Liz. She wrinkled her forehead as she pulled the zipper. "How lovely!" she exclaimed, zipping it up again.

"Yeah, charming—why was she crying?" Liz took the backpack away before Constance wore out the zipper.

Constance shrugged. "She's your mother. Do you not know her burdens?"

Liz stared at Constance, into the mirrors of her green eyes, and finally looked away. Her mother's burdens were everyone's burdens, and no one knew them as well as Liz did. "We're going to miss the bus." Her own heart dropped just a little as she glanced one last time up the stairs to where her mother slept. *Crying . . .*

They walked to the bus stop. Liz grunted when she saw Garrett's family car in the driveway, already warming up.

The morning was cool, but not cold. Liz snorted at the idea of Garrett warming up his car when it was still basically summer.

Liz did her best not to look at Garrett's driveway, but when he called out a cheerful, "Hello," she had to acknowledge him.

"And, hello, Constance." He flashed a bright smile.

It was disconcerting the way he said Constance's name as he greeted her and the way he let himself stare at her a moment longer than necessary.

Then he turned and got in the car.

"He's a very pleasant boy," Constance said.

"I thought you were married."

"I am. Being married does not mean I cannot view the good qualities of another person." Constance fell into step beside Liz.

"Yeah, especially when that other person is *viewing* your 'good qualities.'"

"I beg your pardon?"

"You can beg all day, and it won't make me hand my pardon over." They approached the bus stop, and Liz dropped her voice. "And try to remember not to be weird, okay? No getting all excited about things. Most people are pretty unimpressed with the stuff they see every day."

Constance looked pained. "A world without wonder . . ."

"Yeah, whatever, and remember, you're my cousin visiting from England."

"Is it really right to lie?"

"Better that than go to the mental hospital in Provo."

"You make an excellent point. President Young said we should avoid all hospitals."

Liz didn't bother asking what Constance meant by that.

There weren't many people at the bus stop. Not a huge surprise, since most students who lived in this neighborhood had their own cars. Liz sighed. She likely would've had her own car if things hadn't worked out like they had. The few kids waiting for the bus were drivers' license–deprived sophomores and a dressed-all-in-black junior who always insisted he was a vampire.

Constance smiled at the vampire and asked him how he was. He glared at her and turned away.

Her eyes widened, and she whispered to Liz as they boarded the bus, "It is excessively inappropriate to turn away from another person's greeting."

"He's a creep; don't worry about it." Liz made sure they sat a good few rows away from the vampire and crouched low in her seat as a shiny red BMW filled with girls from her ward passed. Liz glared at them.

"Are you all right?" Constance asked, smoothing her hands over the denim fabric covering her legs.

"Fine."

"You look unwell."

"I'm fine. Quit fidgeting with your clothes."

"They're too tight. Can you tell me you like having your legs bound like a cow ready for slaughter? Who were the girls?"

"I don't feel bound. What girls?"

Constance arched an eyebrow. "The ones that rode past in the . . . car." She had hesitated over the word *car* and rolled the *r* slightly, making it sound funny.

"Becky Dunford and her friends."

"And why does Miss Dunford make you look as though you've swallowed a skunk?"

"She's a cheerleader." Liz's voice was flat.

"And that's bad?"

"That's bad, Constance."

"Why?"

Liz grimaced. "Becky and I used to be friends. She dumped me when she started cheerleading. If being a cheerleader means you can't be nice to your old friends, then that makes it bad." Things went further than that. It was how Becky alienated her when she found out Liz's dad was getting excommunicated.

"I see." Constance shook her head as though she didn't see and stared past Liz out the bus window as the bus lurched forward.

"What's wrong with you?" Liz asked gently.

"I'm wondering who is taking care of my baby, Eliza? Who is feeding her? Who is calming her when she's crying? She'll likely go to some mother who has already lost a child. A mother who still has milk to offer an infant. And . . . I feel guilt."

Liz tucked a stray strand of hair behind her ears and leaned in. "Guilt? Why?"

"I slept perfectly well last night. For the first time in so long, I was comfortable and well fed."

"And that's bad?"

"Was my daughter comfortable last night? I would daresay she has never known a day of comfort in her life. I was so quick to forget her and excessively slow to remember her this morning as I woke in comfort and was privileged to a nice meal. Yes, I feel guilt."

Liz wanted to say something. Something that would make Constance feel better, but she couldn't think of anything. They were silent for a few minutes, listening to the drone of the bus, the sophomore girls chattering excitedly about school, and finally the swish of the doors opening to let them off at her high school.

The first day for the last time.

This was a thought Liz should have relished. She should have been able to savor the moment of knowing she would never have to do another first day in high school again, but all she could think about was the agony of whatever Eliza, her infant fourth great-grandmother, was going through for the day.

Liz thought so much on it during the day that while she was imagining her infant grandmother being cold and unfed and alone with no parents, her English literature teacher had called out her name several times before she finally snapped her head up. "What?"

Mr. Colby rolled his eyes. "I was asking how long your cousin would be visiting us, but perhaps I should've asked how long *you* were planning on being with us."

The class laughed. Had Constance already introduced herself and Liz not noticed? Becky Dunford turned her blond, frizzy cheerleader head to whisper to the girl next to her. They both tittered and looked her direction.

Liz felt her face grow warm, and though she tried to sit up straighter, she ended up sinking lower in her seat. "She'll be coming to school until she has to go back."

More laughter.

"We assumed as much, Liz," Mr. Colby said dryly.

Constance spoke up. "I'll not be returning for a while. And we have no definite plans as to the exact date. A great deal depends upon my family and the choices they make. My stay could be for some duration."

No one laughed at Constance. Maybe it was the cool accent or the authority with which she spoke. Maybe it was just because she was new and no one wanted her to feel out of place, but then that couldn't be it. High schoolers ate new kids for appetizers.

Liz looked at Constance, who really could have been her twin, maybe not identical, but close enough to be noticeable. The hair, the eyes, the slight upturn of their noses all implied that the same blood flowed through them, but the similarities ended there. Constance was a full-grown woman with a husband, a child, and self-confidence. Liz smiled at Constance gratefully, and when Constance smiled back, Liz felt another pang of sorrow at what Constance's daughter must be going through at that very moment in the past.

This is crazy, she told herself. *Eliza Brown has been dead for like a hundred years or more.* She wasn't doing anything at that very moment because she was buried . . . buried where?

Liz frowned. Where was Eliza Brown buried? Did she die along the trek somewhere on the plains, left behind in a shallow, unmarked grave? Did the infant ever make it to the valley? But of course she had to make it, or Liz wouldn't even be here to wonder.

"Miss King!" Mr. Colby's voice broke through her thoughts. Constance stared at her curiously as though trying to understand why she kept ignoring her teacher.

"I'm sorry, what?"

More laughter. Was the whole day going to be like this?

* * *

On her way out of class, Becky made sure to say loudly, "Are things so bad you can't *afford* to pay attention?" Liz felt sorry she'd told Becky anything about her parents' separation and tighter finances. Liz had run to Becky needing someone to talk to—only to discover Becky didn't care. They had been enemies since then, but never before had Becky tortured her outright. Liz was a little bewildered over their personal war coming out into the open.

She tried to shoulder her way past Becky, but Becky stopped her.

"Did I really see you riding in Garrett's car yesterday?"

So that was it! Becky was mad about her being with Garrett. Liz folded her arms across her chest and tried to match the cold sarcasm in her former friend's voice. "Does it matter?"

"It matters because I say it does."

"And that means exactly what?" Constance interrupted.

Becky narrowed her eyes so she was looking through slits of mascaraed lashes. "Excuse me?"

"Are you warning her away from Mr. Mitchell because you have some claim to him? Or is it simply, as I personally believe, that you have no claim on him and have the irrepressible jealousy of knowing he might prefer Liz's good humor to yours?" Constance tilted her head, making her dark ponytail rest over her shoulder.

Becky's fake-'n'-bake tanned face darkened with redness that rose to her cheeks.

"As I suspected: you have no response, as you have no claim. A woman with something to fight for will fight. You possess little more than a fantasy. Pardon me." The cluster of girls opened up to let Constance pass by them.

When they walked away, Becky grabbed Liz's shoulder to spin her around. "Just stay away from Garrett." She turned to Constance. "And you have no idea how Americans fight for what they want."

Constance stood to her full height and leaned closer to Becky. "My dear girl, of course I know. They were Englishmen before they were ever Americans." Constance turned on a heel and sauntered off with Liz hurrying after.

"Why did you do that?" Liz asked.

"Liz, I am a gentleman's daughter. And if I've learned anything, it is this: I am a lady by birthright and never have to step down from my position to satiate one whose connections and parentage are wholly unknown to me."

"Things don't work like that anymore . . ." Liz started to say.

"Do they not? Her mention of your family's financial situation was certainly indicative of the separation of social classes, was it not?"

Exasperated, Liz sputtered, "I don't even understand what you just said. You're not even speaking my language! You shouldn't have done that. The school year is long enough without her gunning for me. And what if she goes and tells Garrett I'm trying to go after him, which I'm not! This is horrible, really—I don't get why you'd do this!"

Constance stopped and stared at Liz. "I have a child to care for. I have a husband who is lost and needs to be found. I have a life with the Saints . . . a journey to make. I set out to find Zion . . . to reach the valley and live there, work there, grow old there, and die *there!* I am here to help you; of that I am certain. If humbling a silly girl in front of her silly friends helps you, then so be it."

Liz couldn't believe her ears. "And what if it didn't help? What if what you just did earns you another decade here?"

Constance stood a moment, thinking. She finally gave a short nod, making her ponytail bob and sway. "Even if it earns me another decade. Can you tell me it was not worth it to put that silly girl in her place?" Constance smiled.

Liz shook her head and finally laughed. That moment might have been social suicide, but could a social life that didn't exist really be killed?

CHAPTER 12

THE REST OF THE DAY was mostly uneventful. At least uneventful compared to picking a fight with the most popular girl in school. News of Constance giving Becky her comeuppance spread like the plague during the Renaissance. To Liz's horror, it even reached Garrett's ears.

How much or how little detail he ended up with and how accurate that detail was, she didn't know. Liz did her best to smile when he called out her name after school as she gathered her things from her locker. She gritted her teeth, turned, and waited for him to approach. All she could do was hope that the inward cringe that crawled through her stomach didn't show on her face.

"Your cousin's earned herself quite the reputation."

"Yeah . . ."

"Reputation?" Constance asked. "Reputation for what exactly?"

Garrett shrugged. "Everyone's just impressed with how you stood up for yourself. Don't worry; they think you're cool."

"My temperament has never been described as *cool*, Mr. Mitchell. And I don't believe I approve of such gossip. I am as warm as the next person. Miss Dunford should have set a better precedence. She provoked me into cool behavior if indeed it was inappropriately cold."

Garrett's forehead was a mass of wrinkled confusion. "No!" He laughed. "I mean they think you're cool as in, you know, cool. Awesome, neat. You did good."

Constance blinked her green eyes. "Oh. Oh, I see. Isn't that an odd thing to say?"

Liz rolled her eyes. "The world keeps changing, Grandma."

Garrett laughed outright. "Did you just call her Grandma?"

Liz froze a moment before saying, "She *acts* like my grandma sometimes. Thanks for stopping by and letting us know that the school loves her. It's made her day, I'm sure. We gotta go. We'll miss the bus." Liz shut her locker and turned away as if dismissing him.

He jumped in front of them. "Hey, you live next door. Let me give you a ride."

Her heart stopped, and she glared at Constance. "I've lived next door to you for the last decade, and it wasn't ever close enough for you to offer before." She pushed past him with Constance following in a bewildered stupor behind her.

"Hey, wait up!" He put his arm out to stop her. "Lizzie, don't go getting all mad at me. I was only trying to be nice. That wasn't exactly the reaction I was hoping for."

"What did you want me to do? Did you want me to get all girly with you and tell you how strong you are?" Liz gritted her teeth. Garrett had abandoned Liz when he had gone out for basketball as a freshman, just like Becky had ditched her with cheerleading.

"No." He looked mad now. "I wanted you to be nice back!"

"He has an excellent point," Constance murmured gently.

Liz goggled at the both of them and stamped back the twinge of annoyance she felt that he liked Constance. "Fine. If you want to drive us home, let's just go."

Constance refused to sit in the front, forcing Liz to sit there instead. She wondered if Garrett was unhappy about the seating arrangement, but he didn't mention it.

"Do you know you've acted mad at me since we left junior high?" he said to Liz once they were driving.

"I haven't *acted* anything."

"So you *are* mad at me, then?"

"This really isn't about you." It was, though. It was about a lot of things, and he was a part of those things. She *had* been mad since junior high. She'd been mad since he'd become taller and popular and since he'd moved on with his life. She'd been mad since she felt stagnant in her own life, yet things changed all around her in ways that were anything but stagnant. Her family had fallen apart. Her father would be married again soon, and now she had to be the new supermom to her siblings.

No. *Stagnant* wasn't the right word. Her life was spiraling into an abyss of black despair, and she didn't know how to make it stop.

To add to all that, she had a visitor from another time to witness her failure and deficiency, a visitor whom Garrett seemed to like.

"So what's it about, then?" he asked, refusing to let it drop.

"It's about nothing . . . nothing at all." She turned, focusing on the view out the window and not seeing any of it.

Constance, on the other hand, was seeing all of it. She twisted and turned in her seat belt. She seemed to no longer be bothered by the speed or the motion but rather intrigued with the situation. She was very much the backseat tourist.

Garrett's blue eyes glanced at Liz. "I think you could try to be nicer to me then, since it isn't about anything and you aren't really mad."

"You need to get over yourself."

Constance gasped aloud. "What are your plans for the future . . . Garrett?" Liz knew Constance was drawing the conversation to something else—*anything* else.

"I'm working until I go on my mission. I was going to go to college, but my dad wants me to save some of my own money to pay for the mission. You know, teach me responsibility and all that."

"Sounds wise." She nodded in agreement.

Liz sighed inwardly. It bugged her that all she did was fight with Garrett while her pioneer grandmother asked questions about him and kept him conversing easily rather than keeping him on the defense. It occurred to Liz that Garrett was infinitely more pleasant Constance's way.

They chatted on about education and books and plans for the future. In spite of being from the past, Constance acted as though she completely understood when he said he was always checking his grades on the Internet to make sure he didn't fall behind. She nodded with pretended comprehension when he said he wanted to fly to California to live with his aunt and uncle for a few weeks to hang out at the beach for his graduation getaway. There was no way her fifth great-grandmother had any clue what he was talking about, but she never gave any hint to that.

Liz conceded a smile. Constance really was the queen of social graces. She worked a conversation so that she always remained in control. She was empathetic and sympathetic, making those she spoke with feel understood. It made Liz feel nothing but *pathetic*. When was the last time she'd had a normal conversation with someone who wasn't her horse?

With some slight shame she realized her social standing in school and church had likely, to some degree, been the fault of her inability to care about what others were doing. Since the separation and following affair, Liz had been too preoccupied with herself to worry about anyone else.

She never asked after Garrett's family. She never wondered over his future plans. The last real conversation she'd had with Garrett had been led by him asking her questions, and she'd spent the whole time talking about herself.

She listened with fascination, learning that Garrett was in love with English literature but hated the woodshop class he'd taken last year. He loved physics but had to work really hard to understand math. He wanted to serve his mission anywhere except the countries where they only ate fish since he hated seafood. In that short ten-minute drive, Liz learned more about Garrett Mitchell than she had in the ten years previous.

* * *

"You were done a disservice to have never had a governess teach you to act better in society," Constance said with a casual air. She waved to Garrett as he walked up his own front step into his house.

"You didn't have a governess either. And sometimes society isn't worth the trouble."

Constance settled her stern green gaze on Liz. "And sometimes . . . it is." She turned toward the house.

"So you think *Garrett* is worth the trouble or society in general?" Liz asked, catching up.

"He is a very pleasant young man."

"Like your William?"

Constance stopped short. "Not hardly like my William, but not entirely *unlike* him either."

Liz opened her mouth to give her grandma a lecture on flirting with someone else when she was married but snapped it shut hard enough that her teeth clacked together when Constance turned back to her. Constance's eyes brimmed with tears that spilled down her face. "I miss him so much!"

Liz hesitated before she finally wrapped her arms around Constance, sorry she'd lashed out and made her cry. Constance let the tears fall, and though she had cried off and on several times since Liz had found her in the stable yard, this time Liz felt the pain in it. She spent half her day worrying about the very same things.

"Has he already found the wagon company, or is he still lost? Who will sing our Eliza to sleep if he fails to return? Who's feeding her right now? She'd already began eating solid food . . . did they continue with solids or has a wet nurse taken over?"

"I'm sure they're fine," Liz said, not sure at all. She wondered and worried right alongside her grandmother.

Liz gasped and abruptly pulled away. "I know how we can find out!" She grabbed Constance's hand, leading her to the front door.

Liz felt so excited, she laughed outright. It made perfect sense! Why hadn't she thought of it before?

She halted when she entered the house and saw her mom. "Lizzie, you're home. I—" Her mother stopped short when she saw Constance. She looked from Constance to Liz and back to Constance.

Liz tucked her hair behind her ear. "Mom . . . um, this is my friend . . . Constance."

"Hello, Constance. What a beautiful name. So unique nowadays. We have some ancestors with that name in our genealogy, don't we, Liz?"

Liz didn't answer, feeling a little stricken by the question and not sure what to say.

Constance inclined her head. "Hello . . . Mrs. . . ."

"Clair. Just call me Clair. Do you go to school with Liz?"

"I did so today, Clair."

"You're from England!" Liz's mom exclaimed.

"Yes, I am." Constance straightened her shoulders.

Liz interrupted before many more questions could follow. "Hey, Mom, we need to do some work on ancestry for . . . an assignment. Do you have any stuff on our ancestors who crossed the plains to Utah?"

Her mother's expression shifted to excitement in almost a blink. "I have all sorts of things! You know that!" She started off from the entryway to the hall. "Were you looking from my mother's line or my father's?"

Liz had to consider a moment. "Which line did the name Eliza come from?"

"My mother's line. Okay! This should be fun!" She ushered the two girls into the study.

It had once been filled with expensive paintings and interesting little sculptures. Her dad took those with him when he moved. Liz tried not to sigh from the disappointment she always felt at the emptiness of the walls. The only thing left was the family history chart on the wall behind the door. She focused on her mom digging through the oak file cabinets that were filled and overflowing from the genealogy work she'd spent her whole life compiling.

She pulled out several files and laid them on the desk for Liz to look through. Liz sat in the leather chair.

"What did you want to know?" her mother asked, bending down to peer over Liz's shoulder.

"I'm not sure. I just wanted to kind of look through it . . . If I need anything, I can ask you later."

Her mom straightened. "You're brushing me off, aren't you?"

Liz blew out a long breath. "Well . . . not really brushing you off exactly . . . just thinking it might be better for me to discover it on my own."

"Fine. I know a brush-off when I see one. If you have questions, you know where to find me." She walked to the door and stopped. "Hey, Liz, have you been on my computer?"

"No. Why?"

"I just—I found some emails deleted in my box that I hadn't read yet."

"Maybe your spam filter deleted them."

"No. They were already read before they'd been deleted."

"I wasn't on the computer. Ask Ali."

"Yeah . . . good idea. I'll ask her." Taking a last glance at the two of them, she shook her head. "You two look so much alike." She shook her head again. "You look more like sisters than even you and Alison. Funny." With that she left the study, leaving the door open. Her mom was weird about closed doors when friends were over. She felt it bred trouble.

"What is it we're doing?" Constance asked.

"My mom's got a pretty complete history of what happened to each member of her family once they came to America. I think she's missing a bunch of stuff from before that, but she probably has what you want to know."

"So she knows what happens to us all?"

"Probably."

"Is it safe to look?" Constance cast a glance at the door.

Liz looked up too. "Don't worry about my mom. She has no idea why you want to know."

"No. You mistake my meaning. Is it . . . *right* to look at a history yet unlived?"

Liz rolled her eyes. "Do you want to know or not?"

Constance paled as though she were making a pact with the devil. Her hand reached toward the emerald earring on her right lobe.

Of all the crazy things, Liz thought. To have a chance to know your future and to worry about seeing it! She shook off the thought that were it her, she might worry too.

Liz licked her thumb and shuffled through more pages until she found the name Eliza Julia Brown.

Constance's breathing became shallow and fast as she peered over Liz's shoulder. "Lynnette," she whispered.

Before Liz could ask what that meant, Constance touched a photocopied picture on the page of a young woman holding the hand of what looked like a three-year-old girl.

Liz scanned the papers.

> *Eliza Julia Brown was born September 11, 1851, to William and Constance Brown. After the loss of her mother and father while crossing the plains, she was given to and raised by Lynnette Nielson. Eliza married Jonathon Keller March 15, 1869, and moved with him to settle the southern Utah region. They had eleven children but raised only six to adulthood. Matthew Graham Keller born June 23, 1870 . . .*

Liz's throat tightened, and she skipped the part of the loss of Eliza's parents. She read Constance the rest to prove to her that at least Eliza came through everything okay.

Constance paled as Liz read. "My Eliza had children and their children had children : . . It all happened without me."

"You don't know it happened without you," Liz said, feeling sick over knowing how the history did mention that both parents were lost. But Liz didn't know what else to say. She looked down so Constance wouldn't see the lie.

CHAPTER 13

CONSTANCE LISTENED, EVERY WORD STRIKING a deeper pang of something she didn't immediately recognize further into her heart. She slapped the papers down from Liz's hands to the table. "Where is any mention of me?" Her hand flew to her mouth, and she gasped. Her eyes widened. "I don't return!"

She shouted loud enough that Clair called out from the kitchen, "Everything okay in there?"

"Fine, Mom!" Liz called back, then dropping her voice to a hiss, she turned back to Constance. "What is your damage? What do you mean you aren't going back?"

"You saw the picture. Why would Lynnette be in that picture with Eliza if I were to return? Your history would mention my return. It would say that my daughter was raised by her mother! I'm trapped here! And William never returns! If he had, the history would mention that as well!"

"We were reading Eliza's history, not yours. These things are never complete. You said Lynnette was your dearest friend . . . Why wouldn't she be in a picture with your daughter?"

Constance stopped listening and turned to the window that looked out into the backyard. She wrapped her arms around herself, needing to hold onto something solid, and she was the only solid thing she could trust right now. Everything else seemed like the wisps of memory from a dream after you'd been awake long enough to forget.

"I'm being punished," Constance said finally, still staring into the backyard where Matthew was now playing with one of the neighbor children.

"Punished for what?"

"The prayer I uttered before finding myself here. I told the Lord . . . I told Him He was not worth suffering my pains for. I was horrible, and for that He has answered my apathy by reciprocating with His own."

"Oh, stop it! God does not act like that."

"The absurdity of it all," Constance went on, ignoring Liz's admonition, "is that I made my daughter an orphan. And what am I to do here? I can't function properly in a world so foreign to me. You use words that have no meaning to me. Your teachers lecture on events I've never heard of. I live in a world of candlelight, and you live in a world of . . . *magic*. Magic I do not understand!"

Constance did not find herself equal to the emotions swirling about her. She was losing her self-control again. She was terrified she would go mad entirely and swoon like so many fragile women did. She had never considered herself fragile, but it seemed, since her arrival in this new time, she gave over to hysteria with little provocation. She had no idea how to resolve the situation. No idea how to steel herself against the black void in her heart so that it did not engulf her whole soul.

But the Lord told her she had to stay, that helping this family was her mission.

This family, not the family in her past.

She took a deep breath and tried to focus on the scene outside the window as Matt and his little friend dug in his mother's garden. *This family.*

She tried to find joy in that part of her posterity, the part where she knew she was not being punished but blessed. How many people were allowed to see the fruits of their womb forwarded several generations as she was doing at this very moment? Lizzie was her granddaughter, Matt her grandson, and the twins . . . surely there were others. Eliza's mother, Clair, could not have been an only child. Eliza likely had aunts, uncles, and cousins.

Constance did feel joy in that, but the black ache existed still. She never felt the joy of raising her own child, and nothing could replace that. She was a phantom trapped in between worlds but taking part in neither, simply watching like some helpless bystander.

Liz waited for her to speak; Constance could feel the worry in Liz's silence and steeled herself again. "I'm fine," she said finally. The words sounded far lighter than she felt.

Liz's mother called from the kitchen requesting help.

"I'd better go help her. Want to come or maybe just . . . you know, relax or whatever? I'm sorry I have to help, but she'll freak if I don't."

"Of course you must help. I'll join you. I would much rather not look upon these papers any further. I think maybe in a day or two . . . maybe later my heart will be ready to hear more." She didn't think she'd ever be ready to hear anything more. She felt entirely displaced.

The wonders of the future were as disconcerting as they were inspiring. And with the newness of the future and the joy in her posterity, the ache of loneliness and confusion threaded its way through, causing her emotions to tumble from one to the other. Joy, sorrow, intrigue, pain. Each rolling into her and washing over her so completely, she was drowning in her own feelings.

But at that moment, nothing gave her pause from her pain. She followed Liz to the kitchen. Constance stared at Clair without really seeing her. She felt as though she would die.

Stop, she thought. *Fix this family, and then you can return to your own.*

Determination to do as she was asked forced Constance to really focus on Clair. With Liz, the resemblance had been striking. However, Clair's features were not at all like her own. Though the green eyes were similar, Clair's hair was lighter and cut startlingly short for a woman. Constance had seen more hair on the heads of newborns. She let her gaze fall to the rounded, slumping shoulders and gasped.

Her emerald necklace, nestled in a bed of white gold filigree, hung at the hollow of Clair's throat. Constance absently reached up to feel the pendant at her own throat and ached that it was no longer there. She held her hands still to resist the urge to reach out to Clair's necklace.

It had been in her family for generations, worn only on special occasions and treated with great care. Well, at least until Constance got it.

She found she could best care for it if it was around her own neck at all times, hidden from prying eyes under the protection and privacy of her dress. But the necklace was lost to her . . . and found again on a woman she didn't know.

She could not keep herself from staring, making both Liz and Clair stare back.

"It's a lovely pendant," Constance heard herself say. When she saw Clair reach for the pendant and finger it in that familiar way, she felt a kinship to this woman, this granddaughter at least twice her age.

Clair continued to hold on to the emerald stone. "Thank you. It belonged to one of my ancestors who crossed the plains. It reminds me that if they suffered through everything they had to deal with, then I should be able to deal with anything."

Tears clouded Constance's vision. "I understand." And she did understand. That small link she kept to her family continued to link her family together.

And more. The necklace gave her comfort. Constance knew she had left the wagon camp with that very same pendant around her own neck. This had to mean she'd return to her own time. She had to return to give the necklace to her daughter so it could pass through the generations to Clair.

"How can I help, Mom?" Liz cut in.

Constance shook herself. "Of course, we came to help."

"I was hoping you could help with cutting the vegetables. I'm in a bit of a hurry. I have to go down to my lawyer's and get some paperwork settled."

Constance felt more than saw Liz stiffen. She glanced between the mother and daughter and tried to understand what had happened to create the contention.

Liz inhaled sharply and turned to the counter, picking up the knife and gripping it tight enough to turn her knuckles white.

Clair's eyes flashed with what seemed a warning, but Liz turned away. She chopped with great energy at the carrots. "What are we having for dinner?"

"Stir fry." Clair took a hesitant step forward on the stone floor.

"So how small do you want the carrots?"

"A little smaller than that."

Liz started in on the ones she had already cut.

"Lizzie—"

"No, Mom. Go get it done. The sooner, the better." She ran the knife along the carrot without reaching up to wipe the tears from her eyes. When she carelessly cut into her finger, she didn't seem to notice until Clair jumped forward.

"Honey! You need to be more careful!" She grabbed Liz's hand and pressed a light blue towel to the wound.

Liz pulled away, taking the towel with her. "It's just a cut, Mom. You'd better go. That snake charges by the hour whether you're there or not."

Clair stepped back, looking torn between taking care of her daughter and settling this . . . whatever it was she had to do. The lawyer in their lives was an object of great negativity. Constance felt helpless and curious watching the drama unfold before her.

Clair finally nodded. "I'll be home soon. Constance, it was nice to meet you. We'll talk later, Lizzie."

Liz looked down at her hand wrapped in a blue dishtowel. She ignored her mother as Clair passed one last worried look at her and hurried out the side door that led to the place where they kept the car.

Constance took Liz's wounded hand and removed the compress to peek at it. "She seems terribly sad," she said while inspecting the cut.

"She is sad. Life stinks. Whadaya do?"

"Pardon me?"

"There isn't anything we can do about it right now, so we can't worry about it, right?"

"But you *are* worried." Constance washed the knife off, then finished cutting up the carrots.

"I'm not worried."

"You nearly cut off your finger because you're entirely calm?"

Liz inhaled sharply. "Okay, I am worried, but I can't do anything about it."

"You're wrong. She needs your help, your support, your friendship."

"Friendship? She's my mom."

"And you are incapable of friendship with your mother?" Constance shook her head and began to chop the broccoli as well. "I was great friends with my mother. I think we might have stayed as such had I not met the missionaries, had I not found the gospel. But I see in your mother a great need for friendship. She has lost far more than her husband. When a woman and man marry, they lean on each other and confide in one another. But when they part, the loss is far worse than that of a simple husband. She no longer has a confidante. She is entirely alone. She needs you." Constance wondered as she spoke her thoughts and helped prepare dinner if perhaps Clair had also offered a prayer that night with Liz and Constance. Three women seeking solace.

Somehow Constance felt emotionally sustained to think that Clair might need her too, that she had a purpose to fulfill and that once that purpose was done, she would go back and find her own life righted again. No matter what the family history said, she had to go back and give her daughter the necklace so it could be passed through time to finally settle itself around Clair's neck.

She would have faith that William was well, that her little Eliza was warm and fed properly. Lynnette had made the floured mush many times since Constance had lost her ability to sustain the child through nursing. Surely she would be able to continue feeding Eliza. For the first time since feeling her milk supply depleting, Constance was grateful. It was as though God knew that she would go for a time without being accessible to her child and prepared both of them for that physical separation.

CHAPTER 14

LIZ WATCHED HER GRANDMOTHER SMOOTHLY run the knife over the vegetables, making all the pieces uniformly even. Constance insisted she'd return to her own time, basing her whole knowledge on the fact that Liz's mom had the necklace. She hoped Constance was right.

Constance's faith surrounded them, bringing peace into Liz's heart even though her mom had gone to finalize the fracture of their family.

She got a Band-Aid for her finger and finished cutting vegetables. She asked more about Constance's travels and about her husband, and Constance spoke with animation over their trials on the ship to America and in trying to get supplies to join the wagon company. When Ali came in to check on when dinner would be, she stayed to listen to the stories.

"So what movie was this?" Alison finally asked. Liz had forgotten Ali was there.

Constance blinked, giving the blankest stare of incomprehension Liz had ever seen. Liz hurried to think of something. "It's a remake of one of . . . a book."

"Really, which one?"

Liz thought fast. Saying the word *book* was a mistake since her sister was a total book fanatic. Even if she hadn't read them, she would know a real title if she heard it. "Pride of the P- Prairies," Liz said with a slight stutter.

"I've never heard of that." Ali crossed her skinny arms over her chest.

"Well, it's a crossover between a few different books. You know how directors are. They're always stealing from all kinds of sources." Liz shook her head and turned to get the plates from the cupboard. "Hey, Ali, will you get the forks and knives and stuff out? Mom should be home soon." Liz then went on to ask Ali about her day and to tell some stories of races she and Sassy had won. Anything to keep the subject off of "the movie" Constance had been telling about.

"Where'd Mom go?" Alison flipped her long hair back.

"The lawyer's. Final paperwork to sign."

"Oh." The response was short and quiet, but Alison's hands shook as she turned and opened the silverware drawer. When Liz put a hand on Ali's arm, she whirled around, tears in her eyes. "I hate Patty!" She slammed the drawer shut and fled the room.

Liz sighed deeply and shrugged at Constance, who asked, "Who is Patty?"

"My dad's fiancée."

"Are you not going to console her? Your sister seems a great deal distressed."

"Nothing I'd say could fix things. She'll scream 'get out' and throw something at me. Besides, Mom wants dinner ready when she comes home."

"An unfeeling response from the girl who feels everything and pretends to feel nothing."

"If you think she needs coddling, you go up and babysit her."

Constance opened her mouth, closed it, nodded, and swished out of the room as though she still wore her pioneer skirts. Liz ground her teeth and pushed away the guilt caused by allowing Constance to do what she should be doing herself. She stood in place, deciding what to do next. She felt the pull of Alison's upstairs bedroom but instead returned to making dinner.

* * *

Constance listened to Alison's muffled crying from the doorway before she smoothed her hands over the tight, coarse jeans. She grimaced at the feel of the pale blue denim. Wearing the jeans felt indecent in every fathomable way. Liz's school brimmed with lack of propriety. There were perhaps three girls out of all those people who were dressed with any semblance of quality. The rest looked like women unworthy of knowing, showing far too much skin and acting in manners that shamed Constance to witness. In many ways, after going to school with Liz, she felt grateful for the clothing she had. At least she was covered. Most of the other girls in the school could not boast the same. Could a woman's respect for herself have fallen so far?

She grimaced and entered the room. "Are you all right?"

"No! Yes . . . I need to be alone for a while."

Constance stepped farther into the room anyway. She settled on the bed without being invited and smoothed a hand over the young girl's hair. "I daresay today has not gone quite well for anyone. It cannot improve if everyone ignores their pain."

"Are your parents divorced?" Alison's voice was muffled by the pillow.

"No, they are not."

"Then you don't get it."

Even through the pillow, the accusation came out harshly. Constance did not let it offend her, though. She and Liz had had an identical conversation the night previous. "I believe I do. You feel as though you're isolated. You feel abandoned."

Alison sat up, forcing Constance to drop her hand. "I do not! I feel mad!"

Constance smiled. "You see? I do understand. I have felt angry for quite some time now."

"Why are *you* mad?"

Constance wondered how much she should tell. Would it be inappropriate to share intimate details with this girl? But she also knew she needed to help this family and knew of no other way. "I am a convert to the Church. My father put me out of the house. My mother acts as though I've died instead of finding the Savior's gospel. She has never returned even one letter. My parents are not divorced. They still have one another. But they have very much removed themselves from me." Constance let out a low, bitter laugh. She really did feel angry over the loss of her family.

Part of her blasphemy in prayer the few nights previous had been due to the anger she had allowed to build up. It was a huge relief to confess the sin of anger to this young girl. She almost felt like she could breathe again. *And to think all this time I thought I was handling it so well. I had fooled myself into believing I was quite all right. Perhaps I didn't fool myself after all; perhaps I simply was the fool.*

"That totally bites; I'm really sorry."

Constance didn't understand the phrase but understood the feeling behind it. "I do not share this to give you cause to pity me. I share this to help you know I do understand your pain."

"So if your parents don't let you live with them . . . where do you live?"

Constance hesitated before answering. "I have no home."

* * *

Liz felt terrible for each minute she stayed away from her sister's room. But her feet were like lead every time she moved to join Constance in comforting Ali. When they both came back downstairs, all smiles and chatter, Liz felt worse than terrible; she felt jealous. Jealous on both sides. She turned away from them, not wanting them to see her agitation. *If I'd just gone up, Alison would have talked to me instead, and she'd be laughing with me. If I'd gone up, Constance would respect me for making the better choice.* Liz frowned. She hadn't gone up and had to face the fact that it was her own fault.

Liz pushed aside her feelings and focused on finishing the meal. She wanted her mom to come home and see it all done. They could all sit as a family and focus on dinner, and on each other, and forget that this was a black day in the King household.

* * *

Dinner sat cold and untouched on the stove top. Liz tried to keep it warm while they waited for their mom to come home but ended up burning the bottom portion of the food.

"But I'm hungry, Lizzie!" Nathan's whine was louder and less patient than Matt's. He wandered into the kitchen where she stood guard over the meal and did his best to look like he was being starved. He moaned and held his stomach as though in significant pain.

"Mom isn't home yet," Liz recited like a mantra.

"Do you think she got lost?" Matt asked. He sat under the table after forming two rows of dinosaurs around the chair legs. He peeked out at her.

"Of course she didn't get lost. Grown-ups don't get lost," Liz snapped.

Constance gasped and left the kitchen. Liz felt bad for saying it and certainly hadn't meant to offend Constance by implying anything about William's condition, but she was getting worried too. Her mom seldom came home late from anything. She wasn't the type of person to wander into shops and lose track of time, especially when she knew that dinner and her kids would be ready and waiting.

"Liz, I'm going to Sean's house." Nathan grabbed his jacket.

"Mom didn't say you could go to your friend's house."

"Mom didn't say I had to starve either. Sean's having dinner right now."

Liz shot a glance out the side window to the empty driveway. She strained hard to hear the sound of the garage door opener grinding as it lifted the door.

Silence.

Well . . . silence unless you counted Nathan's tirade over hunger and Matt weeping that Mommy got lost and wouldn't ever find her way home, in perfect beat to Alison telling them all to quit being so dramatic since no one was starving and no one was lost and her insisting she was going to move to a different country to get away from all of them.

"Everybody, shut up!" Liz shouted. "We'll just eat now. Mom can eat when she gets home." Liz turned and yanked a bowl out of the cupboard. She poured the stir fry into the bowl, careful not to scrape across the bottom of the pan and end up with the burnt stuff. The last thing Liz needed was one more night with the whole family refusing to eat.

She microwaved the stir fry, and microwaved the rice, making it rubbery, and after slapping the plates on the table, she demanded that the entire family sit. Even Constance hurried to take her place at the table. Nathan said a swift prayer, as though he really were starving and couldn't waste time on being too grateful, and they ate.

No one spoke.

The only one who seemed remotely normal was Nathan, who piled his plate high and shoveled as fast as his fork would move.

The grandfather clock chimed the new hour. Constance shifted. "Tell me of your interests, Alison."

"Interests?"

"Yes. What do you like to do? I know that Eliza's interests are equestrian. But I do not see you in riding clothes."

"I don't like horses." Alison sketched a glance to Liz and then quickly amended, "I like Lizzie's horse, but I don't want to have one for myself. It's more fun just to visit hers. I like music."

"Oh, yes! Liz told me! You are fond of the piano. I hear you play well."

Alison blushed. "I play okay, I guess—"

"Mom's home!" Liz announced at the sound of the garage door opening.

Matt jumped up and ran to the door, where he swung it open fast enough to startle their mother. "You got lost!"

Liz stood and glared at her mom. "She didn't get lost; she just didn't come home."

Clair dropped her purse on the stone tiles of the kitchen and picked Matt up. She kissed his cheek. "Did you finish eating already, honey?"

"Yeah, but it tasted like a campfire."

"Since you're done, why don't we go read a story?" She walked past Liz without saying anything at all about being late or giving any indication that Liz was even in the room.

Liz leaned on her chair, taking deep breaths. All that worry and her mom didn't even apologize! She didn't explain or anything.

"Are you okay?" Alison was standing, too, now. Nathan was the only one at the table mopping up the last of his meal. When he finished, he picked up his book and was already reading when he exited the kitchen.

Liz didn't answer Alison. Alison shrugged and said, "I'll do dishes tonight."

Liz turned toward the table to start clearing.

Constance moved to help her, but Liz took the plate out of her hands. "No, thanks. I can do it myself."

Constance's eyes widened in confusion. "But why should you when there are others willing to share the load?"

"Because I want to!" Liz shouted.

Alison's mouth gaped open. "You shouldn't talk like that to your friend. She's only trying to be nice."

"It's all right, Alison." Constance's eyes look pained. "Your sister's only angry."

"I don't need a shrink deciphering my moods, okay?" Liz turned her back on them and ran the hot water, scrubbing furiously at the plates in the sink, ignoring the fact that her Band-Aid had come off and her finger was bleeding again. "She didn't even say she was sorry for not calling. If I did that, she'd ground me for a month! I can't believe I was worried about her. She sure as heck wasn't worried about us! She just hands over her dishtowels and diaper bag and expects me to make dinner and mother her kids and clean her stupid house." Liz inhaled sharply. "This *stupid* house! We should just *move* from this *stupid* house and these *stupid* neighbors! We should just move, and then they can stop feeling sorry for the poor, *stupid* Kings who can't hold it all together!"

"You're shouting loud enough—I'm sure the neighbors heard you." The three girls turned as one to look in the direction the words had come from. Clair stood against the doorframe, her arms folded across her chest and her eyes blazing. "Did you have something to say, Liz?"

Liz dropped her head. "No."

"An outburst like that will get you grounded. You should be embarrassed to act like that in front of your friend."

Liz looked at Constance then back at her mother. "It's like I'm grounded anyway with all the stuff you expect me to do."

Clair stiffened and turned to Constance. "It was nice having you over, Constance, but you can see we're having a few problems right now. Maybe you can come back some other time."

Constance frowned but moved toward the door. "Of course . . ."

Liz was horrified but unable to speak. What could she say? In what way could she stop her mom from kicking Constance out? "I'll walk you out," she offered.

When Liz started to leave, Clair put up her arm to block her. "You need to stay here. Constance can find her own way out."

"Mom! You're being rude!"

"No more rude than you."

The two glared at each other. Liz shot one more despairing look toward Constance as she left the room.

CHAPTER 15

ALISON FOLLOWED CONSTANCE OUT OF the room and to the front entry hall. "My mom's not normally like that."

"I'm sure she is not."

"She's had a bad day."

"So it would seem," Constance said.

"Anyway, I'm sorry. Things'll be better when you come back." Alison shoved her hands into her pockets and stared at the stone-tiled entryway.

"No need to apologize, Alison."

Alison shifted. "If you don't have a home, where do you sleep?"

"I've slept on the roadside for these many months since coming to America."

Alison gasped, and Constance gave her a tired smile. "Don't worry. I am quite all right." She patted Alison's shoulder.

When Constance was outside the house, she pondered over the lie she had told Alison. Sleeping on the roadside in her wagon with her husband to protect her was one thing. Sleeping on the roadside in the open in a foreign land with no protection at all was most certainly another. She feared the world outside the Kings' doorstep. Fearful and fascinated all at once.

She took a deep breath and determined that walking around the street and circling back after a bit would be the only solution. There was nothing else to be done. Perhaps Liz would come for her after her mother went to sleep.

Whatever happened, she knew she couldn't stay out all night alone. She needed to remain close to the family. Her great-granddaughter was her only link to returning to her daughter and husband. She pushed aside the fear that her husband was never mentioned again in the family history Liz read. He never returned to the wagon company. Like her, he had disappeared from the records.

Her heart quickened. Maybe he had been spirited to the future as she had. Perhaps they had both stumbled into something that transported them through time and he was here too.

She became almost giddy with this thought. Though it wasn't a sensible thought, it gave her hope. Were he only here, she could search for him! They would be together, and then she knew she could face this future with all its newness.

If she was never able to return to her proper time, and had to face this alone, she would not survive it. This world was far too strange to her. She felt her mind would go quite distracted if she was put against the modern world on her own.

Besides . . . she had no skills that would be useful to earn wages. She had no money to pay for lodgings at an inn or to pay for food. She could not forage for food as she had in England when her father expelled her from the house. She had observed no farms or orchards anywhere in this new time.

Where did food come from for these people? Liz opened the cold box in her kitchen and food was magically there, but how did it get there? She hadn't seen any of the family making the necessary daily trips to the marketplaces that must exist somewhere, and they had no servants to make those trips. Even if Constance had money, she'd never be able to traverse the marketplaces of this strange place. Constance worried over this as she turned at the sidewalk and started in the direction of the Mitchells' house.

A rhythmic pounding came from the side of his home, and when she got close enough to see, she realized that Garrett was bouncing a ball and throwing it into a net at the top of a long pole.

"Good evening, Garrett!" Constance called out. She couldn't stop herself from staring at the ball as it flew through the net. Her calling out made him stumble when he went to catch it. She quickly hid her grin and wondered that a full-grown man would be out playing with a child's toy.

"Well, hey there, neighbor! Where's your cousin?"

"She has remained inside this evening."

"I don't blame her. I'd love to kick back, but I have to practice."

"Practice?" She arched an eyebrow. What could he possibly be practicing?

"Basketball." He gave her a sideways look when all she could do was stare blankly at him. "Don't they call it basketball in England?"

"I . . . couldn't say . . ."

"Well, that's one thing you have in common with your cousin. She's not all that impressed with sports either. Course, I don't think anything impresses her . . ." He muttered the last part of his sentence as he aimed and jumped, the ball falling through the net again. This time he caught it when it came back down.

"Do you care about her good opinion? To . . . impress her?" She felt intensely curious and knew to be caught asking such a brazen question would displease Liz terribly.

He shrugged and took aim at the net again. "She's all right, I guess. It wouldn't hurt her to act nice, though, would it?"

"No. Indeed it would not." Constance frowned. He didn't really answer the question in a way she could decipher, but she let it go. "There are other girls more to your liking then?"

He was about to jump and throw the ball but stopped. He turned to Constance, his eyes blinking as the sweat rolled into them. He tucked the ball under his arm and took a few steps closer. "Why are you asking?"

He was entirely too close to be proper. She stepped back. "Merely curious, I suppose. Liz has tried many times to explain how society here differs from society in England. I am merely trying to make it out."

"I'll give you a little lesson then." He grinned. "Come with me to Stomp."

He waited.

She waited, trying to puzzle out what he was asking, afraid that if she asked what he meant, she would expose her own ignorance. "I . . . Stomp?"

"Yeah, Stomp. It's, you know, a dance."

She stepped back again. "You're asking me to a dance?"

His shoulders twitched with a shrug. "Yeah. Don't you dance in the UK?"

"I . . . cannot. I thank you for asking. However, I feel I must tell you I am quite attached."

He shook his head. "Attached . . . to what?"

She felt her face grow warm. The very idea of having to explain such a thing to someone who should be asking her own granddaughter to the dance was horrifying in every way. "Another man, of course."

"Oh, you're already going with somebody. Well, that's too bad. My loss." He threw the ball into the net and made no move to catch it when it fell through to the ground and bounced to the grass.

"Perhaps, Liz . . ."

He laughed and put his hands up. It was his turn to back away. "Oh, no. She doesn't do dances. Besides, she doesn't really like me."

"You may be mistaken in that."

"After years of being her neighbor, I couldn't be more right about anything. She doesn't like anyone."

"I hardly think that true. She and I get along splendidly!"

"But you're related. You have to get along. It's like a law or something."

"A great many people are related and despise one another in every way. I rather think we get along because she is so much like me."

"Funny, you don't seem alike at all to me." He retrieved his ball from the lawn where it settled.

"I've had time to get used to my life. She is still so young."

"Oh, yeah . . . and you're so old. What are you? Like six months older than she is?" He laughed, and Constance blushed. This conversation was far too intimate, and she was too far out of her comfort zone to be discussing anything with him.

"I am not so much older than her in actual years lived." Well, that was true enough. "I do believe you've misjudged her. She wants very much to be social but fears it as much as she desires it. She is a very kind person."

"She's better when you're around."

A small girl poked her head out his front door. "Garrett! Mom says it's time to come in!"

He looked over his shoulder. "Coming." When he looked back to Constance, he was all smiles. "See you around." He walked to his door, bouncing the ball as he went.

Constance looked from his house to the King household where she believed her family was still bickering. She wondered if she should go back but decided against it. Better to wait a bit longer before trying to work her way back into the household. So she pressed on down the street.

As it grew darker, the city lit up like the stars in the sky. Lights twinkled down below in the valley. Such a miracle . . . to light up a household without the flicker of one candle flame. It was odd to her to see the things that families had and what they didn't have. There were cars in almost every driveway and space to store cars attached to every house. The spaces for their lawns and gardens were small even if their houses were quite large. She wondered where all the children played.

She had imagined the time when she would be settled in the valley, growing gardens and working alongside her husband to make a living. She imagined her children playing in the fields and helping with the chores.

She sighed. So much hoped for . . . all of it as far out of reach as the moon. The two nights after William's disappearance, Constance looked at the sky and took comfort that he was under the same stars. Here in this future, she looked up and could find no satisfaction in such a thought. She ached to hear his voice, and her arms felt the emptiness from not having her child there to fill them.

Constance had made it quite far and passed down many streets—so many that she hoped she would be able to find her way back in the darkness now enveloping her. She thought for a long time of her daughter and her husband and the wagon company. She thought of her parents and her sister and all the things in her life that had led her to this moment.

A baby cried from across the road. A young mother removed the baby from a brightly colored basket from her car. Constance watched longingly as the mother cooed to the infant.

"Where is my baby right now?" she whispered. The phrase had repeated itself through her mind so many times it felt like a mockery to her. She closed her eyes and inhaled sharply. Lynnette was a good woman. She was strong and capable. Lynnette loved Eliza and would care for her no matter what happened. But that did not guarantee safety or comfort. The trail was a harsh place for an infant.

"She is safe," a voice said from behind her.

Constance whirled around to see who was speaking, but the walk behind her was empty shadow. Her eyes darted from the yards and houses nearby, but there was no one in sight. The woman with the infant had already gone inside her home.

"*Is* she safe?" she begged the emptiness to confirm.

"She is safe."

She ached to believe this phantom voice and knew such knowledge could only come from the Lord. "Is my William safe as well?"

The emptiness remained empty. Constance pressed her lips together to hold in the sob. She missed him so much! She missed speaking to him about their future, their plans, his opinions on life. She missed his smile and the quiet songs he sang as they put the baby to sleep. How could anyone understand how alone she felt? How could anyone know how—

She whirled to stare back down the street she had come from. The lights spilled out from the windows of all the homes onto the lawns as though searching the twilight for her.

"*Go back,*" said the voice.

I can't go back now, she thought. *It is not possible that Liz has the ability to sneak me into the house.*

"*Go back.*"

Her mother will surely still be awake . . .

"*Go back! Now!*"

Her feet moved to the command until she was running.

CHAPTER 16

CONSTANCE'S INSISTENT KNOCKING FINALLY BROUGHT Clair to the door. Constance's heart was racing. Her breath came in rapid, shallow spurts. She looked behind her as though followed by a pack of wolves.

"What's wrong? Are you okay?" Clair's face expressed all the panic Constance felt in needing to return. "You look as if you've seen a ghost! Come in! Come in!"

Constance hurried into the room. Clair closed the door tightly, and Constance breathed a sigh of relief to be inside. "I felt as though I were being chased by the devil himself!" she declared as she tried to catch her breath.

"What happened?"

"I hardly know! I was walking and then I felt I had to return. I felt danger. I don't know if it was for myself or for you, but I felt I must return, so I hurried and feared I would not be fast enough. Are *you* all right?"

Clair looked at the floor, but her face was pale. She didn't answer.

"What's wrong? You must tell me what happened. Is there an intruder in the house? Has one of the children been hurt?"

Clair's whole body shook. She wrapped her arms around herself and rocked back and forth as though soothing an infant. "Nothing . . ."

"What? What happened?"

"Nothing happened. Nothing at all. Everything is fine." Tears brimmed her green eyes, illuminating the emerald color.

"But I was sure . . . I felt—I *heard* . . ." Constance felt bewildered standing there in the foyer with this woman who looked as though *she* had seen a ghost while at the same time insisting that all was well.

"I'm sorry," Clair mumbled, rubbing at her arms as though she felt a draft. "I'm sorry . . ." As she rubbed at her arm, a small bottle fell from her hand and crashed to the floor. It bounced several times against the stone tiles before settling near the door.

Clair covered her mouth with a trembling hand, tears flowing freely down her cheeks. She hurried to collect the bottle. "It's a prescription." She sounded defensive to Constance. Clair placed the bottle in the pocket of her black jacket. She ran a hand through her short, dark hair, making it stand straight out in many places, like sticks caught in a muddy bog. She laughed, low and strained. "Do you want something to drink?"

Constance had no idea what was happening. Was she mistaken in rushing to return? Everything seemed normal aside from Clair's odd behavior, but it certainly didn't seem as though it were any type of emergency.

"Where's Liz?"

Clair smiled through her tears. "She's been difficult enough. I'm ready to lock her up for a year."

"Where is she now?" she asked carefully, in case Clair *had* done exactly that.

"She's in her room. She insisted she had to go find you. We got into a pretty bad fight over it. She said you didn't have anywhere to go and accused me of . . . well, basically of *killing* you for making you leave. She's such a drama queen sometimes." Clair turned away and walked through the dining room it seemed they never used and into the kitchen. A glass of water was on the table.

Clair opened the cupboard and took out another glass. Her hands trembled so much, Constance feared she would drop it, but she managed to hold it and fill it with water without too much difficulty. "Ice?" she asked.

"Yes, please."

"You have great manners." Clair put the water glass into a hole in the cold box. Three chunks of ice rolled out and into the glass. Constance loved the cold box with the ice maker. She'd played with it earlier when Liz made dinner. But now, Constance's sense of wonder was overtaken by her growing concern. Though everything seemed perfectly normal by outward appearance, something was wrong, and Constance could not make sense of it at all.

"My mother took great care with matters of etiquette. Forgive me for asking, but are you . . . unwell?"

Clair sat without answering. Her hand rested over her pocket. She took a long drink of her water and set it down hard on the table. "I'm fine. Why would I be unwell? I'm forty-two years old and get to start my life over. I should be celebrating. But I can't, 'cause I'm too old to celebrate. The only thing worse than restarting my adult life would be having to go through puberty again on top of it all. *That* would be worse." She nodded and bit the inside of her cheek. "That would be the only thing worse."

"Are things *so* bad?" Constance had no concept as to how to make the situation better. This woman was unraveling mentally, but most of what she said made no sense.

"I'm alone. You know . . . I haven't ever been alone. Not ever. I went straight from high school to marriage. From my dad's house to my husband's." She lifted each hand as though weighing something and then folded her fingers into her palms as though what she weighed had been nothing of substance after all. Constance felt the woman's pain and wanted to embrace Clair and explain how well she understood it.

Clair folded her arms. "Girls today are so much better off. You're encouraged to learn and grow and develop yourselves. We were encouraged to get married and be good wives and mommies. Take advantage of the opportunities given you in this life, Constance. You'll never know when you'll need to fall back on them. Make sure you learn how to be strong on your own."

"Surely you know how to be strong . . ."

Clair nodded sharply. "I've always been like the plastic couple on the wedding cake. If I wasn't attached to the groom, I'd fall over." She bit her quivering lip. "See me now . . . falling over!"

"You are not falling over," Constance said, desperate to say anything that might be helpful. She felt entirely unnerved to have this woman divulging such personal details. "You have been forced into a new situation. But you'll adapt and find happiness in time."

"Happiness? I wasn't ever really happy before. You know? It isn't that I really liked having him around. He'd become so quiet that the silence of his absence was way better than the silence of *him*. I just . . . I just wasn't good enough . . . to make him happy, you know?" Clair took a deep breath and picked up her glass again. It was empty when she set it back down. "You don't know. How could you know? You're what, seventeen?

Here I am, exposing my stupidity and flaws in front of a perfect stranger, a teenager, no less, who will likely have to seek counseling by the time I decide to let her leave."

"I'll not be leaving. I'll stay as long as you require company."

"The thing is I do require company. I so totally hate being alone."

Constance swallowed her own tears back. How *she* hated being alone as well. "I do understand. You feel there is no one left to turn to since you can no longer turn to him. You wonder at the start of each day how you will make it through without him, only to wonder how you *did* make it through once you reached the end of the day. You fear that you, alone, are not enough to sustain your own emotions."

Clair's face shone in the sheen of tears. "Yes. That's it exactly. And I miss him. Is that stupid?"

Constance shook her head. "Not at all. I miss—" She almost said she missed William the same way, but what would Clair think of such confessions?

Clair surveyed Constance, seeming to wait for Constance to finish her statement. When Constance remained silent, Clair said, "Your accent is pretty."

"Thank you." The comment was bewildering. To go from confessions of the heart to compliments in the blink of an eye seemed irregular. It was an odd conversation to begin with, and Constance wasn't sure what to make of it. Never had anyone shared such confidences with her aside from Lynnette, whose life was filled with girlish dreams. She felt foolish for having divulged so much information herself.

* * *

Clair tilted her head, and the slightest frown tugged at the corners of her mouth. She couldn't believe she'd just spilled her guts to a teenager. *I must be crazy*, she thought. Wanting to steer the conversation away from herself, she asked, "Did your parents just move here?"

"No. They stayed in England. I came to America without them."

"So who are you living with?" Clair couldn't believe how irresponsible this girl's parents were, letting her roam the world with no one to supervise.

Constance looked like she was having an internal battle on how to answer the question. "I am not living with anyone at this time."

Clair gasped, completely shocked by such information. "You're not staying with anyone?"

Constance shook her head.

"What were you going to do? Where were you going to go when I told you to leave earlier?" She felt immediately guilty for not listening when Liz said Constance had nowhere to go, but then . . . Clair couldn't remember the last time she'd really listened to any of her kids. She felt like she was going through all the motions of motherhood, but all the feeling had seeped out of her with nothing left. She placed her hand in her pocket again to feel the bottle there. At least she'd sleep tonight.

She'd debated on whether or not to take the pills again but decided she couldn't do another day at work walking around like a zombie. If she didn't drug herself to sleep, she knew she'd spend the whole night trying to find a way to make her body take up the whole bed so it didn't feel so empty. She wasn't an addict or anything. They were only sleeping pills.

Constance looked at the table. "I had no way of knowing where I would end up or what would happen. I am still a bit unsettled as to what this night will bring."

"But how did you end up here? In the U.S., I mean. Where are your parents? What happened?" Clair leaned forward. It felt good being able to worry about anyone else. She'd been afraid her ability to care about anyone else had gone too.

"I am a convert to The Church of Jesus Christ of Latter-day Saints. When my father learned of my baptism, he refused to allow me to live in his home any longer. So I saved my money until I could pay for passage to America. I wanted to join the Saints, so here I am."

Clair closed her eyes feeling more tears welling up in them. They were tears of pity, but for the first time in a long time, they weren't tears of *self*-pity. She reached to her necklace . . . her emerald a reminder that worse things could happen. Didn't a few of her own ancestors face similar trials as this teenager? "You poor thing! I can't imagine what you must have been through!"

Clair thought of their entire conversation and couldn't remember the last time she felt like anyone understood her the way this girl seemed to. Clair had been glad to have Constance to talk to, and in that moment she realized she couldn't let Constance live on the street. The girl had given Clair a gift of real understanding. The least Clair could do in return is let her have a place to sleep. "You can stay with us . . . until you get your feet under you. I can't believe Liz didn't tell me about this. If she'd have just said something—"

"I did say something," Liz said from the doorway.

Clair looked her daughter over and felt instantly annoyed. "You have your running shoes on and my car keys in your hand. Did you have plans?"

"I was going to look for Con—Constance?" Liz crossed the room, seeming relieved that Constance was there. "Are you okay? I was worried something happened to you."

"I worried something happened to *you*. I had the most terrible feeling that there was something amiss . . ."

Clair stood abruptly. *Does Constance know how I'm feeling? Did she know how much I wanted to swallow this bottle whole and just sleep forever?* "But everything is fine." *I wouldn't have taken the* whole *bottle,* she thought. *Wanting to do something and actually doing it are two different things. I wouldn't have taken the whole thing.*

"You don't look fine, Mom," Liz said.

"Well, I am. Were you here long enough to hear me say Constance could stay with us for a while?"

"Yeah?" Liz looked suspicious.

Clair sighed inwardly. *Have I been so out of it that my daughter believes me entirely heartless?* she wondered. "Great, well, make sure she's comfortable. There are blankets in the closet. I'm off to bed now. You girls better do the same. It's a school night." She knew her voice was too high, too pleasant. It sounded distinctly false and belied the conversation she'd had just moments before with Constance. She hoped Constance didn't tell Liz everything they'd talked about.

As she left the kitchen, she stole a glance back at the new teenager in her house and found that Constance was staring at her. *No,* she thought. *She won't tell Liz that I'm a basket case.* Clair believed this because in that look shared between her and Constance, they understood one another. Clair knew that Constance had lost her sense of identity too. Granted, Constance hadn't lost a husband. *But,* Clair supposed, *losing your parents when you're still so young has to be close to the same thing as losing a spouse. Poor Constance . . . Poor me.*

* * *

"Well, I guess we don't have to hide you from my mom anymore," Liz said as soon as they were back in her room. She kept her voice low, just in case. Who knew what noises carried through the heating vents?

"Your mother is unwell, Liz." Constance settled into a pair of pajamas with ducks all over them. The pajamas were a gift from an aunt who remembered what size Liz was but apparently forgot her age. They were brand new. Liz hadn't even bothered to take the tags off until she handed them over to Constance, who accepted the offering gratefully, which made Liz feel guilty for being so *ungrateful*.

"Yeah, she's unwell; she's psychotic. Did you see the way she yelled at me? As if I was the one who had done something wrong. I spent the whole evening making dinner and watching her kids, and I'm the one that gets yelled at. Nice!"

"Be serious."

"You think I'm not being serious? I'm totally ticked at her. And then she sent *you* out into the neighborhood alone. Anything could've happened to you out there. The world's not a safe place for pioneers. There're murderers and rapists and gangs out there. You coulda got hurt! And when I tried to explain about you being all alone, she sent me to my room! That's like the tenth time this week, I swear it is."

"Something is *wrong* with her."

"You don't have to convince me!" Liz slid under her comforter and propped her head up on her arm as Constance slid into her blankets next to the bed. Liz was so mad she could scream. Not that it would do any good, but she wanted to just the same.

"I ran all the way back. I felt if I didn't arrive soon enough, something horrible was going to happen. When she answered the door, she looked . . . ashamed—as though she'd been caught doing something naughty."

"She should be ashamed! She kicked you out!"

"No!" Constance frowned. "She looked nervous, and she had this bottle she dropped. She appeared horrified when she noticed that I saw it."

"Bottle?" Liz sat up. "What bottle?"

"I don't know. It didn't break when it dropped as I thought it would. It bounced."

"Probably plastic. Plastic doesn't break very often, unless it's a jug of milk and you're in a hurry and don't have time to clean it up." Liz grimaced.

"Truly, that is an irrelevant detail. What is important is that your mother is not herself."

"How would you know? You just barely met her." Liz didn't add that her mom wasn't usually late coming home from anything before and that she really wasn't acting like herself. Her mom had all but slept through the last month. She always said she was tired and took more naps than a baby.

"There's something about that bottle. It rattled like a child's toy, and she was not pleased to have me take note of it."

"Probably just ibuprofen. She's had a lot of headaches lately. Don't worry about it. What you should be worrying about is you. Where did you go when you left the house?"

"I walked."

"Just walked?"

"Well, I spoke to Garrett before he was called in to his house, and then I continued walking."

Liz sat up straight. "Garrett?"

"Yes. You know, Liz, you should really consider being kinder to that boy. I think he would enjoy some attention from you."

"He'd enjoy attention from any girl who'd ask to feel his biceps. And only girls like Becky do things like that. I refuse to act like that Barbie-doll drone!"

"He is a far more decent person than you give him credit for," Constance insisted. Liz noticed she didn't take the bait to start a rip session on Becky.

"Did he tell you I was a creep or something?"

"He said you never looked at any person without scorn. I told him he was wrong, that you were kind to me, but he indicated that your kindness toward me was only because we are related."

Liz looked at her hands, feeling guilty that Constance had defended her from the truth. She knew she really didn't like other people very much anymore. Other people were always disappointing . . . like Becky, like Garrett, like her father.

When she was little, she had followed her father everywhere, loved being near him, but she eventually realized he didn't want her around the way she wanted to be around. He was always pawning her back on her mom. *Go find something to keep Lizzie busy . . . Clair, Lizzie was in my papers again! . . . Not now, Snow White, I'm busy . . .* Seventeen years later, he was still pawning her off as he moved away and found someone else to occupy his time. "Do you think I'm kind . . . really?"

"You are kind to me. But it does seem strange . . ."

"Are you calling *me* strange or something else?"

"You have no friends at school."

Liz blew out a breath between her teeth. "I have friends."

"The only person you spoke with was me. At least the only person you spoke to with any hint at civility. When you spoke with other people, you were rather sharp, I think."

"Oh, please!"

"Your sister has portraits all about her room of other people," Constance continued over Liz's protests. "You have drawings and portraits of animals . . . horses."

"And that's a problem for you?"

"I would think it a problem for you. I simply don't understand."

"You're only trying to psychoanalyze me so you can fix my problems and go home."

"That's not fair. It could be that I do care about your happiness."

Liz looked away. *What's wrong with liking horses? So what if I don't like the people at school. They don't like me, either. And dang it all, I am very happy! And there are people I say hi to in the halls and eat lunch with sometimes.*

"Don't be angry. I do care, and I believe you do as well. I see in you the potential to care a great deal for others . . . if you would let yourself."

"I let myself," Liz said sullenly.

Constance laughed. "I'm sure you do, Liz." The way she said it was condescending, as though she were sure of the exact opposite. "But this isn't about you. This is about your mother. I'm concerned."

"Do you have to use my name in every sentence?"

When Constance looked confused, Liz rolled her eyes. "Everything you say seems to start and end with a very snooty *Liz*, like you are always giving me a lecture."

"I'll try not to. Aren't you even the slightest bit worried over your mother?"

Liz grunted. "Let's worry about it tomorrow. We have to get up early." Liz flipped the nightstand light off and snuggled deeper into her blankets.

"Liz?"

"Hmmm?"

"Do you not think we should have our evening prayers?"

"Oh! Right." Liz didn't turn the lights on but slipped out of her covers and knelt by her bed. A rustle from the floor indicated Constance did the same on the other side.

Constance offered the prayer, and again Liz was struck with how innocent and filled with faith Constance was. She thought about all the nights she determined herself too tired to pray and all the nights she didn't think about it at all. She felt a little guilty and made a silent vow to do better.

CHAPTER 17

CONSTANCE SHIFTED UNEASILY IN THE darkness. It was only moments before Liz was asleep and softly snoring. Constance thought about the previous night when she had heard Clair crying and wondered if she would be crying again. It pained her to see the broken fragments of this family.

Matthew was affected by the general mood of the household, but he was young and oblivious to most of what took place. Nathan handled himself well enough, but Constance believed the young man to be hiding in the pages of his books. Alison was overly needy of attention, and Liz was outright hostile to human contact. And Clair . . . Clair was simply sad.

Constance waited a while longer and finally got up, unable to sleep. Between her worry of the family she had left, and the worry over the family she had come to, her stomach twisted in a way that hurt. A glass of water might settle her. She crept out from Liz's bedroom and down the stairs.

She loved to move the handle to the faucet and have water run out in a clear, cold stream. She twisted the handle a few times, making the water flow and then stop again, flow and then stop again, chiding herself for being silly and finally putting her glass under the spigot. As she filled her glass, she noticed light coming from down the hall. Constance turned and wandered toward the light. She peeked into the study. Clair sat at the desk, looking over the files left from when Liz and Constance had gone to make dinner.

A pair of spectacles sat low on Clair's nose as she peered at the papers and made notes in a little book. Her eyes were red and swollen as if she'd been crying again.

Constance shifted at the doorway. She wanted to leave but knew she was to help the family. That meant Clair, too. "Finding anything of interest?"

Clair jumped as though startled and tugged on her spectacles so that they hung around her neck on a chain. She smiled, making her eyes disappear in the puffy folds. "Can't you sleep?" Clair asked.

"I must not be very tired."

"Me either. I actually came in here to do some studying on my family history. Your story of converting to the Church and then getting kicked out sounded so much like one of my ancestors that I wanted to find the story and show it to you. I think it might help if you knew someone else had gone through the same thing."

"Thank you for worrying over me."

"It's nice to have something to do."

Constance looked at the papers in front of Clair. "Do you spend a great deal of time searching out your ancestors?"

"As much as I can, but, you know, not as much as I should. I had more time before the di—well, I had more time before. It wasn't hard at first, doing genealogy, I mean. There were so many records ready to be found and put into place, but I'm stumped now, no matter how many times I go over it."

Constance smiled softly. *Stumped* was a word she'd never heard, but she was able to gather that Clair was unable to continue her work. Constance tried her new word out. "What is it that has you stumped?"

"My family disappears once I get to England. I can't find the names of the ancestors there at all. It's like there was nobody before that."

"Does it please you to find these names?" Constance was in awe of the idea. She had been lectured on her grandparents and great-grandparents from the moment she could speak. In her home, it was important to know where you came from so you understood your place in society. She had found, upon her arrival in America, that no one cared who anyone was before, or at least few did. Most only cared who you were now and what it was you were doing. She was glad of that since she had hated memorizing the names and social rankings of the portraits lining the hallways of her father's home. Those people in the portraits were dead, well . . . most of them anyway, and they made little impression on her.

Clair shrugged. "It makes me feel . . . complete, you know? Like I'm connected to something bigger than I am. You should study your history. It'd be fun for you to see where you came from. I can't tell you how nice it was to see Lizzie come home wanting information." Clair gave a light laugh. "I swear she gets that glazed-over look every time I mention her ancestors. It would be nice to have her excited about her family."

"I do believe she is a great deal more interested today than she was yesterday." Constance smiled.

"She's a good kid. She never gave me much trouble until now. I'm glad to see her hanging out with you, though. Friends are good to have."

"Indeed. I appreciate you letting me stay. You're very generous."

"It's the least we could do. I'm just sorry I asked you to leave. I feel terrible about that. That was hardly any way to treat a guest."

"Oh, please, no. Don't be uneasy. I feel very welcomed. I feel like . . . family." Constance smiled again. "I'm glad to see you're better." She nodded and turned to leave.

"When I find the story, I'll let you read it," Clair said from behind her.

"I will be glad to read it." Constance didn't know how glad she really felt. A part of her wanted to read everything there was to know about her life. Another part of her feared finding out anything. She wanted to believe she would go back and that she would find William when she got there.

"Hey, Constance?" Clair called.

"Yes—" Constance had almost called her Mrs. King but thought better of it. She'd never met a woman actually divorced from her husband. It was quite the scandal when things like that occurred, and she'd heard of it mostly though gossip. She had no idea how to address a formerly married woman. She'd have to ask Liz in the morning.

"Do you need me to sign any papers for school or anything? Like a guardian or whatever?"

Constance hesitated before choosing the only answer that made sense. "I am my own guardian."

"Oh. Right . . . sure." Clair's head bobbed in understanding. "Being over sixteen, you would be able to, wouldn't you? Great. Well, I'll see you in the morning."

"Good night." Constance left but was back after a moment of deliberation in the hallway. "You may believe there is no one to turn to, but you're wrong. You have your children. You have Liz. I think she wants you to talk to her, to be open with her. You're a strong person, and you will triumph over this moment in your life and find that the moment will be cause for gratitude for the growth and strength it offers. Forgive me for speaking so boldly. I merely wanted you to know my feelings." Constance turned away from Clair's puffy eyes, now widened in surprise, and hurried up the stairs to Liz's bedroom. Her heart pounded in her chest for speaking so freely.

She had let many of her "absurd proprieties," as William called them, fall to the wayside when she met him and sailed to the states. But she still harbored them in her heart, and without William there to tease her out of her formal behavior, she found herself afraid not to maintain the level of respect one should when speaking to a person of greater maturity.

She felt foolish for trying to maintain her propriety in a society that had obviously cast those notions away generations prior. And she felt even more foolish for worrying when she, too, cast them aside. It wasn't as though anyone in this time or place noticed. She sighed. Perhaps her pushing a mother and daughter to heal their relationship was a mistake. She should let it heal on its own. But Constance was torn.

Two families to worry about. She couldn't bear to see the family breaking up around her, and she wanted them to heal faster . . . not for their sake but for her own. If she could make the world right here, she hoped to get the opportunity to make her world right.

* * *

"You're not really leaving the house in such attire?"

Liz could actually feel scandal in Constance's gaze as she surveyed her. "This is my favorite shirt. I wear it at least once a week—more if I can find time to do laundry—so I don't see the problem."

"Half your body's hanging out of it. You should cover yourself."

Liz blew out a breath. They were already running late since Matt had insisted on a cold lunch today, and the only way to shut him up had been to hurry and make him a sandwich. "It isn't bad. You're being neurotic, and we're late so we gotta go." Liz herded Constance out the door before another word was said about the shirt that showed a little of her stomach.

Liz hated having to drag Constance to school. No pioneer should have to deal with high school. High school destroyed innocence. The making out in the halls and the lewd words called out made Liz want to slap her hands over Constance's ears and eyes.

Liz cringed at every cuss word. And it wasn't like she was innocent of the crimes she was now so ashamed of . . . Nobody belted out a cuss word and slammed their fist into a horn faster in traffic than Liz did. She was just more aware of them than she ever had been in her life, and she found herself cutting off her own sentences to keep from saying anything that might shock her grandmother.

She also found herself tugging on her shirt all day to cover up the flash of bare stomach it revealed. She tried to do it when her grandmother wasn't looking, but she knew Constance could see her discomfort. Liz hated that Constance would sniff with that finishing-school arrogance every time she caught Liz tugging on the bottom of her shirt.

"It isn't that bad," she grumbled under her breath. The shirt had been an impulse buy at the mall last summer. It was a black stretch top. It went with everything she owned and made her look like she had a figure. Not that she cared that anyone knew she had a figure, but *she* liked knowing she had a figure.

But now that Constance was sniffing in disgust and shaking her head like some bobblehead doll, Liz hated that she hadn't worn something else. The shirt was a little short and probably a little tight too. But she'd be darned if she would change now. She had a point to prove, and even if it made her miserable, she was going to prove it.

By the end of fifth hour, she couldn't remember what the point was. She only knew she wanted to change more than anything in the world.

She received a few glares from Becky in the couple of classes they unfortunately had together. And Liz glared right back. Becky's shirt was shorter than her own. Why wasn't Constance giving Becky lectures? But Constance picked no fights with Becky, who seemed eager to steer clear of Constance. Garrett, on the other hand, appeared to be everywhere they turned.

He was there at lunch, offering to sit with them, scooting in next to Constance at the same time that Constance scooted away. He was there after gym class, commenting on how cool it was Constance had such a great tolerance for running and suggesting she join the track team. And he was there again after school, offering another ride home. Liz wanted to strangle him.

She was married, and he was a *jock*, certainly not worthy of Constance's attentions even if she were totally available, which she *wasn't*. Liz determined to give the boy some well-meant advice to get lost.

Liz sighed as they walked out to his car. She couldn't understand why her feet moved that direction. She hadn't been friends with Garrett for years and certainly didn't want his attentions now, but as he talked a mile a minute to Constance, Liz felt a twinge of . . . annoyance. Was she jealous? No, of course not. She didn't even like Garrett. He was a show-off with biceps, his intelligence comparable to the ball he bounced around the basketball court. Besides, as her next-door neighbor, he'd heard most of her parents' screaming matches when her dad came home late. Garrett and his family were firsthand witnesses to the fall of the House of King. Garrett's knowledge made him very much an enemy to Liz.

"I finally finished the paper I was doing for physics on kinetic energy. I could use a second opinion before I turn it in. Would you want to look at it and tell me what you think?" Garrett raked his fingers through his dark hair.

Liz looked away, even further annoyed. Asking for help with home-work was a truly desperate ploy. No girl would fall for that.

She found her jaw dropping as Constance said, "I would be very interested to read your paper. I'm afraid I may not be much help on the topic, but I have excellent grammar skills, so I can certainly be useful there." Constance smiled sweetly at Liz. "And my dear Liz would be able to help on the content. I am sure she knows all about kinetic energy."

As Liz was about to refuse, she felt the backs of Garrett's fingers brush her arm. "Would you do that for me, Lizzie?"

She *did* know a thing or two about kinetic energy. She knew that the energy caused from the motion in his fingers as they brushed her skin left her feeling like a snowman in a heat wave.

She couldn't even yell at him for calling her *Lizzie*. All she could do was nod dumbly and get into the car. She turned to make sure Constance was putting on a seat belt and felt grateful Constance did so without being told, since Liz found herself incapable of speaking.

Did Einstein have an equation for what just happened? Did Newton have a theory?

Garrett was in fine spirits as he explained the project that would accompany the paper. Liz stared at him. Yes . . . she had completely misjudged him. He hadn't traded his mind for a set of basketball sneakers. He wasn't like the Barbie drones that hung on him and asked him to all those dumb dances. Garrett was truly intelligent.

What kind of girl would Garrett ask out? Constance spoke up from the backseat. "Steam-propelling an engine in a boat would be considered kinetic energy, then?"

Garrett beamed at Constance in his rearview mirror. "Exactly! And you said you wouldn't understand my paper." He winked at her. Liz knew at that moment exactly what kind of girl Garrett would ask out if given the opportunity.

Liz sighed. His simple T-shirt and jeans made him look clean and freshly scrubbed. The wink was kind of cute. His getting excited over a science project was kind of cute too, and all that cute was being directed at her sesquicentennial fifth great-grandmother and none of it at her.

Liz looked back at Constance, who had gone silent and looked surprised at the wink. Her hands folded and refolded in her lap as though she finally realized she was being flirted with and wasn't sure what to do with that information.

"Hey, you okay?" he asked after he realized that his passengers were quiet.

"I think you made her uncomfortable." Liz sighed for what felt like the thirteenth time that day.

He looked in his rearview mirror again. "Oh, don't worry. I'm not asking you out again. But if you dump the other guy, you know where I live."

These words were said as he pulled up in front of Liz's house. Liz had to swallow to bite back the yelp she felt forming in her mind. He'd already asked her out? When had this happened? And why hadn't Constance mentioned it?

Once they were deposited on the sidewalk, Liz noted thankfully that he had driven away down the street and around the bend and not to his own house, where they could be overheard. Liz turned on Constance. "He asked you *out?*"

Constance folded her arms across her chest and arched an eyebrow. "I thought you didn't care for him."

"I don't," Liz said as she tugged hard on the black shirt.

"Then what difference does it make if he asked me to a dance?"

"You're married! And he asked you to Stomp?" Liz whirled around and stalked to the house.

Constance kept up with Liz. "Of course I'm married, which is why I declined the invitation. If you were nicer to the poor boy, he would have extended that invitation to you, but you're so intent on being a nit to everyone you meet, he hardly would have the courage to ask you, would he?"

"Did you just call me a *nit*?" Liz fumbled with her key at the door.

"Someone needed to!"

Liz pushed the door open, and the two of them stumbled inside, Liz trying to get some distance from Constance, and Constance refusing to give her that distance.

"I am not a nit! I don't even know what that is, but whatever that is . . . I'm not it! And we are *not* taking any more rides home with Garrett. He's too big a distraction."

"Only a distraction to you. For my part, he is no distraction at all."

"I don't mean for *me*. You! You are a distraction for *him*, and if Becky finds out we were with him again, she'll key my mom's car!"

"She'll what?"

"Never mind!"

"Lizzie . . ." Constance's voice had grown soft. It was the first time she'd ever called Liz the pet name everyone else used for her. The sound of it was comforting and made Liz want to cry for reasons she couldn't understand. Constance took her hand. "I am not vying for the affections of Garrett. You know I am not. But seeing you like this gives me hope that perhaps you are not altogether lost as to the ways of women. He seems a dear, sweet boy. Stop hating him long enough to let yourself like him."

"I don't hate him."

"I know that. But he doesn't."

Liz wanted to glare a little longer, but she couldn't be angry with the gentle touch of her great-grandmother holding her hand like that. Liz looked down at their hands. Hers were soft and smooth. Constance's were rough and reddened by the sun and elements. From the way they spoke, it seemed they should be reversed. With Constance's perfect English, she seemed like she would have the hands of a lady who never knew a day of chores. In their hands they were different.

Liz swallowed and looked into her grandmother's eyes, green like her own. Different . . . but the same. Liz looked away. "I'm sorry. I know you weren't trying to get Garrett or anything. I didn't mean—"

"Of course you did. And there's nothing wrong with that. You just experienced real jealousy for a moment. I think such an emotion is good for a person every now and again. It keeps that person from becoming complacent."

Liz's heart heaved a sigh of relief—at least that's what it felt like. The tears fell before she knew how to stop them, and she impulsively reached out and hugged Constance. She couldn't explain in any way she thought Constance would understand, but never before had anyone told her it was okay to show an emotion.

Not that she never showed emotion. But the only one she felt capable of revealing was anger. And that one emotion encompassed the rest, covering the others up. And here Constance stood, understanding what lay under the anger without anyone needing to explain. "I'm sorry," Liz said again.

"As am I." Constance hugged her back. "Now forget this and tell me something important."

"Tell you what?"

Constance linked her arm through Liz's and led the way toward the kitchen. "Do you have any bananas left?"

CHAPTER 18

LIZ HANDED A BANANA TO Constance before pressing the flashing button on the answering machine. Constance concentrated on getting the banana peeled but lost interest in what she was doing when the machine beeped and Liz's dad's voice boomed through the tiny speaker. Constance jumped at the sound.

Liz rummaged in the fridge while she listened.

"Hey, guys, it's your dad," he said.

"Good thing he identifies himself," Liz muttered, "otherwise we'd never figure it out."

"Just wondering if I can get sizes for your wedding clothes. Patty has the dresses picked out, and they need to be fitted, and the boys need the tuxedos ordered at the rental shop. The wedding's coming up pretty quick, and I need this stuff . . . like yesterday. Love you kids. Bye."

Liz glared at the machine. The message was meant for her mother, but he never mentioned or acknowledged her in the message.

"Patty is such a cow. The last thing I need is to be forced to see her kissing my dad under an arbor."

Liz had expected a lecture on being polite. But Constance ate her banana without comment. A car pulled up in the driveway, and Matt bounded out of Mrs. Hammond's car. She'd babysat him until Liz came home. He entered the house and dumped a pile of papers in Liz's hands as he talked a mile a minute about the school snack. She nodded, and uh-hmmed, and acted excited for him when he showed her the paper plates stapled together with beans inside. He finally ran out of things to say and hugged Liz tightly. She hugged him back, grateful he wanted to hug her. Over the last couple of months, her relationship with Matt had turned into nagging on her part and whining on his.

Constance smiled at him as he wandered away. "I think you'll look lovely in a dress."

Liz made a face. "What?"

"Your father said you needed to be fitted for a dress. I think a dress would be a considerable improvement."

Liz tugged again at the black shirt and tried to ignore Constance's raised eyebrows.

"If the garment worn requires adjusting every few moments, it is far better to choose another to wear in its place, do you not agree?" Constance placed her banana peelings in the trash can and waited for Liz to reply.

Liz didn't reply. She spun on her heel and stomped off to change shirts.

* * *

Liz's mom came home shortly after all the kids, even though she wasn't expected for another few hours. She listened to the saved messages, said nothing, and went to her room without talking to anyone. Alison jumped when she heard the master bedroom door slam. "Do you think the dresses will look okay?" she asked, looking more than a little worried.

"Alison!" Of all the things to worry about! Liz wanted to just scream. Another happy night in her happy home. She waited a few minutes before realizing there was no way her mom was coming back downstairs.

She finally went upstairs and knocked on the door. "Mom?" Silence answered her. She knocked again. "Mom?"

A muffled, "Whaddaya want?" came from behind the door.

"I need to go exercise Sassy. I have my competition on Saturday. Can I borrow the keys?"

There was another pause of silence followed by a loud thump of keys hitting the door and sliding down to the floor in a jingle. "Nice," Liz hissed. She opened the door, retrieved the keys, and looked to the bed, where her mother lay folded in the fetal position. Her mom's back was to her so there was no way to know if she was crying or just trying to nap. Her mom still had her black heels on. Liz considered removing them but hesitated. If her mom were trying to sleep, the shoes would make her uncomfortable. If she were just pouting, the shoes would still make her uncomfortable, but if Liz said anything about it, she'd likely get her head chewed off.

Her mom couldn't be asleep yet . . . she'd just thrown the keys at the door. Liz decided to leave well enough alone and shut the door behind her.

"What's the matter with Mom?"

Liz jumped. "Matty, don't sneak up on people. Mom's tired."

"I didn't sneak. I just walked. Is Mom okay?"

"I said she was tired. She's fine."

"Can I go in her room?"

"I don't think that's a good idea right now." Liz groaned when his face fell in disappointment. "Hey, bud, why don't you come and help me brush down Sassy?"

"Can I?"

"If you promise to stay out of the way." Last time she'd taken him to the stables, he'd dumped out a bucket of pellet supplements. When Liz yelled at him for dumping it all on the ground, he'd cried and insisted he was just trying to make himself a chair. Liz wouldn't have cared as much if all of Sassy's supplies didn't come out of her meager earnings from the competitions she won and from the random odd jobs she took around the neighborhood. That was the only way she was able to keep her mom from selling off Sassy the way she had sold off Alison's piano.

Liz knew her mom didn't need any excuses to sell off her horse. Every time Alison passed the empty space in the living room where the Steinway had been, she moaned and looked like she'd just been kicked. It was a constant reminder to Liz to keep Sassy and supply costs out of her mom's mind.

Liz grabbed a small fold-up camping chair, hoping it would keep Matt from getting any ideas about dumping anything else out.

"Where are you going?" Alison asked as Liz hauled the chair to the garage.

"I have to get some practice in before Saturday."

Alison followed Liz around to the back of the car. "Cool, can you drop me off at Steph's house?"

"Did Mom say you could go?"

Alison's face darkened. "Is Mom even talking? She's been weird ever since she went to sign the papers."

"She was weird way before that."

Nathan poked his head in the garage. "Where you going?"

"Is everybody going to ask me that?" Liz put the chair in the trunk and slammed it closed. "I'm going to the stables."

"Cool, can I come?"

Liz stopped and stared at her brother. Nathan never wanted to go anywhere. "Why?"

"There's nothing to do around here. Mom won't let me ride the scooter, and all the guys are going to the movies tonight."

"Why aren't you going with them?"

When Nathan shrugged and looked at his feet, Liz felt her whole body compress with the weight. Of course he couldn't go—how would he pay for it? For the same reason he didn't try out for freshman basketball when the guys did: there was no way he could afford the cost of uniforms and basketball camp. "Yeah, you can come. I'll let you warm her up while I clean the stall."

Nathan blinked. "Really?"

"Well, if you'd rather, you can clean the stall while I warm her up."

"Yeah, like that'd happen." He had his book tucked under his arm. Liz really did feel bad for him—for all of them. Nathan's sandy hair was tousled and looked like he'd run his fingers through it so many times it would never be able to lie flat again. She knew Alison was going to her friend's house to escape their mother's silence and to complain about how much she hated Patty. And Matt was desperate to hang onto anyone who would let him. Liz was actually glad to have Constance and Nathan along so that she wasn't worried about keeping Matt out of trouble.

As they all piled into the car, Liz shot a last look at the garage door, wondering if their mother would even appear when she heard them leaving.

The door remained closed.

* * *

"Can I choose the station?" Alison reached through the middle to start messing with the knobs before anyone could tell her no. She settled on a tween station that Liz would never publicly admit to listening to, even though privately she knew all the words to most of the songs they played. She left the music playing but turned the volume down so as not to freak out Constance. Although Constance adjusted pretty well to new situations, Liz wasn't taking chances.

"I was listening to that!" Alison protested. She reached to turn it back up, but Liz caught her hand.

"I'm the driver, so I get to pick what plays and how loud. Those are the rules of the car. If you don't like it, you can get out and walk."

"At least leave it on the station!" Alison's whine was loud enough to sound like an emergency vehicle.

"You're such a baby," Nathan said. "It's hard to believe you're four minutes older than me."

Liz grunted. "Guys, no fighting! I did leave it on your station, and quit calling people babies. Let's make this ride pleasant, okay? All this babysitting, and I'm not even getting paid," Liz muttered.

"I thought you said we couldn't call anyone babies." Matt looked upset.

"I did, and I mean it! That goes for you too, Matt."

"But *you* just called us babies."

Liz turned on her blinker. "I did not!"

"You said you were babysitting."

Liz's lips quirked up into a smile. "Don't get into semantics with me, Matty."

Once they were pulled up in front of the Meyers' house, Alison gathered her bag and got out of the car. She leaned her head back in. "How long can I stay?"

Liz looked at her a moment before answering. This same scenario had placed itself in their lives a million times before, but it was always her mom driving the car and answering the "how long can I stay" questions.

"I'll be coming back through in about two hours."

"Two hours? That's all?"

"Don't whine, Ali. Mom only gave me the car to practice with Sassy. She might not let me use it later. If I don't win my competition, Sassy's stable will cost too much, and then I'll have to—"

"Fine." Alison cut her off. "Two hours." She slammed the door closed and bounded up the lawn to the Meyers' front door.

"You'll have to what?" Constance asked when they were driving again.

"Sell Sassy." Liz ground her teeth hard. Selling her only friend in the world was not an option.

When they got to the stables, piled out of the car, and into the Little Barn where Sassy was housed, Nathan had the tack cabinet opened before Liz could even remember why she was there. "Can I saddle her?" he asked.

"Nope. The last time I let you help with that, you put the saddle too high, and it rubbed against her withers."

"You told me to."

"No. I told you to put the saddle a little higher and then pull it back into place so the hair on her back was smooth. You didn't push it back."

Nathan shrugged, plopped himself down in the hay, and started reading. He'd always been able to tune out everyone, especially Matt, who was practically screaming as he ran around the stables. Liz had to grab him several times and remind him that they'd all get in trouble if he spooked the other horses.

Sassy never got spooked. She could deal with Matt's antics all day and do nothing beyond swishing her tail at him. He loved it when she whinnied and stomped, and he imitated her when she did. Some of the other horses housed in the Little Barn weren't so friendly. A couple of hot bloods a few stalls away seemed to spend more time reared up on their back legs than they did on all fours. Liz tried to never take Sassy out at the same time those two were out.

She finished tightening the cinch and adjusted the stirrups for Nathan's legs. He wasn't much shorter than her anymore, but if she didn't adjust it and there was a problem, she knew she'd feel guilty forever.

"She's ready," Liz said, holding the reins out to Nathan.

He dog-eared a corner of his book and swiped a hand through his hair before looking at her with a grin. "Thanks, Lizzie."

"You sure you don't want to muck out the stall?" She grinned at him.

Instead of answering, he hurried to hop up into the saddle. He clucked his tongue the way Liz always did, and Sassy trotted off with him bouncing on her back. Liz chuckled and went to work on cleaning. Constance was quick to pitch in and even got Matt to help out. Liz was thrilled to have the job done so fast.

She slid her feet into her riding boots. When Nathan got back, Liz took over the reins and readjusted the stirrups. She led Sassy out and climbed up on her back then made a kissing noise that told Sassy to canter. She left the boys and Constance at the barn entrance while she rode through her paces.

Liz took several deep breaths. Life thrilled through her when she was riding. The sheer height of being on Sassy's back was enough to empower her to do anything. She urged Sassy faster so that they were galloping. She needed a little more speed to get Sassy to leap the first fence, and when Sassy cleared it, Liz let out a laugh. It was like flying, and she never got over the excitement of it.

Sassy performed with perfection. The competition was hers if she wanted it. The first place winner won four hundred dollars, which wasn't much, but it would make a difference.

Liz returned to the Little Barn feeling triumphant. It didn't matter what else was happening in her life—Sassy was always there to make it go away. Liz dismounted and looked over to where Nathan stood waiting for her. His book was in his hands, but it was closed. His blue eyes were tight, his mouth set in a thin line. "Alton came by; Mom called."

Liz felt her own smile slide off her face into an immediate frown. "What's wrong?"

"We have to meet Patty to get tuxedos and to get you and Ali dresses for the wedding."

"Oh," Liz said flatly. "Right. The wedding."

Matt stood in Sassy's stall with the medium brush in his hand. "Can I help brush her?"

Liz stared at his little face. Matt likely didn't understand why getting tuxedos and dresses made Nathan unhappy. He likely had no clue what was going on, and Liz didn't want to be the one to try to explain it. She sighed. "Sure, bud. You can help, but do it so her hair lies flat. It bugs her the other way."

They curried the horse in silence. Constance tried at several different conversations, but the only one willing to talk was Matt. So she had to find satisfaction in hearing about the rainbow song he'd learned, and they all had to bear his uneven voice singing the song twice. Matt seemed annoyed with the little response he got back for his vocal efforts and wandered off to look at the other horses. Liz cautioned him to stay away from the Arabians several stalls down.

The last thing she needed was Matt ticking them off. The owner was as hot-blooded as the animals, and if he even thought Liz had anything to do with his horses being bothered, he'd likely skin her. He was a surly sort of guy who wore a big cowboy hat and a bigger belt buckle. Sassy was an Arabian and was a total sweetheart in spite of the hot-blooded reputation her breed had. And Liz had known lots of other people who owned Arabians and found their horses to be very mild tempered. She figured his rotten disposition had something to do with his horses being so mean-spirited.

With Matt gone, the silence settled in between them like winter. Liz finished cleaning her tack and putting it away. She oiled Sassy's hooves with corn oil. It was cheaper than the hoof oil she used to buy from Alton. When he realized she was trying her best to save money, he gave her little tips like the corn oil to keep the hooves from cracking. Alton understood how much she needed Sassy, but he also knew how quickly Sassy could become a burden to the family. Little tips like the corn oil were implemented where they could be. He also let Liz muck out the stall herself to save on boarding fees.

After she'd finished and locked up her tack, a loud voice yelled from where the cowboy's Arabians were kept. The yelling accompanied the shrill whinny of the horses. Even Sassy back-stepped a little at the noise.

"Get outta here! You stay away from my animals. You understand?"

Liz, Nathan, and Constance hurried out to find Matt. When they got out, they found him backed up against the wall of the Little Barn, tucking his head into his shoulders as though he were a turtle trying to hide in his shell. The cowboy let out a line of expletives that made Constance stand taller.

Liz was furious, but before she had the chance to make the cowboy leave her brother alone, Constance had marched right up to him and jabbed a thin finger into the man's chest. "What right do you have to scold this child? Is he your child? No, he is *not*! I would daresay you have no cause to bring any such discipline upon him!" She looked at Matt. "Matthew? Were you doing anything you ought not to do?"

"N—no. I was just looking. They didn't start making noises and crying like they did 'til he came over." Matt pointed at the cowboy.

"Just keep him away from my animals!" the cowboy bellowed. Constance wrapped an arm around Matt's shoulder and led him away from the cowboy. Liz hurried to lock Sassy's stall.

They hadn't made it quite to the doors when the cowboy yelled out, "I'm filing a complaint with Alton! You'll be hearing about this!"

Liz groaned. Alton had helped her out in so many ways; he would be unhappy to hear she was involved in causing any trouble, even if it wasn't her fault. "Matt, I told you to stay away from those horses!" she said as she unlocked the car door to let the boys climb into the backseat.

"I did stay away. I was just walking by! He was the one that made them cry like they did."

"It wasn't just the animals he's made cry," Constance murmured.

Liz turned to see tears rolling down Matt's face. She felt a stab of shame for making her brother feel bad. "Don't cry, Matty. That crabby cowboy isn't enough to worry about." It wasn't exactly an apology, but it was the best she could manage after dealing with the cowboy and knowing she still had to deal with the tantrum Alison would throw as soon as she found out where they were going.

CHAPTER 19

"I AM NOT GOING ANYWHERE without Mom!" Alison shouted as soon as Nathan told her they were going to get fitted for wedding clothes.

"Mom told Nathan she didn't want to go, but we have to do it today because Patty needs it done."

"Since when do we care what Patty needs?"

"Dad cares," Matt said.

Everyone fell silent and stared at Matt. It was Constance who finally responded. "Your father does care. It is best not to disappoint him."

"Yeah, 'cause we'd hate to let him know what *that* feels like." Liz kept her voice low so only Constance heard her.

Constance scowled but didn't lecture. And before any one of them had time to truly fume over their situation, they were at the boutique in a strip mall. Patty waited inside. Liz could see her through the window sitting in an overstuffed blue chair with her fake blond hair hanging loose around her shoulders, her sandaled foot tapping impatiently.

When they opened the heavy glass door, the bell at the top tinkled, and Patty looked up. She didn't look exactly happy to see them, but then . . . they weren't exactly happy to see her either.

She stood and hurried to greet them, a smile pasted to her tanned face. She tried to hug Alison, who stiffened and pulled away abruptly. Patty's smile fell, and she bit her lip before shrugging and trying at a nervous laugh. She moved closer to Liz, but instead of trying at a hug, she wrinkled her nose. "Oh, you smell like horses."

"I just came from cleaning the stable."

"Maybe you should have gone home and cleaned up first."

"We were told we needed to meet you as soon as possible. *This* was as soon as possible."

Patty stepped back a bit to distance herself from the smell, and Liz moved in closer. It was Patty's own fault they were forced to come straight from the stables.

"We'd better get going on this, or we'll be here all night," she said, backing up even farther. An older woman in a nice black pantsuit claimed Nathan and Matt to get their measurements for the tuxedos while another less tidy woman in blue jeans and a pullover claimed Alison and Liz. For a moment, Patty stared at the leftover in their group. Constance stared back.

Patty frowned. "Wait . . . are there—" She shook her head, and Liz could almost see her brain counting the children in the shop. Liz didn't bother to explain and wondered if Constance would finally give in and say who she was, but Constance waited until Patty spoke again. "I'm sorry; I can't remember your name."

Constance nodded. "Of course you cannot. I've not yet given you my name. Liz, would you mind making a proper introduction?"

For a moment Liz believed Constance was just being snippy to Patty, and Liz was glad to watch Patty get a chew-out like Becky had. But Liz felt the sting of admonishment in Constance's voice. "Right. Patty, this is Constance. She's staying with our family for a little while."

Liz felt like that was enough, but Constance gave a small shake of her head. For a moment Liz was confused and unsure what she was supposed to do next. "And Constance, this is Patty," she said slowly.

Only then did Constance step forward and say, "It is a pleasure to meet you."

Patty didn't seem to know what to do with such good manners but seemed grateful that someone was going to at least pretend to be pleasant. Liz would have felt sorry for Patty if she hadn't already been determined to hate her.

"Are you related?" Patty asked. Liz knew she was wondering if she had to get the visitor a dress too.

"She's just visiting," Liz said. "She doesn't need a dress. She'll likely be home before the wedding."

"No way!" Alison said a little louder than appropriate in such a little boutique. Ali stomped out from the back dressing room she'd just been to, dragging a pale pink gown behind her. "I can't wear this."

"But I thought you liked pink—" Patty looked pale.

"It's sleeveless! My mom would never let me out in public in a dress like that. *Dad* wouldn't either!"

Liz smirked. Girls' camp this year had been one huge lesson on modesty. Liz was glad to see the lesson strike home in Alison, especially when that would lead to an even more uncomfortable Patty. Liz tried to look sympathetic but shook her head too. "Alison's right. Mom would never allow us to wear dresses like that."

"I'm sure your mother won't mind just for this special occasion—" Patty started.

"Even if my mom did allow it, *I* would never allow it. I don't ever wear clothes like that. And I *won't* ever wear clothes like that. If a person drops their standards for even a minute, who knows where that minute will lead them?"

Constance raised her eyebrows at Liz's declaration, but Liz plowed on, hoping Constance would stay quiet about the black top she'd been wearing earlier.

Liz touched the dress like it was a greasy oil rag and dropped it again. "You wouldn't really want us to dress like *that*, would you?"

Patty twitched her own bare shoulders in her candy apple red tank top, and Liz knew they'd struck the right nerve. Patty had *totally* meant for them to dress like that. Why would she even ponder that they wouldn't want to when she dressed like that every day? This little trip to the bridal boutique allowed them to slam Patty discreetly, in a way she couldn't even run home and complain to their dad about later. Liz enjoyed the moment more than she would a caramel cheesecake.

Patty frowned and tried to respond in some way to make them see reason, but they'd won when the first noise Patty uttered came out like a whine.

They ended up with dresses that were pale blue instead of pink, since they were the only dresses that were in the two girls' sizes that had decent sleeves and weren't cut low in the back. Patty looked deflated over it, and that made Liz like the blue dress even if it wasn't something she'd normally wear. Patty seemed grateful the boys were no trouble.

When Liz got home, she went straight to her room and threw away the black top. She'd never wear clothes like that again, not if it meant a possibility of her becoming as shallow and morally desensitized as her soon-to-be stepmother.

She pitched the shirt into the huge city trash can in the garage. When she entered the house again, she realized she hadn't seen her mother at all when they came home.

"Mom?" she called. "Mom?"

"She's asleep in her room," Alison said. "I already checked on her and had to get Matt out before he bugged her."

"I was just gonna kiss her g'night," he said in his own defense.

"She sleeps a lot," Alison said.

"Maybe the new job keeps her on her feet a lot." Liz knew that even though she was the one making up the excuse, the excuse was in no way valid. Her mom slept too much before the job. "Anyway, let's just do cereal tonight. I don't want to make anything."

"I could make mac-and-cheese," Alison suggested. "Nathan won't eat cold cereal for dinner."

"He used to."

Alison shrugged. "He said it's too weird to eat breakfast for dinner and won't do it. Weren't you there when he freaked at Mom for doing French toast a few weeks ago?"

"Nathan doesn't freak. You're exaggerating."

"Try making him eat cereal and you'll see."

Liz watched Alison getting the stuff she'd need for Nathan's dinner and gave a halfhearted smile. They fought a lot, but they stuck together a lot too. *It must be nice being a twin,* she thought for the gazillionth time in her life. "If you're going to make some, make enough for everyone."

Alison rolled her eyes. "Whatever." But she pulled out another two boxes.

Liz let the kids eat in front of the TV. It wasn't that anything good was on, but they all found a kid's sitcom and seemed content with that.

Liz and Constance ate at the table with all of Liz's homework spread between them. "I'm worried about you," Constance said as she pushed the food around on her plate. She apparently wasn't a fan of processed cheese.

"Why?"

"Alison went to visit her friends today. You went to visit your horse. I have the impression that this is a common scenario in your lives."

"So?"

"We've discussed this before. In Alison's room, there are pictures of her with other girls. In yours there are pictures of horses."

"So?"

"You need to be with people. I think your horse is a fine creature, but it doesn't take the place of real human friendships."

Liz smiled. "Maybe that's what you're here for. You can be my real human friendship."

Constance shook her head. "You flatter me. But I am entirely serious."

"And you think I'm not? Look, don't worry about me. I'm fine. Really."

But Constance didn't look convinced that Liz was fine. Liz wanted to think it was only the dinner that made Constance frown, but she knew Constance was worried about far more than just mac-and-cheese.

CHAPTER 20

CONSTANCE DIDN'T WANT TO GO to school. She claimed her head ached, that she was tired and wanted to just stay home. Liz was tired too but couldn't find a way to use that as leverage in making Constance go to school. "What if my mom finds out you stayed home?"

"I'll explain I'm unwell."

"What if something happens and you need help?"

"I'm not an infant. I'm quite capable of caring for myself. I promise not to leave the house. But you'd better hurry; you'll miss your bus."

Liz threw a withering look in Constance's direction. Constance had been living in modern times less than a week and was already making sandwiches for Matt and waving Liz off to the bus. In a way she had taken over as the mother so that Liz didn't have to. Liz felt grateful and guilty all at the same time. Grateful she didn't have to and guilty because she felt like she should.

As Liz walked through the front doors to the school, she wondered when her mom would be normal again. It was like she'd shut down the night she'd signed the papers. All she did was go to work and then come home and sleep. Liz wasn't even sure she was eating. Could someone survive for very long without eating? Liz hoped her mom at least got lunch during her workday.

It was while she worried about her mom and worried about whether or not Constance would really stay put like she said that Liz walked past Becky Dunford's locker.

Becky stood in front of her so Liz couldn't pass. "Where's your cute little English cousin?"

"She stayed home today." Liz hated getting cornered without Constance. She felt safer when Constance was around, like she had her own personal bodyguard, but then . . . maybe that wasn't such a great thing. Becky hated that Garrett liked Constance even more than Liz hated it.

Becky's torture used to be little more than a flippant remark that could be taken as kind or cruel depending on your interpretation. These were comments she could get away with in front of Sunday school leaders and Young Women advisors.

But from the moment Constance had shown up and Garrett had shown interest, Liz had become target practice.

"That's too bad. We were becoming such good friends."

"You're more than welcome to go visit her after school."

"No need. You can give her my message."

Liz didn't bother to ask what message. She knew if she waited long enough, Becky would get frustrated and tell her anyway.

Becky waited a few moments longer than Liz would've expected before saying, "Garrett asked me to Stomp."

Liz almost laughed. That was her big news? Could a dumb guy be so worth all this fanfare? But then there was a side of Liz that boiled at the news since she knew he wasn't a dumb guy. "So?" Liz said. "That must make you feel kinda bad."

"Why would that make me feel bad? It means the American won."

"By forfeit. He already asked Constance to go, but she turned him down. *I'd* hate taking someone else's reject."

Liz's heart pounded. Sure, she'd disliked most of the student body from day one of entering Alta High, but this was the first time she'd actually handled a direct confrontation. She saved her confrontations for her family, where they'd have to accept her either way. At school, she tried to keep her head down. Liz smiled, shrugged, and waved good-bye to Becky's reddened face.

She ended up late for her class. By the time lunch came, and the unavoidable Garrett along with it, Liz wanted to howl.

"Hey, where's your cousin?" he asked, plopping himself down next to her. His long legs stretched out to the next tables. Liz scowled at that. If he'd been considerate, he'd know that people used the aisles to pass through. She scowled even deeper when he hurried to offer a quick apology to someone wanting to pass as he tucked his legs back in.

"She's at home."

"England home or the King home?"

"The King home. She's sick." Liz stuffed a roll into her mouth. *Maybe he'll just go away.*

No such luck. His face brightened with the news. "That's great. Do you think she'd mind if I stopped by after school?"

Liz couldn't believe her ears. "You think it's great she's sick?"

"No! I mean great she's still in town."

Liz snorted. "You know—and I don't mean this to sound mean, but—yes, she would mind. No, you shouldn't come over."

He paused before speaking, scrubbing a hand through his thick dark hair. *He needs a haircut if he wants to go on a mission,* she thought.

"Is it that she'll mind or that *you'll* mind?"

"She'll mind. *I* couldn't care less."

He huffed at that. "I've noticed. Why would she mind?"

"She's—already got a guy. And she doesn't cheat. You should take a lesson." Liz started gathering up her lunch tray and backpack.

"What's *that* supposed to mean?" He stood up at the same time she did, blocking her escape.

"You're going to Stomp with Becky." She knew her tone sounded accusatory, as though he were out skinning small animals or something, but once a stupid thing was said, the only thing left to do was make a run for it. With that she dodged around him, but in the effort her tray slipped. She could only keep a hold with one hand and so created a slide for all the tray's contents to crash to the floor. The spaghetti landed with a sickening splat.

Why were there a million eyes to witness the event when something truly horrible happened? The applause from the cafeteria made Liz want to melt into the ground and disappear down one of the cracks in the floor.

She stared in horror at the mess and in greater horror that Garrett was still there watching her. He looked mad, likely not as mad as she felt, but mad just the same. *He* was the two-timer hitting on her *married great-grandmother* and then making out with Becky behind the bleachers in the gym. Okay, so she didn't *know* he was making out behind the bleachers, but it seemed like a logical conclusion to draw, and Liz was always logical. Or at least she was until he started popping up everywhere.

"Are you gonna clean that up?" he asked.

"I might." Liz put down the tray, now dripping with red sauce, and hefted her backpack up on her shoulder so it didn't drop into the mess.

"It'd be easier if you put the pack down too." He was still standing there watching her.

"It'd be easier if some guy in my ward who blesses the sacrament every week would help."

"I don't bless it every week. We take turns. And just so you know, going to a dance with someone doesn't make us exclusive."

The blessing-the-sacrament slam must have hit home, because he was now bent over with a wad of napkins he'd pulled off a nearby table. He mopped at the sauce with a great deal of agitation.

"Well, Constance *is* seeing someone exclusively." Liz finally put her backpack down.

"That's okay with me. I didn't ask to come over and marry her. I just wanted to come over and say hi. You said she was sick; maybe she could use some cheering up."

"She has me for that."

His eyebrows climbed his forehead. "Exactly my point!"

Liz wasn't sure what happened in that moment. She had a modest-sized handful of dripping spaghetti noodles, and the next thing she knew they were flying through the air and landing on Garrett's shirt, splattering his face and making him flinch to avoid getting any in his eyes.

Liz covered her mouth with a spaghetti-sauce hand. "Oh! I am so sorry! I swear, I didn't mean to do that." She didn't know what she expected, but she wasn't ready for him to stand up and pick the noodles off his shirt and then walk away saying nothing at all.

She remembered again that she was in a cafeteria filled with students. She wondered how many of them noticed the exchange. When she looked up and a ton of faces hurried to turn back to their trays, she figured plenty had noticed. She was grateful Becky had second lunch—not that she wouldn't hear about it and torment her over it. Even if Becky never said a word, just knowing she'd know made Liz want to die.

And worse was the stone face of Garrett. She'd never seen him walk away like that. Even when they were kids and they got into fights, Garrett was always the first one standing on her porch, forgiving her and asking if they could play with his new action figures.

* * *

Constance's day rejuvenated her, offering a mental respite as well as physical. She wandered the house, inspecting light switches and touching things she knew she should not. But when there was no one around to tell her not to be curious and no one around to put up such pretenses for, she felt like she'd been set free. She used the bathtub to scrub out her dress and underclothes and hung them out over the curtain rod to dry. She sincerely hoped they dried before anyone came home to inquire after them.

It grieved her that Liz had been right regarding the clothes. It was a rare woman who wore a skirt in this century, and the ones they wore scarcely covered their bodies. No one seemed concerned if they showed off half their leg to public scrutiny . . . or more in some cases. Even women of little means in her time respected themselves enough to cover up. Constance shook her head at the tragedy.

She spent a good hour looking over books in the bookshelves and was struck with the irony of it all. These were books that hadn't even been written yet. If she didn't read them now and was suddenly pulled back, she'd never get to! Not wanting to disappoint herself, she pulled a few off the shelf and perused the back covers. Most were books about things and places she'd never heard of, and after reading the back covers, she returned them to the shelf.

But then she found a black, leather-bound book. There were no pictures of odd machines on the covers, or pictures of muscled men on horseback riding into battles. The black book cover had few words on the spine, but the words made her heart pound the way it had the day the missionaries had found her so long ago.

THE BOOK OF MORMON.

There were other words written on the spine too—THE DOCTRINE AND COVENANTS and THE PEARL OF GREAT PRICE. Her body shivered with the delight of seeing the book that had inspired her journey to the moment in which she now stood. She eased it off the shelf with reverential awe and held it to her chest for a long time before opening its pages.

She was again reminded of the tender mercy of the Lord. Had it not been for this book, she would have never met her William. She would not have her small Eliza. Were it not for this book, the home in which she stood and the lives that now surrounded her would not exist. They would be replaced by something else. She would have married Daniel and been a meek, absurd little wife like her mother. Even if Eliza's spirit had still been sent to her, Eliza would never have known happiness in a household like Daniel's . . . a household like the one Constance had been raised in.

She fell to her knees. "Is this what you wanted from me, Lord?" she asked. "Were you searching for my gratitude?" She waited, but no answer came. "I *am* grateful," she continued. "I am not sorry that my life led me to your word, to your gospel. I do not mourn the life I had in England. I would not go back to that. I am only uncertain that I can return to a life without William." And she felt instant shame at the words. She could not take them back, for they were truth, and the Lord would know a lie.

She wanted to say she was sorry for her lack of gratitude, but the resentment over her loss of husband and child had not enabled her to such a disposition. She sighed, feeling her own failure and simply knelt there, holding the book that meant so much to her and harboring the enormous resentment that came with her current situation. How one could feel resentful and grateful at once bewildered her, but there it was and there was nothing to do but recognize she was not ready to apologize.

She read for some time, stopped for a bit of food, and took a brief walk. She hurried along the walk. She had promised, after all, not to leave the house but hated feeling trapped inside when the world outside was so full of wonder.

Watching the modern world carry on was fascinating, and walking helped to alleviate her anxiety about what she could do, or should do, to return to her own life. Clair had called and left a message admonishing the children to stay away from her computer since many emails of hers had again been deleted.

The message sounded like gibberish to Constance. So many things in this time sounded foreign to her that she wondered how she could help a family when she herself felt so entirely helpless. How was she ever to get back to the wagons when a simple sentence threw her into a quandary?

A few people said hello to her as they clipped their lawns and pulled at weeds. Others ignored her entirely. Society was certainly altered. And how one determined their place in society was a puzzle.

She returned to the house and her reading. She pulled two bananas off the little bunch and took them, the book, and a little blanket to the couch where she cuddled up, ate, and read. The words on the page were a calming salve, and soon she was engrossed in the plight of the Nephites as they warred, made peace, and warred again. Surely if the women who taught their sons to be brave and to fight for righteousness could withstand their troubles long enough to be such mothers, her own troubles, which paled in comparison, could be handled.

She jumped when she heard grumbling from the side of the house—wrenching, grinding noises that sounded like pain had been given a voice. Constance let the little blanket fall to the ground as she hurried to scoop up the banana peelings. She quickly tossed them in the waste bin and stepped toward the garage door and put an ear to it.

The sound stopped.

Then there was a slam. She opened the door, thinking maybe Liz had returned early. A man stood at the bottom of the garage stairs. He jumped and let out a cry of surprise followed by a string of expletives. His startled reaction gave cause to her own, and the next thing she knew, she was falling.

A scream and a few loud crashes later, Constance found herself at the bottom of the three stairs, looking up at the man. Her knee hurt.

"Who are you?" he asked, frowning.

"Since I am supposed to be here and no one has mentioned your coming, I feel I should be asking that question," she said as she used the shelving near the stairs to pull herself up.

"It's my house. Tell me who you are, or I'm calling the cops."

Constance crossed her arms over her chest and raised an eyebrow at that. She moved up the stairs and stood at the top to block him from entering the house. This man was likely Liz's father, and though she wasn't one to cause contention, she wasn't one to allow deception either.

From what she knew of Clair, the woman would never have allowed him to enter the house without her being present. He knew Clair worked during the day, and the children were all in school. He was here, no doubt, for mischievous reasons of his own.

He glared at her for taking the strategic high ground and moved to pass her anyway.

She blocked him. "What is your business here?"

"I came to get some things. It's my house. What are you? The guard dog?"

He smelled horrid to Constance, like soap perfumed too heavily. She wrinkled her nose. "I live here, and this is Clair's home. She would have spoken of your visit yesterday were you expected or welcome."

"Look, kid, I could easily pick you up and move you, so let's just make this easy and you move yourself."

"I can call Clair using the cell phone. I will lock the door until I have her approval for your entrance. If she approves, then you need not worry as I will admit you to the house. If you fail to meet with her approval, I shall be forced to keep the doors locked and take whatever precautions she may feel to be necessary."

His mouth hung slack as she offered up the options to him. He scratched at his ear just under his sandy blond hairline. "This is stupid," he said. "You don't live here. My wife and kids live here. I don't know who you think you are, but I'm—"

She wasn't sure if it was reading about the boldness of the Nephite warriors, or if it was her own agitation at having witnessed the family try to manage their pain, or if it was simply the fact that this man was at fault for making her fall down the stairs and then treating her like a child, but Constance was ready to turn this brute of a man over her knee! "You chose to break the connection to your family. They now undergo a great deal of pressure to maintain this household without the support of a loyal father and husband. This is no longer your home, by your choice. And I most certainly belong here. I've been invited to stay for as long as I desire. I belong here. You, sir, do not. Now, please step down before you force me to cause you harm."

"Did Clair get herself a British Nazi?" he muttered to himself.

"You stay here. I'll call Clair. If you really have a right to be here, she will tell me and I will promptly apologize for detaining you."

His eyes narrowed, but he stepped back off the stairs. "Fine. Forget it. I'll come back when Clair gets home." He returned to his car and got in, pausing for one final glare before he started the engine and drove away.

Constance worried that maybe Clair had wanted him there and didn't stop worrying until Liz came home.

CHAPTER 21

"YOU KICKED OUT MY DAD?" Liz asked, horrified and satisfied all at the same time. He wasn't a bad guy, not diabolically anyway, and she really did love him, but she was mad at him too. It felt good to see him stymied.

"What else could I do? He provoked a tumble down the stairs and then didn't even bother to help me up. A proper gentleman would offer assistance in such a circumstance!"

Liz could only shrug at that. Constance had a point. "I hope my mom doesn't get mad about this."

"Do you think she'll be angry?"

Liz shrugged again. "Doubt it. I don't see why he was here anyway when no one else was. I hate to be suspicious of him, but it sounds weird." Liz tucked her hair behind her ear. "Actually . . . not too weird. Dad's a control freak. He probably just likes to feel powerful by still having control in some way. You know, Mom's message said she'd found deleted emails and told us to stay off her computer. Do you think he's spying on her and reading her emails and stuff?"

"Liz, I can scarcely comprehend what you just said."

"Well, never mind. I'll talk to Mom about it. So you wanna know what happened to me today?"

When Constance turned her full attention to Liz, she spilled the news about Becky, the math test she only got a B on when she needed an A, and finally the disaster in the cafeteria with Garrett.

Constance stared at her when she was done explaining. "You threw your food at him?"

"He was just so . . . argh! He was lucky I didn't pop his ribs in half!"

Constance laughed out loud. "Aren't we a pretty pair? Willing to wrestle a man to the ground if need be to save our pride from their insults!"

Liz laughed too. If you looked at it the right way, the situation could be sort of funny. Sort of . . .

They lowered their voices when Matt came home so he couldn't hear them debate on what to tell Liz's mom when she got home from work. Matt came in and bugged them a few times but seemed content to pull potato bugs from under the rocks in the garden most of the afternoon.

Nathan and Alison came home, but Nathan immediately disappeared to the living room couch to read, and Alison left for her friend's house.

It made for a quiet evening.

As they sat on the back patio in the cooling autumn air, Liz thought to ask, "Besides kicking my dad out, what did you do all day?"

"I read the Book of Mormon."

Liz smiled. "We have other books, you know."

"I saw them. But when I went to choose, that was the only book I cared to read. It filled me with peace."

"It's a little weak on the romance." Liz yawned for emphasis.

"Weak on the romance? You sound like one of those girls sitting on pillows and eating chocolates. Pampered, spoiled . . ." Constance said softly with a mischievous grin playing across her lips.

Liz tossed her a dirty look, but she was smiling too. "Arrogant, over-bred . . ." she retaliated.

"Overbred! That's hardly a compliment!"

"And *pampered* is supposed to be a compliment?" Liz thumped her lightly on the head with a fluffy chaise pillow.

Constance returned the attack with a pillow from her own chair, and they ran around the yard, tagging each other with pillows until Matt came from the side of the house to see what the noise was. They turned on him and chased him around until they all three were too tired to run away and too tired to give chase even if one of them were to run. Matt went back to bug collecting. Liz and Constance sat on the cool grass.

Constance sighed. "If William and Eliza were here, I don't think I'd ever return to the wagon companies. I'd stay and get complacent and lazy like my granddaughter."

"If Eliza were to turn up here, you wouldn't ever have a grand-daughter. Just remember that."

"True. And that would be a tragedy. She is much better off where she is. I'll see her soon enough."

Liz heard the longing in her voice and felt bad over it. At least Constance wasn't crying anymore. Well . . . not as much anyway. She'd still get teary eyed and sniffle every now and again, but for the most part, she'd succumbed to the new circumstance.

"I am glad to see you dressed better today," Constance said, surveying the green Gap shirt and blue jeans. "You still look like a boy, but at least you're not showing your skin."

"Are you going to give me a daily update on your feelings for my clothes?"

"Likely."

Liz laughed and stood up. "I gotta make dinner. Mom'll be home soon."

"Will she read to me?" Matt popped over from where he was putting his potato bugs in a row along the cement crack of the patio.

"I dunno. Maybe. Ask her when she gets home."

As Liz was heading through the back door, she caught sight of Garrett over the fence. He hurried to look away then disappeared around the side of his house. She cringed. What he must think of her . . .

* * *

Her mom didn't come home in time for dinner. They had tacos. Constance felt it was a bit spicy and drank a ton of water to wash it all down. Matt giggled as she waved her hand over her mouth. "She's like a cartoon!" He immediately mimicked her.

Alison beamed when she sat at the table. She barely made it home in time for the blessing over the food. "I can take piano lessons again!" she announced as soon as the amens echoed around the table.

"How?" asked Nathan.

"Stephanie's mom is letting me use her piano to practice! And Sister Rowley is giving me free lessons if I babysit for her on Saturdays."

"That isn't free," Nathan said. "That's bartering."

"Whatever. Either way I get to keep playing until I can get a new piano! Isn't that so cool?"

"Yeah, that's really cool!" Liz showed more enthusiasm than she felt. Now she was down one babysitter, but she understood how Ali loved the piano. She loved it like Liz loved Sassy. Maybe she could find a way to bribe Nathan to watch Matt when she went to her competition. Taking Matt was out of the question.

"Yay," Nathan said in a monotone voice.

"Don't be a creep, Nay-thing," Ali said.

And the two were off in insults, private jokes, and pretended hurt feelings. They got loud enough that Liz sent them to eat in front of the TV again just so they could take the noise somewhere else.

Her mom dragged in an hour later just as Liz was trying to wrestle Matt to the bathroom to brush his teeth. She didn't even bother to look in the kitchen and said a few halfhearted hellos and good-nights to the kids before trudging up the stairs and closing her bedroom door.

"She's not reading to me, is she?" Matt asked.

"Nope, I guess not." Liz felt irritated and worried all at the same time.

"Does that mean you are?"

"You bet I will. At least if you brush your teeth. Mom can't afford to fix your teeth when they rot out of your head."

"She fixed your rotten teeth."

"Mine weren't rotten; they were crooked. It's not the same thing. And that's when Dad was home."

Matt didn't argue further and mimicked his mom's trudge as he made his way down the hall to the bathroom.

Alison frowned as she made her way to the bathroom. "She sleeps a lot."

"Maybe she's doing drugs," Nathan said, passing her so he got there first. "Guys before girls, huh, Matty?"

Matt and Nathan hit their fists together in their male bonding ritual as Alison glared, realizing her idea of ever getting into *that* bathroom had been quashed. She harrumphed all the way to the downstairs bathroom. Liz felt grateful no water accompanied this night's episode.

But she did turn to look at her mother's bedroom door when Nathan said the word *drugs*. She shook her head.

No.

No!

There was *no* way her mom, her be-righteous-like-the-pioneers mom, would ever involve herself in something like that. Would she?

No. Of course not, but Constance had seen something that fit the description of a pill bottle. And she said that Mom looked—*No!*

Liz shook her head again to clear her mind, but she let her fingertips trail across her mom's door as she walked by. *Please don't screw our family up more,* she thought.

Matt insisted on reading the Berenstain Bears *The Spooky Old Tree.* Halfway through he stopped and laid a small hand on her cheek. "You're skipping pages again, Lizzie."

How the kid knew she was skipping pages, she had no idea. He couldn't read yet, so it wasn't like he was following along. But when he knew every place to give a violent shudder as the bears got the shivers, she figured he had the thing memorized. He wanted a second round, so she gave in then made him get under the covers. She flipped his light off and made her way to her own room.

"Remember that bottle my mom dropped the other night, the one that bounced?"

Constance looked up from the Book of Mormon. Her loose hair cascaded down the back of her duck pajamas in long dark waves. "Yes?"

"Tell me one more time what it looked like."

"It was brown with a stripe of white. There was writing on the white stripe. There was a white top."

Liz exhaled. "Just a prescription then."

"That's what she said. A prescription." Constance looked down at her book but then looked up again with a quizzical look. "Is this important?"

"No." Liz pulled out the elastic that kept her hair in a ponytail. "If it's a prescription, then it's not important at all. It's probably just ibuprofen for her headaches." Liz plopped herself down on the bed. "Wow. You're almost done?"

"I've had all day to read."

Liz crossed her legs under her. "Are you coming to school with me tomorrow?"

"Do you need me to?"

"I dunno. I got into so much trouble today."

"Would anything have changed had I been there?"

"I probably wouldn't have thrown spaghetti all over Garrett."

Constance smiled. "I think your interaction with Garrett is encouraging. At least you're communicating. And what if your father returns?"

Liz dropped her head in her hands. "He's not a bad guy. What harm could he really do?"

Constance didn't answer. She was obviously tired and didn't want to be bugged. Besides, Liz was tired too. Another long day stood before her, and she needed some sleep.

* * *

Liz tapped her foot. She stood over Alison's sleeping body and fumed. This was the third time this morning she'd been in this same room waking up this same girl! "Alison, now!"

Alison moaned and put a pillow over her head. Liz stripped the pillow and most of the bedding off the bed and threw it onto the floor.

"Lizzie, you're such a freak! I'm tired."

"I'm tired of you, so we're even. Get dressed, or you'll miss your bus."

Constance was up and wearing an outfit she'd picked for herself from Liz's closet. The outfit consisted of a blue, ankle-length skirt and a white, button-up blouse. It was something Liz wore to church every now and again, but she hadn't worn it in months. Constance also had sandals on.

Liz whistled. "Don't you look pretty."

"Another day of boy's britches, and I would begin to question my own gender. I feel much more like myself today. I do miss the stockings, however. I tried to wear them with these shoes, but the appearance was not appropriate."

Liz laughed, imagining Constance wearing sandals and tube socks. "You ready then?"

They hustled the other kids out the door and walked to the bus stop. They were the first ones there. Liz was glad that even though the Mitchells' car sat warming up in the driveway, Garrett was nowhere to be seen. But that bit of luck didn't hold out for long.

He drove slowly to the stop, rolled down the passenger window, and leaned over toward Constance. "Hey, little girl, want a ride?"

"Why would he refer to me as a little girl?" Constance whispered in confusion, but Liz turned away, her face hot with embarrassment.

Just go away! She prayed with all her heart he'd leave and never talk to her or look at her again.

Liz wasn't really surprised that he didn't talk to her; all his comments were to Constance.

"How you feeling?" he asked.

"Fine, thank you. How are you?"

He chuckled. "Great! Liz said you were sick yesterday; I just wanted to make sure you were better."

"I'm much better, thank you."

He seemed ready to offer a ride when his glance slid in Liz's direction and his expression darkened a shade. Becky shattered his focus entirely when she drove by and honked. She revved her engine, and Garrett drove off after her.

"You didn't apologize!" Constance scolded. "I gave you many opportunities, but you stood there as though you were a piece of art instead of a human girl."

"It doesn't matter. He's got Becky to make him feel better." Liz smiled but still felt the perverse sense of jealousy she'd felt earlier. *Do I like Garrett?* She stamped the thought out as quickly as it entered her mind.

School with Constance was a relief. Liz felt normal with another person by her side and wondered if this was what Constance meant when she said Liz needed human companions, not equestrian ones. Liz wondered how she'd managed without Constance around. She worried over the day when Constance would go back and secretly hoped that day would never come.

* * *

Constance took joy in the day she spent with Liz. Wearing appropriate clothing cheered her considerably. And though Liz seemed immature in so many ways, she made an amiable companion. Constance found herself loving Liz as much as she'd loved her sister Julia. Having Liz near her to laugh with and speak with had been a salve to her lonely heart. Less than a week away from the hard trails and cold winds that whipped through the plains, and she felt herself melting into the comfort of the modern world as though it were a bed of down.

Though the people around her were different from those she was accustomed to, different did not mean unpleasant. Constance found that a good many of the girls she met were very pleasant, and as Constance spoke to them, Liz became emboldened to speak as well.

All in all, after having spent a day in scripture and prayer, Constance still worried that William had never returned to the wagons. She worried but would not allow herself to get desperate over that fear. She would have faith they were all well and hoped she would be with them again soon. She knew her daughter, Eliza, was in good hands, and though she ached to hold her own child, she had evidence of that child's well-being in the posterity sitting next to her in the cafeteria.

Three girls had joined them, wanting to hear all about England. But she quietly ebbed from the conversation as Liz became more involved. Constance smiled as Liz described the sheer beauty of her horse to the girls.

"We should go riding sometime. That would be kinda cool." Tami tugged a strand of strawberry blond hair back behind her ear.

"Sure." Liz shrugged and Constance rolled her eyes at the gesture. That girl had the twitchiest shoulders she'd ever seen.

"Hey! There's a stake fireside tonight. You guys should come. We'll save you seats!" This declaration came from Crystal. Her dark hair was in a twist that spilled out from the top. Hairstyles had changed throughout time as well.

Constance wondered what her hair would look like twisted up like that and then spilling loose in a messy topple. When her mother's maid had fixed her hair, it was always done in elaborate braids pinned all over her head. She'd always wished William could have seen her in silk dresses with flowers and ribbons braided in her hair.

William met her after she had learned to make a rudimentary bun. He'd never really seen her when she looked resplendent. And as things stood, he'd never see her that way whether she returned or not. She felt far prettier today than she had in a very long time. She was scrubbed clean, and her hair had been brushed until it shone like a polished chestnut.

"What's the fireside on?" Liz asked.

"It's a Jenny Phillips fireside on her album *Journey to Zion*." Crystal's eyes lit up with excitement. "It's about pioneers. But don't let that freak you out. My sister said it was really cool."

Liz gave a little laugh and a half smile. "I like pioneers." She sketched a glance at Constance, who gave her a wink.

"Yeah, they're doing it because we did a pioneer trek this summer. Are you coming, then?" Tami asked.

"If I can get a babysitter for my little brother."

"Where's your mom?" asked Melanie.

"Working," Liz said with a dramatic sigh.

"Ugh! My mom works too! I hate getting stuck doing all the babysitting while she's gone!" Crystal shook her head so violently that her hair fell out of the clip holding it in the twist. She hurried to twist it back up and clip it in place.

The girls were off on their different lamentations of chores and responsibilities. Constance listened with fascination at each of the complaints. They were all so dissatisfied with their lives that she was tempted to take a paddle to all four of them, and yet they sounded strangely similar to her own midnight rants with her sister Julia. Some things did not change. No matter where one chanced to be in life, there was always something with which to find fault.

She was sorry she and Julia hadn't found joy in as many things as they'd found fault.

"Is the fireside for all the youth?" Liz asked.

"I think so," Crystal said.

"I'd probably have to bring my brother and sister, but I might be able to find someone to watch Matt for a little while. It sounds like fun."

And so the plans were tentatively set in place. Constance was pleased to see Liz branching out and forming new acquaintances. Garrett walked by, saw the girls, and continued walking. Constance sighed. How aggravating for his attentions to be entirely misplaced. If he only saw what Constance saw in Liz, he'd be dancing with a far better girl than the one he was taking to Stomp.

Constance sighed again. That was another thing that had not changed in modern times. Men were foolish in every century.

CHAPTER 22

GETTING SOMEONE TO WATCH MATT was harder than Liz imagined. When Alison insisted she was going to her friend's instead of the fireside, Liz said Alison could stay home and be the babysitter if she didn't want to go.

"You're not the mom!" Alison retorted, her voice nearly a scream.

"I'm the closest thing you've got right now, so . . . either come with us and get some spiritual insight or stay home and babysit."

Alison really did scream then. "I hate you, you know!"

"I care?"

"Fine. I'll go, but Stephanie's coming too, and you're picking her up!"

"Fine." Liz turned away before Alison saw the tears. Alison had never said she hated her before. Liz squared her shoulders and took a sharp breath of air to keep from crying over those stinging words. She didn't want Alison to hate her.

Since Alison had decided to go, Liz was left without a sitter. Happy was the moment when Abby from down the street called and asked if Matt could come over and play. Liz asked to talk to Abby's mom and pled her case of really wanting to provide a deeply spiritual evening for her brother and sister but that Matt would make it hard. Abby's mom sympathized and said she'd take Matt during the fireside.

Next was the matter of the car. She thought about calling her mom but couldn't do it. Her mom was so unhappy that asking her to do anything was like asking her to put another ten tons of brick on her back. Liz couldn't, so she asked her dad instead. He was in a good enough mood that he agreed and dropped off his car while he and Patty went to the tanning beds to get ready for their honeymoon.

When he dropped off the car, it was an effort for Liz to be pleasant and smile.

"Hey, Dad?" she asked as he got into the passenger side of Patty's car.

"Yeah?"

"Can I keep the car until tomorrow? I have a competition, and I need a way to get there. Alton's going to truck Sassy over, so I don't need to worry about that."

He shrugged. "Since it's Saturday, Patty and I were planning on spending the whole day together anyway. We shouldn't need two cars to do that, should we, babe?" He laughed like he'd said something funny. "Sure, Snow White. You can actually keep it 'til we get back from our honeymoon."

"Thanks," she managed to squeak out before his door closed and they were gone. She stood at the curb with his keys in her hand and said, "I wonder why he doesn't have to work."

"What?" Alison asked, having come out to say hello to their dad.

"Didn't he always work on Saturdays when he lived with us?"

Alison bit her lip. "I don't think he *had* to. I think he wanted to." The two girls stared down the street where the car with their father had disappeared around a corner. Alison leaned into Liz. "Were we so bad?"

"No. We just weren't enough." Liz repeated the thing she'd heard her mom say to Constance a few nights before. But even as she said it, she knew the words weren't true. They *were* enough. He just hadn't taken the time to get to know them. She tried to take the words back, but Alison had already slipped away from her and was in the house before Liz could fix what she'd said.

* * *

When Liz slid the dress over her head, Constance stared. "You're a beautiful *girl!*"

"Oh, stop! I don't look any different now than I did ten minutes ago."

"That's where you're wrong. You look like a lady instead of an insolent boy."

"Did you just call me an insolent boy? I don't know that I can ever talk to you again after a cut like that."

Constance laughed.

"Want me to put your hair up for you?" Liz asked.

"Why?"

"It's a fireside. Sunday-dress type of stuff. I mean, your hair looks fine the way it is, but I thought you might like it different."

"I think I'd like that."

Liz had fun putting Constance's hair in the twist. She curled the toppled ends over so they looked elegant instead of messy and put in a few bobby pins to keep it in place.

Constance looked like she might cry when she finally gazed at her finished reflection in the mirror. "William would have liked my hair this way."

"Then you'll have to do it for him when you get home."

"He's not there, Liz. We both know he's not." Constance sounded without hope.

Liz pressed her lips together. She had feared he wouldn't be returning to the wagon company. But she hated to admit that and take away all hope. And she didn't want to see Constance cry anymore about it. Constance flitted back and forth in her emotions. Liz was pretty sure Constance was *always* sad, but most of the time she seemed to be putting up a good front. Knowing Constance had to fake her happiness made Liz feel even worse for the prayer she uttered that brought her ancestor forward in time. Constance had lost so much, and Liz had no idea how to make things better for her.

Liz couldn't think of anything proper to say one way or the other, so she looked at the clock and tsked. "We're late!" She wrote a note in case by some miracle their mom came home before them and cared that any of them were gone. Then they piled into the car. They dropped off Matt first so they could pick up Stephanie and not have to share laps. Liz suspected Nathan had a crush on Alison's little flibberty-jibbit friend and didn't think Nathan would mind having Stephanie sit on his lap, but she kind of figured Stephanie *would* mind. Besides, it was better they were all in seat belts. If any of them were hurt in an accident, Liz would never be able to forgive herself.

The stake center gym was packed with teenagers and leaders all sitting on the hard metal chairs the priesthood had set up before the program. Liz looked at her watch—only three minutes before the thing started, and she wanted seats before that happened.

She scanned the crowd for any sign of Crystal, Melanie, or Tami. She spotted them up close to the front and made her way up the aisle, leading her siblings and Constance along. When she sat, and the lights dimmed a little, Liz smiled to herself. It was the first time in three years she had attended a church function—well, any function, really—at the genuine invitation of another girl.

Constance leaned over and whispered, "Where will they put the fire?"

Liz stifled a chuckle. "They just call them firesides, but there aren't any real fires anywhere."

"Then why call it that?"

"Shh!" Liz straightened again in her seat when the music started. Men and women in black shirts stood behind two girls, also in black. The girls were at microphones, singing as the screen off to the side flashed images of Saints starting on their journey to Zion.

> *Armed with their faith and courage, they began their journey across the plains. Many of these faithful men and women would never make it to the Salt Lake Valley, and thus, some view their story as a tragedy. Though their story is marked with sorrow, it is one of triumph and discipleship, of faith so strong that it invokes a remembrance of what it means to truly be a Saint.*

Liz stiffened as the blond girl, whom she later learned to be Jenny Phillips, sang out the first words—*Lord, I will come . . . How could I stay . . . After what you have done . . . Lord, I will come . . .*

Jenny's voice was clear and perfect, and the words of each song filled Liz's whole soul. Without even realizing what she was doing, she reached over and took Constance's hand. She squeezed tightly. Constance was transfixed on the words and images that faded on and off the screen. Tears streamed down her face. Liz wept too when the words "reminding me what a Saint should be" were sung out in clear, soft notes from a song about a nine-year-old girl who came to America alone, crossed the plains, and froze to death in the snow.

You do remind me what a Saint should be, she wanted to tell Constance. *Strong and righteous, and yet you're so much more. You're funny and real too. You're real . . .*

But Liz didn't say any of those things. She just held Constance's hand and ached over the losses and sufferings of her own pioneer ancestor sitting next to her.

* * *

Constance listened to the performance, enraptured. Sniffles sounded from all around, so she knew she wasn't to feel ashamed of her tears, but she still feared that if she looked at anyone, she'd burst into sobs. She remembered so well her prayer from less than one week previous, the bitterness she felt as she uttered such rebellious words. *It isn't worth it, Lord,* she'd said. *I don't care what Zion is anymore. It could be more beautiful than Eden, and it would not be worth it.*

But as she felt the embrace of generations yet to come, she knew she'd been wrong. Her sufferings were great, but even her sufferings were not so great as some of those from these handcart companies. And as much as all the early Saints had suffered from cold and heat and hunger and fatigue . . . there truly had been a purpose to it.

Their suffering bred faith in their unborn posterity. How could anyone have foreseen such a thing? And yet Constance was certain the Lord *had* foreseen it. She knew He'd allowed the pain, and the triumph over pain, to continue to ensure an entire generation could be raised up to His standard.

She glanced around then and saw the rows and rows of boys and girls. They were stronger because of the trials their ancestors had gone through.

Was it worth it? She thought of William and felt her throat catch. But she also felt the warmth of Liz sitting next to her, clutching her hand so fiercely. Constance felt the connection. *Oh, William,* she thought, *How wicked I've been!* The pain was worth living through if that meant others would be strong. Yes . . . it was worth everything to be in the moment she now sat in, with her heart full to exploding. Her mind finally understanding.

The words of the program coming to a conclusion made her entire body tremble.

> *The mountains we cross today may not be visible, but it will require all of our strength and all of our faith to make it over them. Step by step, we write our own stories of faith and courage. We are changed by those who have gone before us. We feel their strength. We are blessed by their examples. May we live up to their legacy.*

Constance closed her eyes and shook her head. What legacy had she left? She thought of Clair holding the emerald stone of her necklace for strength. The strength she drew from the small jewel had nothing to do with monetary value but with the representation of the trials and sufferings of Constance Miles Brown. Clair believed that Constance was a woman of faith and strength. Was it truth Clair believed, or was it a deception?

Constance felt humbled with that question. *Am I anything like these Saints they revere?*

She didn't know for certain. Constance looked to the youth around her and hoped she could be the type of person they would respect.

Her mother had always said the hardest trials in life would be the ones we were most grateful for because of how they made us see ourselves. Constance saw herself and for the first time understood what it was she saw.

CHAPTER 23

AFTER HEARING THE MUSIC, LIZ decided Jenny was her favorite singer ever. She hadn't felt the Spirit like that in . . . well . . . ever. She went through all the motions of being a member of the Church. She'd prayed, fasted, read her scriptures . . . sometimes, but she always did so with half a heart and only believed the gospel because her parents did.

Through the last week, something shifted. Having Constance there to pray with her, and just *be* there, made Liz remember all there was to love in the gospel. Constance was proof of its truthfulness, not that Liz was out seeking signs or anything, but she'd be a fool to deny what she was experiencing. She took a deep breath. She felt like she was flying—soaring over the kind of hurdle that Sassy would jump in their practices. She felt *light*.

After the fireside was over, the youth snacked on store-bought cookies and lemonade as everyone talked about how cool the program was and how cool the pioneer trek had been in general. Liz felt a stab of shame that she had chosen a riding competition over going to trek. She had planned on the trek until she discovered Becky was going. After that, the competition moved up in importance.

Crystal and Melanie talked a mile a minute about the rain during the trek and how the wheel of their handcart had broken and had to be fixed twice. Constance listened with interest but didn't venture into the conversation. Her face was flushed, and her eyes were wet, but she didn't seem to be having any kind of a breakdown. Liz decided Constance's flushed face was due to the power of the program they had just seen. She figured her own face was likely streaked, too, and dabbed at her eyes in the hopes that mascara trails didn't stain her cheeks.

Liz looked toward where Jenny Phillips had a line of fans talking to her. Liz wanted to join the fans to say thanks, but knew she'd sound lame if she tried to explain why the performance was so moving to her in particular. She could just imagine it: "Uh, yeah, one of my pioneer ancestors was in town visiting, and we really thought you portrayed the Saints in an awesome way . . ." Yeah. She'd be sent to a psychiatrist faster than you could say "shock therapy."

Alison, Stephanie, and Nathan had eaten their refreshments and talked to their friends long enough. So Liz went to say good-bye to Melanie, Crystal, and Tami. She was surprised when they hugged her and wished her luck at her competition.

"How'd they know about the competition?" Liz asked once Stephanie was dropped off and they were on their way to pick up Matt.

"I told them." Alison didn't bother looking at anyone. She answered while staring blankly out the window.

"Why?"

"'Cause it's cool that you do what you do."

Liz almost swallowed her tongue from surprise. "You think I'm cool?"

"I didn't say *you* were cool. I said what you *did* was cool."

It was close enough to a compliment that Liz decided to let it stand. Warmth blossomed in her chest, completely erasing Alison's angry words from earlier.

Out of habit, Liz reached up to the visor and punched the garage door opener. When she realized she was in her dad's car and the garage door lifted up to admit entrance, she realized what she'd done and pulled the opener off the visor with a snap. The opener had gone missing a few weeks after her dad moved out, and no one had ever suspected he'd taken it. They had, in fact, blamed Matt and chewed him out for losing it.

So that's how Dad got in the other day. She stuffed the opener in her pocket and stamped down any guilt she felt over stealing from her dad when she realized he had stolen from them by taking the opener in the first place.

She thought about telling her mom who was probably coming in and messing with her computer and emails but figured she'd gone weird enough and that this kind of news would send her over the edge.

Liz shook her head. His coming in when no one else was there had to be some kind of power trip for him, but Liz wasn't going to make it easy for him. He wasn't getting in this way again. He could ring the doorbell like everyone else.

Liz tugged on Matt's arm to get him out of the car. He'd fallen asleep on the way home and was folded in half like a human taco. When he did get out, he blinked at the cars in the garage. "The garage looks better with both Mommy's and Daddy's cars in it." His voice sounded thick with sleep.

The garage did look better—normal even—but nothing was normal anymore. Liz herded Matt into the house and shut the kitchen door on the two cars sitting benignly next to each other. She got Matt upstairs and made him brush his teeth before she allowed him to fall into bed. Liz ran into Nathan on the way out of the bathroom. "Where's Mom?" she asked.

He shot a glance down to the end of the hall and her closed bedroom door and grimaced. "Take a guess." He shut the bathroom door a little harder than he needed to. Liz decided he had the right to slam doors and chose not to chew him out. She'd slam a couple, too, if she thought it would do any good.

"Where's Mom?" Alison asked when Liz got back downstairs.

"Sleeping, I guess."

"Do you think she's okay?"

Liz didn't answer. What was okay to any of them anymore? "We'd better get to bed. I have my competition tomorrow, and I need you and Nathan to do your chores."

"I was going to Stephanie's house."

"You still can. Just get your chores done first. Nathan already said he'd watch Matt, so at least you don't have to do that."

"But—"

"Ali, I know this is a lot to ask of you. I know it seems unfair, because it seems unfair for mom to ask it all of me too. I can't do everything. I'm only one person. We're only one week into school, and my grades already suck. The house looks scary. If anyone were to come over, I'd die of embarrassment. I can't clean it all by myself. And you do a really good job at making things look nicer."

Alison looked like she was prepared to argue but seemed to soften with Liz's explanation and compliment. Constance smiled at Ali's departing back. "That was a very nearly civil conversation."

"Yeah. Maybe you're rubbing off on me. I'm having a bowl of cereal. Want one?"

"No, thank you. Unlike your sister, I believe I've reached my end for this day." Constance raised her arms in a stretch as she yawned.

"Sleep good."

"Sleep *well*."

"I will when I get there."

Constance laughed. "I meant you should have said sleep *well*, not sleep *good*."

"Why should I say it like that? I'm not from England."

"But you do speak English. It hurts nothing to speak correctly."

"Whatever. Sleep *well*, then."

Constance hesitated before leaving. "Thank you for taking me to the performance. You've no idea how much better I see things now. Before I found myself here, I told the Lord He was not worth it—all my suffering. But I was wrong. Seeing this program helped me see I was wrong. The Lord had not abandoned the Saints in our adversity. We suffered for the faith of our future posterity. Like Nephi being commanded to smite the head off Laban to save future generations. It *was* worth it, Lizzie. I believe this more than I believe anything. *You* were worth it."

Liz felt the tears well up again. Constance once again proved to her how a Saint should act. Liz knew she'd never be strong enough to face what Constance faced. She pulled Constance into a tight embrace. "I hope I am," Liz said.

They held each other for several minutes before Constance pulled away, bestowing a very grandmotherly smile on Liz.

"I'll leave you to your meal."

Liz smiled. "Sleep well," she said again as Constance left. She heard Constance chuckle from the hallway.

Liz fixed herself a bowl of cereal and moved to sit at the table. She was a little bored now that she was alone. And her mom had taken to buying those bagged cereals instead of the boxed ones so there was no back of the box to read. Liz finally wandered down the hall to the study. All the genealogy still lay on the desk. The papers had new meaning with the presence of her own ancestor. Liz sat down, for the first time feeling interested in her own past. She took another bite of cereal and idly sifted through the papers while chomping on Marshmallow Mateys.

She stopped scanning and started reading when she saw Constance's name. She stopped chewing and swallowed everything in her mouth whole. For the briefest moment, relief flooded though her, and she almost ran upstairs to show Constance the proof that Constance would get home eventually. But then Liz dropped the spoon in her bowl and covered her mouth with her hands as realization struck her.

"No!" she whispered. "No!" The little bit of food she'd eaten soured in her stomach, and the room seemed to be doing cartwheels around her.

The words felt like daggers to her heart. It was a partial entry taken from Lynnette Nielson's journal photocopied on the page.

> *I've thought all day about the things Constance told me yesterday. Sickness has become so commonplace that there aren't any among us who can boast an entirely healthy family. My mother and I helped to lay out three children from the Preet family. They lost their children in the night.*
>
> *Not a day passes where someone isn't coming down with a cough or fever. But today my sorrow is for myself only. I cannot believe she's gone. I am overwhelmed with what all of this means in my own life and terrified to continue without my one true friend. Constance passed in the night from cholera. Brother Smoot gave her baby, Eliza, to me to care for. Sister Rawlins was angry that I should get the baby, but Brother Smoot stood firm. Sister Rawlins lost both of her children in four days due to fever. I understand why she wants the baby, but I am so grateful I was the one chosen to care for her. Constance made me promise I'd take the baby, and I would have fought to keep my promise. Constance was the best friend I ever had. I am afraid that I won't be able to do what she asked me. She said to take Eliza to see the valley, and I promised I would. But there's so much sickness all around us, I can only pray the Lord lets me keep my promise. Dear Constance, how I will miss you!*

"She dies!" Liz lamented, trying to stifle the sob that seemed to come from the depth of her heart. Liz looked up toward the ceiling in the direction of her own bedroom, where she knew Constance already slept.

She wanted to throw up, to scream, to break something, but she could only sit there rocking back and forth with her hands covering her mouth. Tears streamed from her eyes. "She can't die. She can't die. *She can't die!*" Liz chanted and then she slipped forward off the chair, landing on her knees. "Please, God. You can't have this happen. She can't die!"

"Who can't die?"

Liz's head shot up. "Mom!" She jumped to her feet and almost knocked her mother over as she threw her arms around her.

Her mom had to pry Liz's arms off to be able to step back and survey her daughter. "What's wrong? What happened?"

"I—" She what? What could she possibly say that made sense? "I was reading our family history, and some of the stories are just—so sad. I guess I got too into it."

Her mom lifted an eyebrow. "You're crying over family history?"

"Yes—no, not really. We went to a fireside tonight, and it was really incredible. I think that, plus reading about my own ancestors, threw me over the edge, you know? I mean, things have been kinda crazy around here. I guess I'm just stressed."

"I'm sorry, baby." Her mom's eyes were ringed by dark circles, making it look like she was getting anything but tons of sleep. Her hair stuck out in every possible direction as though it had been done by a deranged beautician. And her mouth looked like it had been drawn into a frown with a permanent marker.

"Where have you been all week?" Liz asked. Bringing up this subject when her emotions were so raw was a bad idea, but she needed to know. Liz tried to keep the accusation out of her voice, but her tone was tainted just the same.

"Work, mostly."

"I mean after work. You come home and go to your room and don't say anything to any of us."

Her mom shrugged. The thin cloth of her nightgown made a rustling sound with the motion. "I've been here."

"No, you've been in the Twilight Zone."

"Things'll be better."

"I don't believe that." The accusation was in full force now.

"Well, I started taking some medication—"

"Oh, my heck! Nathan was right! You *are* doing drugs!" *Not now. Her mom couldn't really be doing this now!*

"What? Drugs? What are you talking about?"

"Constance said you had a bottle of pills, and Nathan said you were acting like you were on something. What are you taking?"

"You guys are insane. I take a week off to redefine my life, and you think I'm an addict?"

"Well?"

Her mom snorted. "I haven't taken anything. I mean, nothing illegal. I've been seeing a counselor for the last few months and went to talk to him the night I signed the papers. He prescribed something to help me sleep since the antidepressants are giving me insomnia. It's no big deal."

"You saw a shrink?"

"No, I saw a counselor."

"Same thing."

"Let's not get into semantics."

"What? I'm just saying . . ."

Her mom raked her fingers through her already mussed hair. "Anyway . . ."

"So you're taking antidepressants *and* sleeping pills?"

"Yeah, but it isn't a big deal and really not any of your business."

"Stop taking the sleeping pills."

"I need to sleep sometime."

"Not all the time! And you should sleep at night . . . like *now*. You shouldn't be sleeping during the evening hours when we're awake. While you're off with the sandman, it's like you've checked out of our lives. I can't hold this family together. That's your job."

Her mom bit the inside of her cheek and nodded. "I know—I'm sorry. But just because I'm the adult doesn't mean I can handle everything!"

"And you think I can?"

"I know you guys need someone for you. I know that. But I need someone to hold things together for me too. I try to email my old friends for help, but they either don't respond or their emails get sent to my trash bin. Appointment information is getting lost. Everything! I swear my computer's possessed!"

Liz looked at the ground. "Your computer's fine, Mom." And then Liz told her why things were sometimes not quite right when they all got home. She felt angry to have to discuss her father after learning about Constance, especially when Constance was far more important, but she told her mother everything. "But don't worry. I have the opener now."

"He's been sneaking into *my* house?"

Liz nodded. She wondered if it was a bad idea to tell, but there was no backing out now.

"That son of a—"

"Mom!"

"Gun, Lizzie. Son of a *gun*." Her hands covered her face, and she breathed deeply while rocking back and forth. "I am so sorry I blamed you," she whispered through the wall of her fingers.

"It's okay. I understand." Liz felt vindicated to clear herself of the computer blame.

"I didn't realize I was sleeping so much. I'll be more careful."

Liz lifted an eyebrow in disbelief. "Do you have more left?"

When her mother nodded, Liz held out her hand. "Hand them over. You're done doing that to us. If you have trouble sleeping, you tell me, and I'll read the 'begat' section of the Old Testament to you."

"Lizzie!" her mother admonished with a laugh. "You're terrible!"

Liz didn't laugh. "Serious, Mom. No more sleeping through our lives, okay?"

Her mom nodded, looking down at her hands. "They're upstairs. I'll get them before you go to bed."

"Why didn't you just talk to me?"

"You shouldn't have to deal with grown-up problems."

"Yeah, well, in case you didn't notice, I *am* dealing with grown-up problems. Your problems are everyone's problems. When you're nuts like this, everyone in our family is insane right along with you. Matt is clingy and impossible, Nathan reads more books than ever so he doesn't have to deal with reality, and Alison has just gotten mean."

Her mom tilted her head to look at Liz. "What about you?"

"What about me?"

"You gave me a rundown of the family but didn't say anything about you."

"That's because I'm fine."

"You are such a bad liar."

"I'm fine, Mom."

Her mom sifted through some of the pages of family history. "So fine you're crying over things that happened hundreds of years ago."

"I already told you—the fireside was amazing. The Spirit was really strong. I'm fine." Liz repeated it a few more times in case her mom didn't get it. The things bothering Liz had little to do with the divorce anymore. The divorce was such a secondary priority that it seemed not to be on the list at all. *Constance can't die.*

"If you insist everything's okay, I'll have to believe you. How's your friend doing?"

"She's fine." *She can't! Please, God! She can't die!*

"Good. I don't know how long we can really put her up like we are, since money's so tight, but I'm thinking of asking the bishop if a family in the ward could give her room and board."

Liz's gaze slid to the photocopied journal entry. *Constance passed in the night from cholera . . .* Liz's heart felt like someone had reached into her rib cage and pulled it out. *She can't die!* And Liz couldn't let Constance be sent away either. "Give her a little while longer until you do that, okay?"

"Okay, I can do that." Her mom stood and put a fist in the small of her back as she stretched. "Get some sleep, Lizzie. You have a competition tomorrow."

Liz nodded and followed her mom upstairs. She stopped and retrieved the sleeping medication and emptied the bottle into the toilet. She watched the water swirl the little pills down into the sewer and hoped things would be better.

Her mom did remember the competition. That had to mean she wasn't so out of things as Liz had thought. Knowing that gave Liz a sense of security. If her mom remembered dates and schedules, then things would be okay; they'd be normal. And her dad wouldn't be coming in anymore to mess with their personal things. Liz wondered what he could possibly gain from that and decided again that it had to be a power trip for him.

She was creeped out that he'd do something so weird but was glad she told her mom about it. Mom would make certain he knew she knew, and that would be the end of things. Just that little peace of mind would help her mom get her life back in order.

Not that any of that changed anything for Constance. The words from Lynnette's journal entry came back. *Constance also passed in the night from cholera, and Brother Smoot gave her baby, Eliza, to me to care for.*

Liz stared into the inky darkness where Constance snored softly by the bed. *I can't let you die,* Liz thought. *I love you too much to let you die like that.* She prayed that night, and even including her prayer at the stables, she'd never spoken to her Father in Heaven with such fervent need.

"Please, God, leave her here with me! Don't take her from me just to let her die like that!"

* * *

Clair stared in her bathroom mirror for a long time after Liz left with her sleeping pills. She wanted to slam her fist into her reflection. How stupid she felt! Not just for using the pills as a crutch not to think, but for the fact that her seventeen-year-old daughter had to catch her to make her stop. Her oldest child knew what a mess she was. Clair wondered if Liz would tell the other children. She hoped not. She wondered if Liz would tell Constance. It seemed likely she would. Teenage girls shared all kinds of secrets. She felt a deep shame in the poor example she must be to such a new convert. She considered asking Liz not to say anything. But Constance likely knew already. She was the one who had seen the bottle.

Clair sat on the counter and leaned her head against the cool glass. *I'm not an addict,* she said to herself. And she wasn't, but she saw how easily she could have spiraled into one. If Constance hadn't stormed back that night she'd kicked her out, Clair would possibly be dead right now. *NO. I would not have done that.*

But she wondered if she might have. The thought terrified her and made her that much more depressed. What kind of mother takes her own life and leaves her babies to live with a father who can barely care for himself?

Clair let out a groan just thinking of the implications.

She couldn't believe Tom was playing games with her by coming into the house. The more she thought about it, the more furious she became. He'd always been controlling, but his desire to still control her made her want to punch him in the nose. She considered calling him but knew she wasn't up to the emotional battle. Not in a way as personal as a phone call. She eased herself off the counter and listened for noise.

The house was silent.

She opened her door carefully and crept back to the study. She settled into the leather chair and placed her fingers over the keyboard. Her hands shook. She'd never stood up for herself before with Tom. She'd never done anything for herself before. She moved her hands to her lap in defeat. "I can't," she whispered.

She looked up and saw the names of her ancestors typed into their places on her family tree on the wall. She lowered herself from the chair to her knees. "God?" She hated the question in her voice. The question meant she doubted He was there. Did she doubt?

No. Not really—and yet she felt so alone, so abandoned. "Heavenly Father . . ." Warmth filled her chest as she considered this title versus the other one. God was someone cold, impersonal—someone full of wrath. Heavenly Father was *her* Father. And she needed her Father right now. The rest of her prayer was an outpouring of her soul—pleading for strength to endure to the end, pleading for comfort, pleading for her children, and offering gratitude for the things she still had to cling to.

Clair was grateful. She had four perfect children. She had Liz, who had shouldered so much since Tom had come home with the news of his stupidity. Liz had buffered the other children from the pain of Tom leaving. Liz had done it because Clair hadn't been strong enough.

But the warmth in her chest and the peace in her heart helped Clair to know that someone needed to buffer Liz from the pain too. "I will be there for her." Clair uttered the promise out loud as though Heavenly Father wanted a verbal agreement that she would do everything in her power to be strong enough. Not only for herself, but for her children.

Clair knew that His end of that agreement would be to help give her strength. He would stay with her. If she endured to the end, He would be there for her until that end came.

She arose from her prayer feeling renewed.

She went back to the desk, placed her no-longer-trembling fingers on the keyboard, and typed out an email. "Tom. I know about you coming to the house and invading my privacy . . ."

By the time the email was completed, it was four pages long. Clair said she'd be getting a large dog to protect her from any further intrusions and informed him that she had no problem making a civil case out of the situation should it continue. She considered sending a carbon copy to everyone on her email list just so he would know that they all knew, but instead took the higher road. Tom was still the father of her four children. And she still had to deal with him whether she liked it or not.

After reading her email through one more time, she smiled and for the first time in her life felt like she was in charge of herself. She'd never really felt in control. Her dad had taken care of her, and then Tom had.

Now she, alone—with the help of her Father in Heaven—was responsible for her happiness.

She took a deep, liberating breath. *I can do this.* And she knew she could. Her finger hovered over the mouse before she finally clicked and sent the email. "I don't know what game you're playing out, Thomas King, but be prepared. I'm ready to fight back."

She played solitaire for a little while, feeling the irony of the game's name and her current situation. After a continual run of winning, she turned the computer off. "I'll be a better mother tomorrow," she said to the dark screen.

She made her way back to her room, stopping at each of the children's rooms to check on them and kiss their foreheads while they slept. Liz's face seemed wet, like she'd fallen asleep crying. Another stab of shame shot through Clair. How had she let things get so bad that her little girl went to bed crying?

No more, Lizzie. I'll be better. Clair thought about Tom getting his email in just a few hours and smiled. *Everything will be better now.*

CHAPTER 24

CONSTANCE GAZED AT LIZ SLEEPING in the morning light and smiled while shaking her head. She could seldom sleep once dawn broke; the light aggravated her dreams. Liz looked flushed and disturbed in her sleep. Constance determined Liz was having nightmares and considered maybe she'd be helping to wake her up.

But she determined not to wake Liz just yet. Instead Constance went to the bathroom to take a bath. That was something she could not complain about. If she had to be separated from her family, at least she was in a place of certain conveniences—a world of hot water and no muddy, rutted roads. This was close to what she imagined heaven to be like. She didn't know when she would be yanked back into the past and determined she would be ready for it by bathing every day. She would return clean, for who could say when the opportunity to bathe—in hot water, no less—would present itself again?

She'd thought a lot about the performance the night before . . . The fireside and the words, "Lord, I will come," haunted her. Those words carried her exact sentiment when she was baptized, when she had to seek employment to save money for passage to America, every day when she was sick from the motion of the boat as it propelled her to the promised land, when she, alongside William, started her journey on the trail to the valley.

She wondered when those words stopped being her own. *Lord, I will come . . .*

Constance set the water to a little hotter than her skin could stand and held her breath while her body became used to the heat.

Lord, I will come . . . How could I stay . . .

How could she have stayed indeed? She closed her eyes and pondered the words as they became a beating resonance within her. *Could I return?*

She didn't know. She wasn't ready to consider the implications. *After what you have done . . . Lord, I will come . . .*

"I am not worthy to follow," she said to the stream of steaming water pouring from the tap. She thought about this great-granddaughter of hers—Liz and the life she lived every day. Liz lived in a world Constance found very hard. Comfortable, certainly, but comfort at what price? The rhythm of the future beat like hummingbird wings, and though she stood in the midst of this time, she felt it slipping past, leaving her behind, bewildered and afraid. If she didn't have Liz, she'd be utterly lost. She wanted to go back to her daughter and her husband. But how to fulfill her mission to fix this family here in the present?

Lord, I will come . . .

She didn't know. After a night of pondering and contemplating, she wasn't sure she could do what she was asked.

She was not like the bathwater she sat in, steaming hot. She was tepid, neither hot nor cold. And the Lord would spew her out if she could not find her way back to the woman who once said the words, "Lord, I will come," with her whole heart.

* * *

Liz opened her eyes. They hurt, and her head ached from crying the night before. She rolled over to look at Constance and sat up straight in a panic. The blankets by Liz's bed were empty. Could Constance have already been blasted back to the past where she'd die of a horrible sickness and leave her baby an orphan? Liz didn't even know what cholera was, but it sounded really bad. And if Constance was going to leave an orphaned baby, it seemed far better for her to just stay here than for her to go back and die an ugly death. Liz searched the house until she got to the bathroom and put her ear to the door. The bathtub was running, and she heard humming from inside. It sounded a lot like the first song Jenny Phillips had sung the night before.

Liz closed her eyes and breathed out in relief. Constance was still here. Once her moment of panic ended, she thought about her day. She thought about the things she had to get done and then panicked all over again for entirely new reasons. The competition was today.

Liz hurried to her room to get ready. She was careful to braid her hair so it fit right under her helmet, and smoothed her hands over her tan britches as she slipped her feet into her Ariat riding boots. She zipped them up to almost her knees so they fit snug around her calves. She loved her boots. They were the one really expensive part of her outfit—a gift from Dad just before he announced he was moving out.

She buttoned her white shirt and pulled her riding coat from the closet where it still hung in the dry cleaner's bag.

Alison walked past her room and then backed up. "Aren't you going to have breakfast?"

"No. I'm fasting."

"Why? It's not Sunday."

"I just want to do a good job today."

Alison pulled her robe tighter around her. "Oh." She accepted the reasoning easily enough and wandered away down the hall.

It wasn't entirely true. Sure, Liz wanted to do well in the competition, but she wanted things to be good for Constance too. She was fasting so Constance could stay.

When Constance finally emerged from the bathroom, Liz had to rush her through her breakfast and getting ready. They were supposed to be at the arena early so Liz could get Sassy braided and brushed before the competition began. Liz made Nathan promise he'd keep an eye on Matt then hurried to make it to the arena on time.

Constance stood at the edge of the stands to watch as Liz warmed up. Liz wished she'd had more time at the stables to practice, but that week had been weird with her mom working and Constance showing up.

Even without the extra practice, from the moment Liz touched Sassy on the nose, she knew her horse was ready to go. She warmed up with a few jumps and then took Sassy to brush her down a final time.

The event was held inside the arena. Liz counted the jumps—fifteen. A few of them were double combinations and a triple combination at the end with three hurdles spaced close together. She breathed evenly, or tried to. *Sassy's ready*, she thought, *but am I?*

When it was her turn, Liz said a quick prayer and went through the course. Sassy was perfect. They truly moved as one as she took each jump without hesitancy or fear. Liz felt each clap of Sassy's hooves on the ground vibrate through her chest. And when Sassy leapt, Liz was so ready for it, she didn't even get the tickle in her tummy like she normally did. The triple combination included a tricky water jump, but Sassy cleared the poles and moved to the successive jump without missing a beat. Instead of the typical tickle, Liz felt the thrill of victory.

She grinned as Constance clapped from the stands. Liz felt only a little defeated when she scanned the people and then remembered her mom wasn't there. She was at work. Her mom hadn't ever missed a competition. It took the thrill of victory down a notch.

* * *

"I won!" Liz shouted to no one in particular when she and Constance got home.

"Congrats, Sis!" Nathan said before turning immediately back to his book.

Alison grinned almost as wide as Liz figured she was doing herself. "That's awesome! You gonna split your winnings with me?"

"Not in this life. I thought you were going to Stephanie's."

"I did. I got an entire hour of practice in!"

"You're home early," Liz said.

Alison shrugged. "Stephanie got grounded."

"Why?"

"She was supposed to do dishes last night and talked on the phone to that new kid, Mike. Her mom was ticked."

"About her not doing dishes or talking to a guy?"

"Both, I'd think. Steph totally likes him, though. So you got first place?"

"Not only that, but Alton said I should start training a little harder to see if I can get ready for some bigger out-of-state events."

"Sweet! Can I come if you go out of state?"

"If I go, you can definitely come with me." Liz went upstairs to change, feeling pleased to see Alison care. *I won!* It wasn't like she hadn't ever won before, but there were plenty of times where she took second place and plenty times more where she didn't place at all. She put her ribbon by Sassy's picture. Liz smiled and kissed her fingertips, touching them to the glass over the image of Sassy's chestnut face—a very good friend indeed.

Liz changed into jeans again and when she got back down, she stopped short at the bottom of the stairs. "Garrett?"

"Hey, Lizzie."

"What are you doing here?"

"Just came to say hi and see how you did on your competition."

"I won," Liz said with a touch of pride and a big smile.

"Congratulations."

Liz felt confused. Why would he care about her competition? But when she saw him look at Constance, she wanted to grab him by the scruff of the neck and throw him out. He didn't care about the competition. He'd come to flirt with her great-grandma!

"Nice of you to drop by." Liz finally took the last stair so she wasn't towering over him.

"No problem."

"You probably have to be going . . ." She stepped toward the front entryway, hoping he'd follow. He didn't.

"Not really. I mean . . . I do later. I have to get ready for—"

Liz raised an eyebrow. "The Stomp?"

He looked at his hands. "Well . . . yeah."

Constance turned and picked up a book from the shelf near the front entryway and walked to the living room. Garrett and Liz followed. "Are you very well acquainted with the girl you're taking to the dance?" Constance asked as she settled on the couch and arranged the lap blanket around her feet.

Garrett looked from Constance to Liz. His eyes were wide like he'd been cornered. "Sort of. Well . . . not very well," he began. "She asked me to go. Since you'd already turned me down . . ." He flashed a winning smile at Constance. She didn't look up from her book to receive the smile.

"*She* asked *you*? A bit extraordinary, isn't it?" Constance asked.

Liz felt surprised to hear Becky had asked him and not the other way around. She'd just assumed that he'd done the asking. She felt more ashamed for the spaghetti than ever.

So she jumped in to save him. He might not be her best friend anymore, but there was no reason for him to bear the lecture on propriety. Liz had heard it enough over the week that she was pretty sure she could give it herself. "What she means is girls don't ask guys out where she comes from. It's still pretty traditional."

"Oh, right." Then the silence. Constance refused to be helpful in any way to the conversation. She stared at her book with resolution. Garrett finally took the hint and said, "Well, I better be getting stuff done. Congratulations again, Liz." And then he left.

"What was that all about? Why did you ignore him like that?" Liz asked after she saw he was already halfway across the lawn to his own house.

"If he refuses to court you, then I cannot have him here inquiring after me."

Liz laughed. "Why would he court me? I'm his evil neighbor." It was a joke, but she had to admit the idea of him was not as repulsive as she'd once thought.

"Can I go to a dollar movie tonight?" Nathan asked Liz.

"Do you have a dollar?" Liz asked.

"No, but the guys are all going, and I haven't done anything with them for weeks."

"Nate . . ."

"You're saying no, aren't you?"

Liz thought about the money she'd won, plus the little bit she had in a piggy bank leftover from her birthday money from Grandma King. "Fine, I'll pay, and I'll even throw in enough for popcorn, but you owe me three chores." The popcorn was a must. If she sent him without any money for snacks when all the other guys had snack money, he'd look like the charity case they'd all become.

"I did chores today."

"Three on top of your normal chores." She really was starting to sound more and more like her mother. The thought terrified her.

Her mom came home early enough to make dinner and read to Matt. She was pretty normal for the most part. She didn't run to her room and sleep the evening away like she had the whole week previous. She even congratulated Liz on winning her event and hugged Liz tight enough that Liz felt wrapped in safety.

The day and following evening had been perfect, and Liz felt certain things would only get better.

CHAPTER 25

CONSTANCE FELT PURE DELIGHT TO be going to church in the modern Zion. The very idea of seeing how the Church had progressed thrilled her. She couldn't imagine what it would be like. Would the prophet be there to speak? Who was the prophet? She asked questions until she was sure Liz would scream if she were forced to answer another. Constance swallowed down her disappointment that the prophet would not be speaking. Imagining the Church to have grown so vast staggered her.

She dressed carefully and had Liz put up her hair again. Constance felt an absolute burning to attend services. Clair seemed far calmer today than she had ever been before. Clair's calm added to the peace in the family. Everyone readied themselves in relative silence, but not the angry or sullen silence that had seemed to encompass the family. The silence was peaceful.

The family took two cars, both Clair's and Liz's father's, since there wasn't room for them all in just one. The church was an easy walking distance from the house, and Constance wondered why they bothered with the cars at all.

The building was much larger than expected, filling her with great joy. The congregation must be of an adequate size to support such a building. When Liz told her there were three different sessions because the building was so small, Constance was beside herself. Did Liz really think the building small?

Constance's breath caught in her throat as she spied a painting on the wall. She all but dragged Liz to follow her and look. "How lovely. A palace."

"That's not a palace—that's the temple," Liz said.

"But the temple was destroyed."

"What? Oh . . . no. This is the San Diego Temple. You're thinking about the Nauvoo Temple. And that's been rebuilt . . . I think. Anyway, there are tons of temples now."

"Is this true?" Constance felt her whole heart swell.

"Of course, it's true. Would I lie?"

"No, of course not. It's simply so fantastic—too fantastic to believe! Do you know what this means?"

Liz blinked. Constance could only sigh at Liz's lack of comprehension.

"This means so many now have the ability to travel to these temples and receive the gifts the Lord has saved for them."

"Umm-hmm." Liz no longer listened as she focused on shaking the hand of some man greeting the people entering the chapel.

She felt like Liz ignored her purposely with the hope she'd stop talking. *No one else is impressed by the things they see every day*, Liz had said. Constance couldn't comprehend a world so uninterested in itself. But Constance took the hint from Liz's silence and went quiet herself.

She had as much to think about as she did to speak about. She'd save her questions for later.

* * *

Liz was grateful when Constance finally stopped talking. She was also grateful no one had been in earshot when Constance went off on the picture of the temple. Anyone who'd have heard such a conversation would be adding "insane" to the list of Liz King's qualities.

There were several kids on the stand where the speakers sat. Liz knew them—two of them, anyway.

Becky and Garrett. Plus a few kids from their stake were there as well, and though Liz recognized them a little, she didn't know who they were. Becky fidgeted with her skirt, which Liz noted as being too short, and Garrett sat perfectly still, seemingly content to be up there. *He really will be a good missionary someday,* she thought.

The sacrament was passed, and Constance took her portion of bread and water with trembling hands. She closed her eyes, and tears leaked out the sides. Liz watched in fascination.

She hadn't focused on the meaning of the sacrament for so long that she feared she didn't remember it anymore. She always drew pictures on

Nathan's back and made him guess what they were. When Nathan started passing the sacrament, she turned her attentions to playing tic-tac-toe with Matt and Alison.

After the deacons were excused to sit with their families, the bishop announced that each of the youth speakers was there to talk about their pioneer trek experience for a few moments.

Becky stood and made her way to one of the microphones. "I . . . wasn't planning on doing this today. The bishop only just called me this morning. I wasn't planning on doing the pioneer trek either. But I'm really glad I did both. My life's pretty easy, I guess. I mean I never had to bury a baby on the trail or anything like that. I mean . . . I just mean that I really appreciate the examples the early Saints were to us. I don't think I'd make it if I had to cross the plains for real."

It was at this point Liz rolled her eyes and muttered, "No kidding," to which she got jabbed with an elbow by Constance.

Becky bore her testimony, and for the briefest moment, Liz saw beyond the blond, frizzy hair. *High school isn't forever,* Liz thought. She took a moment to wonder if Becky would be a normal person as an adult.

Maybe, Liz conceded. The fact that Becky Dunford had a testimony was something Liz hadn't realized before. She wondered if anyone in their ward knew *Liz King* had one. She was never the type to share her testimony at girls' camp just because everyone else did. Could she blame them for not knowing when she hadn't been sure herself until recently?

Then Garrett took his turn. "I just wanted you all to know I loved being Pa, even when you rascally kids wouldn't listen to a word I said." There were trickles of laughter from the audience. "And I'm still mad about whoever thought it would be funny to make sure I slept over a red ant hill that first night." More laughter. "But really, it was awesome." He shrugged. "Just awesome. It was so wild to see the girls in those dresses taking their turns pulling their handcarts just like the guys. The best part though was the testimony meeting out in the woods. It was totally cool to hear how walking in someone else's shoes had changed us all. Even with the rain and the lack of real food, it was one of my top ten best experiences in life." He also closed with his testimony, which was sweet and to the point.

Liz was sorry she hadn't apologized about the spaghetti. She was sorry it'd happened, but especially sorry she had failed to apologize.

Introducing Constance in Young Women proved a little tricky. They were in church, after all, but the truth would be almost as bad as a lie. So it was the story of, "Constance is here from England. We're not sure how long she's going to stay." Liz didn't mention anything about Constance being a relative. If that got back to her mom, she'd be in huge trouble. Liz was already sorry that Becky and Garrett knew.

Becky was the Laurel president in charge of opening exercises and didn't seem especially happy to say she was glad Constance had joined the class for the day. Sister Peterson must have noticed because when she got up to give the lesson, she was all smiles and gave Constance a more appropriate welcome.

They practiced the song "Families Can Be Together Forever" several times before they excused everyone to their separate classes. Sister Peterson stopped Liz and asked if she'd changed her mind about performing the song.

"No. I just—can't, you know. It doesn't feel right." Liz looked at the missionary letters on the bulletin board while she gave Sister Peterson her denial—again.

Liz fidgeted through the rest of the class, feeling bad for disappointing the one leader who made her feel welcome in church, but she couldn't give in to this. It was the principle. Her dad had broken their family. He had chosen something else. It wasn't Liz's fault the song wasn't true for her. If Sister Peterson didn't like it, she could talk to Dad about it.

Liz was glad when church was out. Constance had a hard time keeping her comments to herself. In Sunday School, she got way overexcited about the lesson on the Prophet Joseph Smith. In Young Women, she blubbered during the entire lesson and kept nodding her head in agreement with the teacher. Liz wanted to bury her head in a hole; or better yet, she wanted to bury Constance's head in a hole.

Liz changed out of her skirt as soon as she could get to her room. Constance sat on the bed, looking like she never intended to change out of the dress. When Liz's mom knocked, Liz braced herself. Her mom only knocked when she had bad news or a chew-out to give.

"Hey, I was wondering if you wanted to take Constance to the temple. You have your dad's car, and she seemed so interested. I thought she might like that."

"Really?" Constance jumped off the bed, making her skirt flutter in the most ladylike way. "Could we?"

"Sure." Liz shrugged with a laugh. Her mom seemed so normal, and the request was so ordinary that Liz was happy to comply. She smiled at her mom and outright grinned when her mom smiled back. Liz had to give her credit for holding it together today. Her dad would get married Wednesday. Liz had no idea if her mom could hold it together after that.

* * *

Liz could barely keep Constance in the car when they parked downtown. She was going to just take her to one of the closer temples but figured Constance would rather see the big one that people she knew helped build. Thinking in those terms, Liz thought again of Constance never getting to the valley with her friends. She'd never get to help build the temple or take part in the whole seagulls-eating-the-crickets deal. Liz had to take several deep breaths to keep from crying. *Please, God. Just leave her with me.*

Constance dragged them all over the grounds of the temple and was horribly disappointed when they couldn't go inside. "You have to have a recommend, and it's closed on Sunday." Liz repeated that statement several times.

She read every one of the historical signs set up along the walls near paintings and panoramas and admired every statue. She spent forever in the room with the *Christus* statue. The longer Liz sat near Constance in that room filled with so much peace, the more peace she felt in her own heart.

"Thank you for a perfect day," Constance said once they were home. She sighed as she settled on Liz's bed, as though she were truly content. "But I can't tell you how ungrateful all this makes me feel."

"Why?" Liz's muffled voice came from under her PJ top as she tugged it over her head.

"When we first met, you said I was not being a very good example. You admonished me for not living up to the heroic pioneer. You said everyone revered them and that I was not making a sacrifice if I was whining."

Liz blushed. "I'm sorry."

"No. Don't apologize. You were right to humble me. I began this . . . journey to your time imagining that I was to help you. What a surprise to see how much you had to teach me."

Liz's face grew warmer. "I haven't taught you anything. Everything you learned today you got from my teachers and from little signs on the walls." Liz laughed.

Constance laughed too, jumped off the bed, and reached out to hug Liz. "And I *have* learned a lot from you."

Please God, let her stay with me instead of going back and dying of cholera. Liz had finally done a Google search before church to find out what cholera even was. The symptoms of cholera sounded like the flu. Liz was shocked at how many people died from such a dumb thing. She was even more shocked to learn that people still died from such dumb diseases.

"How many people do you know who have died?" Liz asked, feeling morbidly curious.

"Many of my acquaintances have already passed on." Constance edged past Liz to the closet so she could change into PJs too.

"Of what?"

"Illness mostly. Few people are truly healthy and fewer still are healthy on the trail. The weather and conditions of traveling seem to breed illness."

"That's so sad."

"Most aren't afraid to die. Most welcome death as a relief and a release from the burdens of life."

Liz picked up one of her miniature horses from her shelf and tossed it back and forth between her hands. She furrowed her brow and shivered at the thought of Constance cold and sick on the trail. "I'm not dying of any sickness." *And you aren't, either, if I have any say in it.*

Constance laughed, though Liz couldn't tell what was so funny. "What shall you die from, then? Or perhaps you plan to live forever?"

"I'm going to die of something cool. I mean think how embarrassing it would be to die of something lame? You'd get to the other side and everyone would ask you, 'How did you die?' What do you tell them? 'Oh, I died from falling off a ladder and dropping a paint can on my head.' Or worse: 'I died from licking envelopes.'"

"Licking envelopes?" Constance scrunched up her nose.

"I saw it on a *Seinfeld* rerun once. Anyway, the point is I want to go out doing something cool, like saving a baby from a fire or flying to outer space to save the planet from aliens."

"Flying indeed."

"We do fly, you know."

"Who flies? Birds, butterflies?"

"People."

Constance felt Liz's forehead. "I do believe you'll die from sickness, after all. That's the maddest thing I've heard you say."

"Airplanes. People fly in airplanes and helicopters—we've even been to the moon. I'll show you." Liz went downstairs and logged onto the Internet.

Constance goggled at the computer screen as pictures of space shuttles and airplanes flashed by. "I don't believe it. Goodness! I simply don't believe it!" she said over and over again. Liz laughed and loved feeling as though she really had taught Constance something new.

CHAPTER 26

"LIZ!" HAVING BECKY CALLING FROM behind her was not the best way for Liz to start out her Monday morning. Liz rolled her eyes and, against her better judgment, stopped walking. Constance crossed her arms and leaned against the school lockers. They waited for Becky to slip through the crowd to catch up to them.

"What?" Liz asked Becky.

Becky's mouth was set in a grim line. Apparently, whatever she'd come to say was not entirely satisfying to her, either. "Sister Peterson thinks—we all think—you should sing in the program on Sunday."

Liz frowned. "I can't."

Becky looked like she had to focus to keep her own eyes from rolling. "Please."

"Why would you care if I sing or not?" Liz wasn't sure this was the best question to ask of someone who had spent her entire life being brutally honest with her opinion.

"I'm the president of the class."

Liz bit her tongue to keep from saying, "Duh!"

"And as president, I feel it's important that we don't sound like a bunch of braying cattle. You know you have a decent voice." This looked like it gave Becky some difficulty to say. Liz noticed she didn't say *good* or *great*, but *decent* was the closest Liz had ever come to receiving a compliment from Becky since she and Liz had parted ways. Becky tossed her head, making her frizzy mane bounce with the movement. "And you know there are some in our class a little less talented in that area. We need you to help balance out those of us who can sing with the others who can't."

It was funny that Becky included herself in the group of those who could sing, but then Liz knew it was true. Becky's voice wasn't terrible.

"Sorry. I can't."

"Can't what?" Garrett asked from behind her. Liz whirled and glared. Getting cornered by Becky was one thing; getting cornered by Becky *and* Garrett was too much.

When Liz turned back, she noticed that Becky wasn't able to look anyone in the eye. "Just think about it," she mumbled and hurried away.

"Can't what?" Garrett repeated.

Liz slid her gaze to Constance, who refused to speak once again. "I can't sing."

Garrett laughed out loud. "You liar. I went to the Christmas performance at church when your mom had you sing 'Once Upon a December.' You were good. Heck, you had half the audience on their feet to make you sing more when you got through."

"Impressing the high priests isn't hard to do. They're impressed when the prime rib's cooked good enough they can eat without their dentures falling out."

"Are you dissing the high priests?" His grin was mischievous.

Liz grunted, her face growing hot. "No. Okay that was harsh. I'm sorry. And I'm sorry about the spaghetti the other day."

He seemed surprised by the apology. Liz was surprised to be giving it. His surprise turned to a grin. "It washed out."

"I'm sorry anyway. I don't know why I did that."

Garrett shrugged and tilted his head into his shoulder like he did when he was little. It was kind of cute.

Liz wondered why Becky disappeared so quickly and to her own horror asked, "How was the dance?"

Garrett shrugged again. "Okay, I guess."

He didn't offer any further information, and Liz was too embarrassed to ask. She guessed from the way Garrett acted normal and Becky hurried to leave that she didn't get a promise ring or a letterman's jacket out of her date. The thought gave Liz some satisfaction. The bell rang. "Oh, we're late!" Liz didn't even say good-bye as she grabbed Constance by the arm and dragged her to class.

* * *

Liz's mom came home in time for dinner again and seemed pretty happy when she got there. She complimented the food, joked with the twins, and held Matt on her lap for half the meal. Things were almost normal again.

Proof of that emerged the next day when Mom was home for the third time before the family sat down for dinner. She didn't argue when Liz asked to go to the stables and even did the dishes for a grateful Alison so Ali could go to Stephanie's house. No one mentioned the wedding taking place the next day. But Liz knew they were all thinking about it.

Constance walked the perimeter of the fields where Liz exercised Sassy, then Liz let her take a turn on the horse. "You didn't tell me you could ride," she exclaimed when Constance reined Sassy to a halt.

"You did not ask. We do not have cars where I came from."

"Oh, c'mon, don't start that whole, 'In my day, we had to walk to school in the snow uphill both ways.'"

"That is absolutely illogical." Constance dismounted and patted Sassy's nose.

"It's a joke, Constance."

"I am aware of that, Lizzie."

Liz laughed and sucked in the cooling evening air. She felt content. Maybe her dad was getting married tomorrow to someone Liz had a hard time respecting, let alone liking, but things felt okay. Maybe they would be okay.

* * *

"Ali, you have to get up and get ready! You'll miss your bus!" Liz banged on the door a few times. She was tired, too, but only because she'd stayed up half the night teaching Constance how to play Monopoly. She still felt grouchy that she got beaten by a pioneer.

Alison trudged from her room. She'd dragged half her bedding to the floor when she got up. Her eyes were red.

"What's the matter?"

Nathan shook his head at Liz as though she were the dumbest human alive for not seeing what was wrong. "Dad's getting married today. Hello?" He put an arm around Alison, and she turned her face into his shoulder. They both looked exhausted. Liz wondered if they'd been up all night talking about the wedding, then felt guilty that she had felt so content when they were still feeling crummy.

When she mentioned to Constance that she was worried about the twins, Constance asked what the worry was over. Liz explained in detail about how having a new mother would affect the kids.

"Don't feel responsible over everything that happens," Constance said later while they were getting off the bus and walking to the school's front entrance. "You aren't entitled to misery that does not belong to you. Find satisfaction with your own misery—heaven knows there will be enough of it in life that you won't need to go seeking more."

She was right, Liz knew. But she also knew Constance was all talk. She knew Constance had personally slipped a small note into Alison's bag before she left to catch her bus. She also knew Constance had taken a moment to compliment Nathan on his clothes since he was acting weird about what he wore. There was no way Constance approved of the baggy pants and untucked shirt, but she handed out the compliment because she was trying to ease Nathan's worry.

And as it turned out, she was right to try. Getting any of the three kids ready for the wedding after school was torture to Liz. Matt ran around screaming, "No! No shiny shoes! Only girls wear shiny shoes!" Nathan wouldn't even get the tuxedo on, and when Liz went in his room to fetch the tuxedo and make him put it on, she found it in a wrinkled heap on the floor. Alison moped about in her pale blue dress and decided she didn't care about curling her hair.

"You always care about your hair!" Liz insisted, wishing Alison were small enough to drag into the bathroom.

"It isn't like anyone I care about will see me!"

"Your father will see you," Constance tried to reason.

"Exactly my point!" Alison crossed her arms over her chest.

Liz had a hard time arguing since she felt the same. "What about Mom? What we do and say and wear represents her. We can't make her look bad."

That did the trick. Alison conveyed the sentiment to Nathan, who even made a halfhearted attempt with an iron over his shirt. The wedding was at five. Then there would be pictures and the reception. And they needed to get going.

The clock ticked off precious minutes, and Mom wasn't home yet. Liz felt a degree of worry. If they didn't show up on time, her dad would freak.

Their mom showed up just before they had to leave.

She let out a deep breath. "You're all ready!" Her eyes met Liz's. The red lines and the extra puff proved her mom had been crying again. "Thank you, Lizzie. You've done so much these last few weeks." She caught herself before crying again. Liz wondered if she'd had to double her dosage on her prescription to make it to this point. She hoped not.

"Aren't you going, Constance?" Clair asked.

"No. I believe I'll stay and catch up on some reading."

"Oh! That reminds me!" Liz's mom clicked back to the office in her high heels. She held a small stack of papers when she emerged again. "I found these for you and thought you might like to read them."

Constance took the papers. "Thank you."

"Well, we'd better go. Your dad hates it when you're late."

Liz looked in horror at the papers Constance now held. "Wait! No!" Her mom checked her watch again and herded Liz out the door. "You can talk when you get home. We're late." Liz cast a despairing glance back as she was swept out of the house in a tide of siblings.

* * *

Constance waved her good-byes as they left the house then wandered to the couch with her stack of papers and the novel she'd started reading the day previous. She found herself wholly engrossed in this book and decided to finish it before moving on to the papers Clair had given her.

The novel was one she'd heard of but never read. Her father didn't approve of fictionalized fancy, so when a friend back in England offered to lend her a copy of *Pride and Prejudice* to read, Constance had dutifully declined. Now she was almost finished and took delight in every word. It gave her a degree of pleasure to know she was doing the thing she'd deprived herself of all those years ago.

It only took an hour to complete the novel. Constance closed the cover and sighed. She found herself smiling over the romance of it all. She thought about William and seeing him for the first time. Her feelings upon meeting him were instantaneous. He'd handed her a flower and tipped his hat. His smile warmed her into puddles. She'd have crossed the world for him . . . and, in fact, had.

Constance covered her eyes with her hands. She worried she'd never see him again, even if she returned to her time, which seemed unlikely anyway.

She shook herself. Giving way to self-pity was hardly the answer . . . though she'd done exactly that several times over the last few days. No. She was resolved to find contentment within herself. The family seemed so much better . . . maybe she'd return soon.

With her resolution firmly in place, she picked up the papers Clair gave her. It was a history of her own life and the lives of her posterity from little Eliza on down. Constance was grateful and fearful of such a magnanimous gift. She both feared and needed the words on these papers. If Constance could not witness these things for herself because her own insolence had led to her entrapment in time, then at least she'd have a record of events.

She read names, dates, and tidbits on people she'd never met and likely would not meet. Some were sad, with children dying; some were joyful with histories of success of family and fortune.

Constance wound her way back in time until she got to the part about her daughter. Eliza had been raised by Lynnette. There was no mention of Constance in Eliza's adult life. And merely a notation that her mother died was the only record of Eliza ever belonging to Constance.

"If they only knew I didn't die," she said aloud to the empty house. "If they only knew I got lost in time." But it scared her to think she'd not be the one to raise her child. Her heartbeat quickened with her growing fear. Surely she would be returning and taking over the rearing of her own daughter. The records must be wrong on that point. They had to be since Constance had no intention of things being any other way.

She scoffed at further proof of the record keeper's ability to keep things and names straight when she noticed Lynnette's last name was listed as Brown, and then she bolted upright on the couch.

William Henry Brown married Lynnette Nielson shortly after his arrival in the valley some two months after his wagon company. Lynnette's journal says this about his arrival: He showed up like a ghost. We were all glad to see him. He told us he'd caught his horse and was injured in the process. He passed out on the animal and was carried for a great distance until some trappers found him and took him to their home. There he was nursed back to health and given supplies to continue his journey. What a blessing the Lord has given us to have him returned safely!

Constance very nearly howled at the words. She stood up, papers spilling to the floor, her heart racing in her chest. *He returns!* The words tumbled in her mind. "He returns!" she shouted. Her agitation was great. How could he return when she was not there to greet him? How could he forget her so soon and marry Lynnette?

True, she loved Lynnette like a sister and had been glad Lynnette would be caring for Eliza until she returned, but to lose her husband and her child to her friend? "No. It is too much!" She shook her head and wrung her hands. She paced until she reached the window and almost turned when she saw Garrett's house.

Her thoughts were far from rational. She had already tried to return home by returning to the stables, yet she could not stop herself. What if it worked this time? She knew she must at least try. The sun hung low in the sky as she approached the Mitchells' house. It was time for Constance to return to her time and claim the husband and child who belonged to her.

CHAPTER 27

"YEAH, I CAN GIVE YOU a ride." Garrett's eyes shined down on her. The smile he bestowed made him look every bit the flirt. Constance smiled over her gritted teeth. He smiled all the wider. "Let me grab my jacket and tell my mom I'm heading out." He turned, leaving her standing alone in the foyer to his home.

She should have written a note to make Liz aware of her leaving, but her need to see William, to be where he was, overtook her power to be sensible. She was a wife and a mother, and she would return no matter what the obstacle.

"Okay, let's go." Garrett shrugged into his jacket. He eyed her with curiosity. "Are you okay?"

"I am perfectly well." She wished he'd walk faster to the car. She looked down and let out a soft gasp. She wore one of Liz's skirts. There was nothing to be done for it; she didn't have time to change. Not now.

He unlocked and opened the door for her with a gallant sort of bow as she got in. She thought the gesture odd, since he'd never done anything like that before. She willed him to make the car move faster as he maneuvered through the streets. Though the car moved faster than any wagon from her time, it felt agonizingly slow.

When they finally arrived at the stables, Constance thanked him over and over as she struggled with the seat belt. He finally unclipped it for her and grinned as though she were a child. The very idea aggravated all sensibility.

He got out of the car the same time as she did. She frowned at him. "I'll be here for quite some duration. You will not need to wait for me. Liz will return to fetch me." Guilt struck her with the lie. Liz wouldn't know what happened to her until Garrett told her. She would be hurt, but Constance couldn't stop now. The family seemed all right enough. They seemed better every day. She had to get back. William was there! She had crossed the world for him, and she'd cross time too.

"I don't mind waiting for you." His tone was mischievous. She wanted to wail!

"I . . . need to be alone right now." She started walking. Instead of going away, he followed. The smile slid from his face. She had to hold her hands to her sides to keep from throwing them up in the air for all the exasperation he'd caused her.

"So something is wrong?"

"No. Nothing at all. I just have a great deal of work to do and truly appreciate your efforts in bringing me here. You're very kind." She knew saying such things would only encourage him in his attachment to her, but such things would not matter when she'd never see him again.

He was all smiles again. "For you . . . always. Well, if you need a ride home or you need anything at all, call me, okay?"

"Of course. I'll notify you immediately."

"Or maybe I'll swing back by later and check on you." He was walking backwards, still smiling. He almost stumbled on a stone sticking up out of the ground as he made his way back to his car. Constance smiled again for him. He was a dear boy . . . pity Liz didn't care one whit for him.

But Liz's romances were quite secondary to her own. Constance nearly ran to the place where she woke up that first morning. She fell to her knees, squeezed her eyes shut, and prayed with her whole soul. She begged for forgiveness. She pled for mercy and stayed there on her knees until her legs tingled and her feet were entirely numb.

She opened her eyes and almost cursed at the view. She was still in the future. "Please, Lord!" she wailed, her tears overpowering her and her shoulders shaking. But she knew in her bones . . . He was saying no. "You cannot leave me here!" she yelled and jumped to her feet.

Constance almost collapsed again under her own weight since her legs felt like water, but she held steady and managed to run to the stable where Liz's horse was kept. "I'll ride back to him! I *am* going back!" She hoped the speed would catapult her to her own life again. With such intentions, Constance knew she was no longer in control of her senses. But she didn't pause for rational thought.

She worked the lock on the stable door and quickly saddled the horse. Sassy whickered and nosed her side. "Don't worry. Everything will be fine," she told the horse, unsure of whether she was trying to comfort the animal or herself.

She led the horse out of the stable and mounted the saddle. She dug her heels in and targeted the animal straight toward the little lean-to next to the maple. She woke up there; surely that was the point of transfer from one time to the next. She heeled the horse faster, her heart pounding in time to the thump of the hooves on the ground. When she was almost to the small structure, the horse slowed enough to show it wasn't interested in a head-on collision. At the last possible moment, the horse veered to the left of the structure.

Sassy leapt.

Constance felt as though her stomach had dropped into her toes as the horse's muscled body took the jump over the ivy-covered fence. Her heart pounded in her own ears, yet the world felt horridly silent as the wind swished her hair from her face.

They landed like a thunderclap on the cement, jolting Constance's entire body with the impact. The hooves still pounded as Sassy kept running.

Constance looked up and saw circular lights rushing toward her. *Was this what it felt like to travel through time?* she wondered until the lights began to swerve and take the form of cars. She screamed.

Cars swerved around her. She tried to pull in on the reins, but Sassy panicked at the blaring noise and the confusing lights. A terrible squealing filled the air, followed by a crunching impact. Constance felt as though she were flying again but knew she wasn't time traveling.

The bushes rushed up to meet her as she fell, landing in a tangle of scratching, reaching branches. She hit hard enough to lose her breath momentarily.

Constance sat there in a pile of bushes, stunned. She ran her hands over legs and arms. She wasn't broken anywhere. She'd ache a great deal later, but she was still whole. The gratitude evaporated before it had time to grow as she stared past the bushes and into the street. People rushed around everywhere, and a horrible noise emanated from the horse, now on its side.

Constance scrambled up. Her stomach pitched and rolled, and her skin felt cold.

Arms were reaching toward her, pulling her gently from her place in the foliage. "Are you okay?" She looked up into Garrett's face as he held her steady. "I was coming back to give you my number when I saw you get bucked. Are you hurt at all?"

"What have I done?" she whispered. She dragged her hand over her face. "What have I done?"

CHAPTER 28

LIZ PRESSED HER LIPS TOGETHER as she herded her brothers and sister into the unfamiliar backyard where the wedding would be held. The yard looked strange with all the pale colors of pink, blue, and lavender. Liz looked back toward the place where her mom had dropped them off. The car was gone now, but Liz wished she could make it come back and carry them away from this.

They were greeted by a lady with a dress that hung too low in the front and who looked like she applied her makeup with a trowel. "You can call me Aunt Grace," she said.

None of the King children looked like they intended on calling her anything. Liz knew she had no intentions of ever meeting her again if such things could be helped.

Liz pitied her younger siblings. At least she was old enough to move out soon and go to college. She didn't have to deal with visitation rights and the garbage that went with it.

Her dad found them almost immediately, looking striking in his black tuxedo and slicked-back hair. "I was afraid you weren't going to make it!" He looked too grumpy to be a guy about to get married, but Liz figured she'd be grumpy too if she were marrying a brainless twit.

Liz knew she wasn't being fair. She knew Patty wasn't diabolically evil. But she couldn't muster the goodwill to like the woman no matter how hard she tried—not that she'd ever really tried.

Her dad fidgeted with his boutonniere in agitation. "If your mother would keep a better schedule, we wouldn't have to rush you guys through this," her dad said.

"If you'd quit messing with her computer, her schedule would be in better order."

He made a sort of grunt of surprise. "Your mother's overinflating a situation. That email she sent to me was totally inappropriate."

"What email?"

"She threatened to call the police on me. What kind of woman threatens the father of her children with things like that?"

"One who won't be walked on." Liz felt him tense and knew he was preparing a retort, but she walked away before he could find the words. Liz smiled. So her mom had confronted him about it. Liz was terribly proud that her mom had the backbone to stand up for herself. No wonder she seemed to be feeling so much better.

Patty's sister showed up and herded Liz to the back to get her own bouquet. "Now, when you walk down the aisle, make sure to smile," Patty's sister said.

Liz took a step back from where the woman started fidgeting with the sleeve on Liz's dress. "I'm not walking down the aisle."

"Of course you are! You all are!"

"What? No way! No one said I had to walk anywhere!" Ali's protest had likely been heard in the next city.

"What's the problem?" the woman who called herself Aunt Grace asked.

"Patty decided this morning that it would be nice if Tom's kids walked down the aisle with him," Patty's sister explained. All of them argued except Matt, who thought walking down the aisle might be fun.

Liz shooed away Patty's sister, took the protesters to a corner, and spoke in a low but firm voice. "He is our father. Whatever we think of this whole deal, he's still our father. And Mom needs us to show people she raised us with good manners. C'mon guys. We're a family. Mom needs us to act like it."

Alison still fumed, but she crossed her arms over her chest and gave a curt nod to show she'd do what she was told. Nathan apologized, Matt clapped, and Liz hugged them all to her. Nathan tried to escape the hug, but she caught his sleeve and pulled him into them. "Thanks guys."

The ceremony was too long, and Liz's feet cramped in her satin-covered shoes. Alison picked at the flowers in her bouquet.

Liz turned her attention to the guy marrying her dad and Patty. Liz thought she remembered him as being Patty's uncle, who was a bishop or something like that. Liz sighed as he droned on about the importance of keeping their vows. What did those words mean to her father? The temple vows he'd made didn't mean all that much to him. Were these going to be somehow more important than those?

Liz tried hard not to look away when they exchanged rings and kissed. She worked to keep her eyes from rolling and bit back her disapproval. She ground her teeth together and smiled until her cheeks hurt.

They took enough pictures after the wedding to make Liz feel like she'd been permanently blinded by all the flashing. The different poses of sitting with just her dad and Patty, then with all of Patty's family too, and all the other different combinations of shifting families around to look natural and loving took way longer than the ceremony, and Liz's feet hurt so much she was sure the back of her heels were bleeding.

Music signaled it was time to be done with the pictures. Liz had never been so grateful for cheesy romance songs in her life. She'd almost made it to the chairs where she'd be able to take off her heels and rub her sore feet when her dad caught her arm. "I gotta dance with both my girls!" he proclaimed loud enough to make him look like the good father.

When he took her hand and danced with her, Liz forced another smile.

Her mind swirled with all the things she could have said then; there were lots of things she *wanted* to say: "Why are these vows more important than the ones you made to Mom?" or, "Do you have any idea how unloved I feel right now while dancing with you?" or, "Don't leave us, Dad!" but she remained silent as they swayed to the music. He seemed so wrapped up in his moment, he'd forgotten the conversation they'd had earlier. When the song ended, he kissed her forehead. "Thanks for being here for me, Snow White."

There were things she could have said to that too: "You should return the favor sometime," or, "Don't call me that when you don't mean it," or, "Why can't you ever be there for *me*?" But Liz just smiled and stepped to the side so Alison could take her turn dancing with their dad.

The colors were all pastel, weird since it was autumn. But Liz figured Patty was a pastel kind of personality no matter what the season. "Stepmother." She rolled the word on her tongue, sounding it out slowly. The word tasted like soap administered after cussing. Liz sighed and watched the dancing. Matt made her dance with him a few times, which meant she was supposed to hold his hands and swing him around. Nathan outright refused to dance and spent most of his time eating finger sandwiches at the buffet.

It grew darker, and someone had flipped a switch, which turned on a million and a half white Christmas lights strung throughout the trees. A few people clapped at the added ambiance. Liz only snorted. She didn't really know anyone there. Most of her dad's relatives left right after the ceremony, and Grandma King flat out refused to come.

Liz sat at a table, picking at a loose thread in the pink tablecloth. She looked up in surprise to see her mom standing over her. Her mom's wide eyes and pale face made Liz feel cold. "Why are you here? What's wrong? What happened?"

"Get Matt. I'll get the twins. We gotta go."

"Why? What happened?"

"I'll tell you in the car." Her mom went to her father first and touched him gently on the shoulder. Liz watched her whisper something to him and watched him frown. He gestured toward the uncut cake, and Liz guessed he wasn't happy to see her mom taking them away already.

Liz was relieved to get out of there. She went and found Matt and then Alison, who was doing the thirteen-year-old version of flirting by taking the tie from one of the boys she'd met there and running from him. Liz grunted, grabbed the tie, and thrust it at the boy.

He took it and wandered off to bug someone else's sister. "What's your damage?" Alison asked.

"Mom has an emergency. She said it's time to go."

Her mom had rounded up Nathan and they were hurrying to the car when Matt whined, "I didn't get to say good-bye to Daddy!"

Liz stopped and grabbed him by the hand. The kids all marched dutifully around to the back of the house, where Matt threw his arms around his dad's legs. "Bye, Daddy!" They each took a turn giving their dad a hug and muttering a good-bye then hurried back to the car where their mom waited.

Liz got in front. "Will you tell me what's wrong?"

Her mom gripped the steering wheel hard enough to turn her knuckles white. "Sassy had an accident."

Liz's body went from cold to frozen.

Her breath was hard to catch, as though someone had shoved her in a deep freezer and left her there. "That's not possible."

"She apparently got out of her stall and jumped the fence. I can't believe she jumped that . . . it was so high . . ." Her mom murmured the last as if musing to herself.

"She couldn't get out. The stall's locked."

"All I know is she got out. Alton said it was bad."

Liz's eyes burned from the tears pricking to the surface. "What's bad? What happened?"

"She got hit by a car."

Liz shook her head slowly. She felt physically ill at the words. Her stomach twisted, and if she hadn't felt the urgency to get to the stables immediately, she'd have insisted her mom stop the car so she could throw up. She couldn't believe it. Her hands trembled and her voice shook. "No. No! There is no way she got out! Her stall is totally secure."

"I'm sorry."

There was no sound from the backseat, none of the usual bickering and banter. The kids stared at her. Matt had tears leaking down his face, which he didn't bother to brush away. Liz realized she had tears on her face too and brushed hers away with an angry swipe. No way could Sassy be really hurt. It had to be someone else's horse. Her horse was in a *secure* stall. Only a few select family members knew the combination to the lock.

"I'm so sorry, Lizzie," Alison murmured.

They arrived to a scene of blue, white, and red flashing lights, washing everything in a kaleidoscope of color. "Stay in the car!" her mom ordered the younger kids as Liz leapt from the vehicle. She searched through the people to find her best friend—her Sassy.

Alton stood with his back to her, his bulky frame silhouetted in the moonlight. And the cowboy who owned the mean-tempered Arabians stood next to him. Liz stared at the cowboy, her mind replaying the events from the other night when the cowboy yelled at Matt. Her eyes narrowed. It had to be him. She ran, her dress billowing behind her. She pushed with all her might against the cowboy with both of her hands. He barely reacted to the shove in time to catch himself. "What the—"

"Why would you do this?" she shouted, cutting him off.

Both he and Alton stared at her like she was some escaped lunatic.

"Why?" she shouted again so loud it hurt her throat.

"I didn't do nothin'." Annoyance filled his cowboy drawl.

"You let her out! I know you did! You're always spurring your own horses so hard, I'm surprised none of them have bolted yet. And now you've hurt mine!"

"I didn't let her out. That girl you're always with. She let her out."

"I'm never with anybody. Don't lie." Liz looked around for a cop. "I'm pressing charges!"

The cowboy stood to his full height. "Your little friend who looks like you. She got in your stall and took the horse for a ride."

"What are you talking about?" Liz asked, her voice lowered a little with uncertainty.

"Liz . . ." someone said behind her. Liz turned slowly.

CHAPTER 29

CONSTANCE LOOKED LIKE A PHANTOM. "How did you get here?" Liz asked. There was no way Constance could be at the stables. She was at home reading. The gashes and cuts across Constance's face and arms were fresh wounds, but Liz couldn't register them properly. The cowboy strutted away, cussing. She turned to watch him leave. Alton and her mom headed toward the Big Barn. She turned back to Constance. "What are you doing here?"

Constance shook her head. Her dark hair, littered with leaves and small twigs, fell over her shoulders with the motion. Tears fell from her bloodshot eyes. "I'm so sorry! I am so sorry!"

Liz felt like the world was upside down and spinning. "No. You didn't do this. You couldn't have done this." The soft rasp of her voice sounded alien to her. She started yelling again just so she could hear her own voice sounding normal. "Tell me you didn't do this to me! Tell me you didn't just destroy my whole life!"

Constance buried her face in her hands.

"Tell me! Tell me you didn't ruin my life!"

"Liz, c'mon, can't you see she's upset?"

For the first time, Liz noticed Garrett standing nearby. She turned on him. "You brought her here! You had to have brought her here. You did this to me, both of you!" Liz shook her head hard to try to change the scenery in front of her. But nothing changed.

"Liz, stop," Garrett chided. "She could've been killed. This could have been way worse."

"Worse? My best friend got hit, and you think it could be worse?"

"What are you talking about? Best friend? That's a *horse*! This is your family!" Garrett's voice was sharp.

Liz put her hand out to silence him. "You don't know what you're talking about, so stay out of this." She whirled back to Constance. "Why would you do this?"

"Lizzie, you must understand, you must know I didn't mean to hurt you. But I had to go back. Lizzie, I have to go back! William's alive!"

The words were like static to Liz. "William's *not* alive, okay? Let's get this through your head. William died—like a hundred and fifty years ago; he's gone, okay? Your baby grew up, and she died too. They're all gone! There's nobody left but you!"

Constance looked like she'd been slapped. Liz wanted to slap her, wanted to hurt her as much as she hurt.

Constance straightened and jutted out her bleeding chin. "I'm sorry to know the same blood flows through us." She turned and walked away.

Liz's bare arms were cold in the night air as she covered her face with her hands. Garrett stared at Liz with incredulity. "You're a real piece of work, Liz King." He raked his fingers through his dark hair and turned to follow Constance.

Liz wanted to call out and make Constance come back. She wanted to hit her and hug her. She wanted to yell at Constance and wanted Constance to comfort her. She wanted to say she was sorry and wanted to hurt Constance more. Not knowing what to do, she looked around to find where Sassy would be.

There were a few patrol cars with their overheads flashing everything in a sick array of red, white, and blue, but the patrolmen weren't close enough to question. She looked at the road, trying to find evidence of blood. A car with its bumper falling off and its front end dented in sat to the side of the road. Liz looked away so she wouldn't see the driver. She didn't want to see the face of the person who hurt her Sassy. There was no sign of her horse. Liz pulled her arms into herself and followed the light of the Big Barn to her mom, bracing herself for the news Alton had about Sassy.

* * *

"She's been heavily sedated," Alton was saying as Liz entered his oak-paneled office.

Her mom looked up to see Liz. "Is Constance all right?"

Liz tried to speak but couldn't make her trembling lips open. She nodded.

Alton's leathered face was creased in worry. "The vet's with her now, in the training stall. They had to get her off the road to let traffic through."

Liz's body jolted. She wanted to race back to see Sassy, but she was terrified. Would Sassy be bloody and road-rashed? Would she be broken and crying in pain? Alton said they had sedated her. Did that mean she was sleeping and not feeling pain?

"What—what happened?" Liz asked, finally finding the ability to speak.

"Your friend was running her, and she jumped the fence. I wish someone had filmed that. I'll bet it was a magnificent jump."

How could he admire the jump at a time like this?

Alton cleared his throat and ran a hand over the leathered skin of his forehead. "Anyway, they jumped into traffic. The horse reared up, which is what threw your friend off, and the car hit Sassy's back legs. Your friend's real lucky she got pitched off the back of the animal or she'd have gotten hurt far worse."

"But what about Sassy? What happened to Sassy?" Liz didn't want to think about Constance. She didn't want to think about the words she'd said and the words she still wanted to say. *How could I have said those things? How could she have tried to go back to a place where she'll just die?*

"The one leg's fractured for sure. The other . . . I don't know yet. Since she was on her back legs, they took the brunt of the force from the car. Her front legs are both fine, cut up from the windshield, I think, but fine. Least that's what the vet said. She's lame though. Even if she doesn't have to be put down from the fracture, she for sure won't be jumping anymore. You won't ever be able to compete with her again. They'll retire her. That's about all I can tell you."

Liz felt a pain shoot through her midsection. *Put her down? Did he just say the words* put down? No way was Sassy getting put down. Not the only friend Liz had. She thought of her other friend. She thought of Constance and the horror on Constance's face at Liz's words. Liz pushed the thought out of her head.

"Can I see her?" Liz's voice quaked. Her lip trembled.

"Sure. She's in the training stall. The vet's working on her. But remember she's sedated, so even if she looks dead, she ain't."

As Liz turned the corner of his office out into the main area of the Big Barn, she heard her mother. "How much will this cost?"

Liz started running. She ran all the way to the main stall in the Big Barn and halted at the door. It stood open. Liz peeked in and saw a woman standing over Sassy's body. Sassy *did* look dead the way she lay there, not moving, not a muscle twitching.

"You can come in," the woman said without looking up from the horse.

Liz jumped at the vet's voice. She eased her way into the stall, the smell of disinfectant mingling with the smell of hay.

"My name's Shannon. You must be Liz."

"Yeah."

"Well, let me tell you what's happened. Sassy fractured her back right cannon. We were worried about the left cannon too, but it looks like it's just cut up pretty bad. We've already immobilized her right leg so she can't hurt it worse. I'm pretty confident we can save the leg and the horse with a good cast, but she'll need to be moved to my clinic."

"How much will it cost to fix her?" Liz hated herself for voicing her mother's question, but she had to know. Everything depended on the price tag.

* * *

Matt cried as they drove home. "Are they gonna shoot her?" he asked.

Liz bit her lip hard enough to taste blood.

"No one's shooting anybody," her mom said, the agitation evident in the way she enunciated every word.

Alison and Nathan remained quiet. Liz and her mom never mentioned that Constance had been involved. There was no reason for the kids to know. Liz felt cold and numb. She doubted she could make a fist if her life depended on it. But she wanted to make a fist. She wanted to pound everything and everyone she saw.

Her mom was far more understanding of Constance's motivations for riding Sassy. "It's amazing what we'll do to impress a boy," she'd said. She really thought Constance had Garrett drive her to the stables to impress him. Liz didn't bother to correct her.

Not to say her mom wasn't angry; she was outright furious. But for her everything remained on the impersonal level. It was just a horse, after all . . . and having the excuse not to stable the horse anymore would likely be a relief to her mom even if her mom didn't say those words out loud. For Liz, everything felt personal. Sassy was *her* horse.

Constance wasn't there when they got home. Liz looked out the window to Garrett's place and saw his dad's car in the driveway. She knew where to find Constance. She made it as far as the front door when she realized she had nothing she wanted to say . . . well nothing she *could* say, anyway. There were tons of things she *wanted* to say.

She sat at the kitchen table and put her head down. It ached from all the yelling and adrenaline. The money was too much. Her mom could never pull it off. Even if Liz got a full-time job bagging groceries or flipping hamburgers, she could never come up with that kind of money either. Her dad was probably on a plane to Hawaii or the Caribbean or wherever he'd taken off to with her new stepmom. Even if he wasn't, he didn't have the money it would take to fix Sassy either.

Liz's mom sat at the table with her. Liz didn't need to raise her head to know who'd joined her; she smelled her mom's Lancome *Miracle* perfume. And she heard the kids going upstairs to bed. They didn't argue at all, which only magnified how bad a day it had been for all of them.

Today, Liz had gotten a new stepmom and lost her best friend.

She felt her mom's hand on her head, stroking her hair. "So what do we do?"

"About what?"

"About everything. Your friend's missing. Should we be worried?"

"She's at Garrett's."

Her mom tsked. "So should we be worried?"

"Should we care?"

He mom's hand dropped from Liz's head. "Eliza Josephine King! How could you be like that?"

Liz lifted her head. "There's one thing in this whole world that makes me happy, and she's gone. I'm never going to brush her coat down or feed her treats or have her nuzzle my face when I'm sad or feel like I'm flying when she jumps . . ." Liz's shaking hands brushed furiously at the tears. "I feel like my whole life is over."

"It's a horse, Liz. I know you loved it, but your life is not over. It's a horse."

"She's my best friend."

"You're being a bit overdramatic."

"So what are we going to do?" Liz looked away when her voice cracked at the last word.

Her mom wrapped her arms around herself as though she'd become suddenly cold. "You know we can't pay to stable a lame horse."

"So you gonna send her to the glue factory? Or maybe we'll just have Alton shoot her."

"Liz, stop!" Her mom pushed back her chair from the table. "You can't think that's how I want this to work out?"

"You didn't care when you sold Alison's piano; why would you care if you shot my horse?"

Stunned, her mom stood. "Alison and I talked things over before I made that choice. It was a Steinway for crying out loud! I was able to pay off my car *and* the credit card. I set aside a little bit so we could buy an upright. Alison goes through the want ads at Stephanie's house every day looking for one that she wants. *She's* been the only thing holding her back from her piano. I told her I wasn't paying for lessons until she finally picked out a piano and had it set up in the house. So she and I made a private deal that didn't concern you at all. And at least Alison was a grown-up about it!"

"What deal are you going to make me?" Liz was now standing too. "And you can't compare the two things. One's a living creature; the other is a piece of wood!"

"I didn't compare the two—*you* did!" Her mom crossed her arms. If her eyes had been daggers, Liz would have been shredded.

"So what are we going to do?" Liz repeated, trying to retreat. She felt horrible that she'd thought her mom had sold Ali's piano without finding a way to make things okay for Ali. She felt horrible she hadn't trusted her mom enough to try to understand things better.

"We need to get Constance to come back. We ought to discuss things with her—and I mean discuss things, not scream at her. Besides, I told her she could stay here until she got her feet under her. She can still do that. I think I want her to get a part-time job so she can pay for things she needs and make some sort of restitution to you. But I can't just leave her out in the street."

"I don't mean what are we going to do about Constance; what are we going to do about Sassy?"

Her mom ran her fingers through her short hair. "I can't make a decision yet. I need to really look at our finances. I don't see how we can justify boarding a lame horse, but I can't say we won't try. I just can't make that decision yet. Let me see what our options are, and we'll see what we can do."

Her mom drew a deep breath. "In the meantime, there is a *human* that needs to be taken care of. Don't make me question your priorities. Because if I start thinking you really care more about a horse than you do about your friend who is all alone in our country and who has been such a good friend to you, I don't know how willing I'll be to really check the options." Her mom didn't bother to say anything more but rounded the table.

She wrapped Liz in a tight embrace and just held her. Liz felt some of her anger drain in her mother's arms. She had no idea how her mom had kept it together for the wedding and the disaster that followed, but not only did she keep it together, but she also was there to try to help Liz keep it together. "Mom?"

"Hmm?"

"I love you."

CHAPTER 30

WHILE CROSSING THE LAWN TO Garrett's house, Liz felt like she was sludging her way through quicksand. She stood at the door for what seemed like forever before she knocked. She hoped no one would hear the halfhearted rap on the door, and then she could go back to her mom and say she at least tried.

But Garrett's little sister answered.

"Hey, Madison. Does Garrett have a friend here?" Liz tried looking around the girl into the foyer but hurried to look away when Garrett stepped into the doorway and slid Madison to the side.

"Coming to apologize?"

"I just came . . . for Constance."

"She's in the kitchen with my dad." Garrett opened the door wider for Liz to follow him in.

When was the last time she'd been inside the Mitchells' house? She took a cautious step inside and silently followed Garrett to the kitchen.

Brother Mitchell and Brother Bunker from across the street stood behind Constance. She sat on a chair with her head bent and her arms folded. She didn't look up.

"They were about to give her a blessing," Garrett said. Brother Mitchell pulled out a vial of oil.

Liz wished she had a chair to sit on as well. The whole world felt like it was spinning. Constance looked a little cleaner than Liz had last seen her, but even with having her cuts cleaned up, she still appeared to have been in a fight with a grizzly bear. Liz wondered if the blessing was for the pain.

Brother Bunker did the anointing. Liz hurried to close her eyes and fold her arms. Then Brother Mitchell cleared his throat and began. He blessed her with a speedy recovery from her accident and with the strength to bear the burdens given to her.

Liz thought about all the times her father had given similar prayers over her head. He couldn't do that anymore since his excommunication. She wondered if he and Patty had kids, who would bless them when they got sick? Would her half brothers and sisters grow up without the gospel, or would he repent sometime? Would he be able to have his priesthood restored someday and bless those kids?

Liz shuddered at the further implications of her father's choices.

When Brother Mitchell closed his prayer, Liz hurried to wipe her eyes so no one would see her crying. Constance stood and hugged Brother Mitchell, thanking him for his generosity. She hugged Brother Bunker, too. She even hugged Garrett.

"It is time for me to go. I appreciate you all for your concern." She smiled softly, making the scrape across her chin stretch out in a sickening way. She winced a little.

"If you need anything at all, you can come back," Garrett said.

Liz knew it was his way of saying she wasn't taking good enough care of Constance. She ducked her head as though she could hide from his insult. If she could hide, would the insults still be true?

Constance didn't say anything to Liz, not even when they were outside and walking back to her house. Liz didn't say anything either. There wasn't anything she could say. Anger still consumed her. And regret had hollowed out a place in her heart, regret for saying things she couldn't take back, regret that she wanted to say so many more hurtful things. Then there was the hurt from the fact that Constance had tried to leave. Wasn't she even planning on saying good-bye?

She left me. And though Liz hated to make the comparison, it felt just like the day her dad said he needed to move out of the house.

Liz followed Constance through the front door, but Liz left Constance standing alone in the foyer the moment the door closed behind them. She took the stairs two at a time to get to her room. Another minute of the silence and she knew she'd break it by screaming again. She already promised her mom she wouldn't do that, but the only way to escape the inevitable screaming was to be alone. Even then, Liz wasn't sure she'd be able to control herself.

When Liz shut her bedroom door and leaned against it to catch her breath, she looked up and saw her room as though seeing it for the first time.

Miniature wooden horses sat on the shelves, posters lined her walls, and stuffed animals took up her whole bed. Her room felt like a huge stable.

Liz yanked the stuffed horses off her bed and off the big beanbag in the corner. She thrust the offending toys into the recesses of her closet. She grabbed a bag she'd made at girls' camp a few years ago for secret sister gifts and slammed the wooden miniatures from the shelves into it. The bag joined the stuffed animals in the closet. In a frenzied rage she turned to the posters and ripped them from the walls.

Her heart pounded the blood through her body. She felt suddenly weak and light-headed, and she fell to the floor and folded her legs under her. She drew the crumpled posters to her chest and hugged them. The back of her throat burned with sobs. Her shoulders shuddered as she gave in to her despair. *She tried to leave me.*

"Lizzie?" Matt's small voice came from her doorway. The hallway light silhouetted his tiny frame.

"Come here, Matty. I need one of your hugs."

Matt crossed the room and plopped into her lap. She tossed the posters to the side, wrapped her arms around him, rested her cheek against the top of his head, and cried.

* * *

Constance stood in the foyer, not quite knowing what to do. Liz brought her back but abandoned her in the same moment. Constance felt like bruises covered her entire body. She longingly looked up the stairs toward the bath. Was she welcome here or merely tolerated?

Tolerated was the more probable answer. Otherwise Liz would try to reconcile the situation. Constance wondered that the other children were nowhere to be seen. She wandered the house to find another breathing person. She wasn't truly ready to deal with Liz yet, and another person might help her sort through her feelings.

Her feelings.

She wanted to howl. William . . . Eliza . . . Liz . . . Liz's horse. So much pain. So much anger. And Constance was at the middle of it all. She hated what she'd done to Liz—hated that she'd hurt this family she had wanted to help. And she hated far more that Liz had been right. William was so far in the past that he was little more than a few words on paper, but he was everything in her heart.

The kitchen, living room, and dining room were all empty. She tried the study and almost retreated when she saw Clair sitting at the desk with her head hanging in her hands.

"Don't go," Clair said.

Constance entered the room cautiously. "I am so sorry for the trouble I've caused your family. I will do what I can to make it right. I just don't know how or where to begin . . ." Her voice trembled. *What have I done?*

"Sit down, please."

Constance sat across from Clair and tried to hold her head up. "I am so sorry." How many times had she said that over the last few hours?

"Tell me what happened." Clair leaned back in her chair and waited to hear the truth—the truth Constance could not give.

"I asked Garrett to take me to the stables. I lost something there and needed to find it. I was in a terrible hurry and thought the horse could get me to the back of the pastures faster than my walking. But I must not know Liz's horse as well as I'd imagined. She jumped the fence and then a car came upon us. The noise was wretched." Her voice caught and she swallowed and blinked to keep from crying. "I am truly sorry. I never intended to hurt anyone."

"I know you didn't," Clair said. Her voice remained remarkably calm considering the situation Constance had placed her in. Clair maintained patient understanding. "I don't know what you were thinking. Taking Liz's horse was *not* a good idea . . . I just don't know what to do now."

"I will work to pay for a new animal." Constance felt like she'd never get home. Surely after causing the family further misfortune, God would be slow to remember her. William was gone to her . . . just as Liz had said. Constance felt grateful that Garrett considered Liz's tirade as little more than hysterics and paid no mind to the details of her words. How would she have given explanation to such things? Her family was gone and she was left to make her way in a foreign world. Life would be far better if no one suspected the awful truth of her origin. Surely she'd settle into this new world and find something she could do to earn her own way and not burden her posterity further.

"Liz doesn't want a new animal. She wants *that* animal."

"But it's been injured. No horse survives such an injury."

"The vet said she thought she could cast the leg and heal it good as new. Well sort of. She's retired from ever competing again. I don't know." Clair took a deep shuddering breath.

"I'm so sorry for the trouble I've been to your family."

"You're not trouble. Well . . . *this* was trouble, but we'll work it out. Things always work out." She shuffled a few papers absently on the desk.

"Your genealogy?"

"Yep. My husband—my ex-husband—called it a senseless hobby."

"I do not believe so. If you do not understand where you came from, how are you to know where you're going?"

Clair gave a depreciative laugh. "That's what I told him. Anyway, it doesn't matter. You need to talk to Liz. She needs a friend."

"I do not believe I am the friend she seeks at this time."

Clair's face fell. "Maybe not, but you're the only friend she has."

Constance didn't hurry to get to Liz's bedroom. She found she'd much rather stay and talk to Clair. However, Clair expected her to talk to Liz. So Constance faced her duty, but she wasn't about to hurry to her duty.

The guilt was all encompassing. Guilt coupled with the loss of William and little Eliza filled her with despair unlike any she'd known. The sting of her granddaughter's words rang in her ears like an eternal echo at the top of a canyon. *William's not alive, okay? Let's get this through your head. William died—like a hundred and fifty years ago! He's gone, okay! Your baby grew up and she died too! They're all gone! There's nobody left but you!* "Nobody left but me . . ." she whispered.

Lord, I will come . . . how could I stay? She was tired but also resigned. She would do what the Lord asked. She felt truly penitent of the anger she'd harbored for these many months since leaving England. The tragedy of the evening gave her understanding as she'd never had before. *After what you have done . . . Lord, I will come.*

But now she feared He didn't want her anymore. Did her repentant heart come too late? Seeing Liz's face crumpled and enraged after the accident filled Constance with the knowledge of her own guilt. For Liz, losing the horse was losing everything, just like Constance had lost everything. Constance felt the girl's pain as acutely as her own, but Liz's pain was Constance's fault.

She stood outside the door listening for noise. Hearing nothing, Constance edged the door open and peered into the darkness. The light from the hall showed the room had been redecorated a bit since Constance had been there last. All equestrian reminders were removed, and the room looked empty.

Liz was under her covers, but Constance knew by the shallow breathing that Liz wasn't sleeping. She left the door open so she could find her night clothes and get changed. When she finally shut the door and burrowed into her makeshift bed, she whispered, "Liz?"

No response. Constance expected the silence. She would be surprised if Liz ever spoke to her again. "Lizzie . . . I know you're awake. I need you to understand. I did not make a deliberate attempt to sabotage your life. The fault is mine, I know, and I'm sorry. I am so sorry."

"My mom's going to put her down. We can't afford to stable a lame horse." Liz's voice emanated angry bitterness in the darkness.

Constance closed her eyes. "She said she would seek an alternative if she could."

"What alternative? There aren't any alternatives."

"If you could but understand," Constance pled, sitting up in her covers. "After you left, I read the papers your mother gave me. The papers said William made it to the valley. He showed up some months after the wagon company. He survived, Lizzie! You were right. He's not alive *now*, but he is alive *there!* He and I started the journey together. We were going to do as the Lord asked and journey to Zion and raise our children unto the Lord. I need to join him there and keep our promises. It felt the right thing for me to do! I tried to go back to the place I awoke that first morning here, but when nothing happened, I thought . . . Oh, how foolish it sounds now, but I thought if I could move faster, I could jump through time. I did not purposely cause injury to your horse; I only meant to do the right thing and return to my own time."

"With all your talk about faith and doing the right thing and *seeking Zion*. What a stupid thing . . . what an absurd thing for you to tell me. You'll never get there. Don't you see that? Even if you go back, you will *never* see Zion."

"What do you mean? What are you speaking of?"

"You'll never get there! You die before you ever reach Zion!"

Constance drew herself back as though Liz had struck her. "That's a horrible thing to say! How could you say such a thing?"

Liz's bedding fell to the side with a quiet rasp. Constance's eyes had adjusted to the darkness well enough to see that she was sitting up too now.

"Because it's true! I read a part of Lynnette's journal. You die of cholera and give your baby to Lynnette with your last words. If you go back, you'll die. That's not what you'd planned on, is it? You could stay here and be safe, but no. You're rushing off to a horrible future—or past, or whatever." Liz fell back onto her pillow and rolled away from Constance.

Constance sat there, unmoving, barely able to breathe for a very long time. *I die?* Impossible! Why would she be put through all this to just die? *I die, yet William lives?* The ache in her burned. Constance thought the history was wrong in saying she died. She thought the history used that to explain her disappearance. But no . . . she would die, and Lynnette would take her place as wife and mother. Constance was to be a replaced member in her own family.

And of cholera! Of all the horrid ways to go! She'd witnessed many die from cholera, and the unpleasantness of such a death was wretched.

She listened in the darkness. Liz's breathing was still shallow, so she did not yet sleep, but her breathing was also short and came in rapid bursts.

So . . . her granddaughter wept . . .

Does she weep for me or for the horse? Constance wondered, then realized it didn't matter. She finally got over the shock enough to lie down.

I die.

Constance continued her prayers, begging for forgiveness for her stubborn, angry, bitter heart. She pled with the Lord for strength to follow His plan for her to abide by His will. *Lord, I will come . . .*

She felt peace through her prayer, peace unlike any she'd felt before. She knew He was watching out for her and that her visit to this future time was not a curse, but a blessing. She imagined being in a field of flowers and running to her Father in Heaven. She imagined Him embracing her and welcoming her home. Constance wondered if she was simply imagining things . . . or if that's what it would be like to die. *After what you have done . . . Lord, I will come.*

She drifted off to sleep, feeling lighter. Feeling forgiven, if not by Liz . . . at least by a loving Father in Heaven.

CHAPTER 31

LIZ WOKE UP BEFORE HER alarm and turned the setting to OFF before it could buzz. She looked at Constance snoring softly in her blankets and hurried to turn away, feeling horrified and ashamed of her words the night previous.

I am a terrible person, she thought.

Sassy's gone. The thought was like a black hole in her heart. She knew there was no way to "look at options" as her mom had hinted. What options were there?

None.

Liz dressed quickly and was surprised to find that her mom had already gotten the other kids up to get dressed. When she passed her mom in the hall, she reached out and grabbed her mom's hand to give it a little squeeze. She let go and continued to the bathroom. She hated the normalcy of the morning routine of brushing teeth and washing her face. This day was like every other day.

The twins were a bit quieter and less argumentative, but they seemed fine. Matt gave her several of his hugs before he left for the bus. Her mom stopped Liz as she opened the garage door. She hugged Liz tight. Liz drank in their support as though it were an antidote for her pain.

This was the first morning Constance wasn't already up, and with a grim realization, Liz figured the night must have been hard on her too. *How could I have said such awful things? How could I have told her she dies in the past?*

But she was going to leave me. She planned on leaving and didn't even say good-bye. It's better that she knows. If she knows, she'll choose to stay.

These were the words she used to ease her own guilt. Liz didn't bother to wake Constance. School would be easier to face alone. Liz went to the garage, grateful to keep her father's car until he came back from his honeymoon. She soured a little thinking about him honey-mooning with her drone stepmom but pushed the thought from her mind.

For the majority of the school day, she kept her head down but had a hard time avoiding Garrett. *Why can't he just go away?* she wondered. *But of course he can't go away; he's the admirer and champion of pioneer grandmothers everywhere.*

He put an arm out to stop Liz from walking past him during lunch hour. "How's she doing?"

"I don't know. I haven't talked to the vet yet today."

He grunted. "Not the horse, Liz—your cousin. Is she okay?"

"Oh. Yeah. Fine."

"Has the headache gone away?"

Liz had no idea Constance even had a headache, so she could only shrug in response.

"She should've gone to see a doctor. But she acted scared of the idea when my dad offered to take her. She said she watched her neighbor get bled by a doctor and that she'd rather die a thousand horrible ways than that one. I think she hit her head harder than she'd admit."

"Hmm." Liz's head hurt too but only because she'd been crying all night. *Constance watched someone get bled? What could that mean?*

He narrowed his eyes. "But you don't care about all that because you're still brooding over your horse."

"I'm not brooding." And she found that she really wasn't brooding over Sassy. She worried about what would happen with Sassy, but she was brooding because Constance had tried to abandon her, and because Garrett had tried to help.

"You *are.*" He shook his head, making a lock of dark hair fall over his right eye. He brushed it back, and Liz felt annoyed she'd noticed such a dumb thing. He confused her when he was around.

"You don't understand." She looked away.

"You're right. I don't. But your cousin is in some kind of trouble. I've never seen anyone so edgy and flat-out scared in my life. I think she could use a friend. If you can't be that friend because you're worried about an animal, then step aside and let someone else do it."

"You don't understand." She wanted to shove him out of the way. He didn't understand. He had no idea what it was like to be abandoned by everyone he loved. His friends hadn't ditched him when they got into high school. His father didn't cheat, get excommunicated, and then leave the family altogether. His fifth great-grandmother who had become his best friend didn't try to leave *him* without saying good-bye.

"What I don't understand is how Constance could admire you and stick up for you all the time when you obviously couldn't care less about her. I'm glad you don't consider *me* your friend. I'd hate to get stabbed in the back too!"

He stomped off. Liz was grateful, grateful he'd kept his voice low enough not to cause another scene, and guilty because he was right.

She hated that he was right. Constance *had* suffered a great deal—and far worse than anything Liz was suffering. "I'm such a jerk!" she muttered to herself. Constance had lost her entire family, been thrown off a horse, and nearly been flattened in a car wreck. And Liz added to her misery by letting her know that she would die when she went back to her time.

Liz closed her eyes and leaned her head on her locker. "I'm sorry," she whispered, wishing there was a way to take it back somehow. She wished Constance knew how to answer the phone so she could call and apologize.

* * *

Constance wandered the house. The peace from her prayer the night previous stayed with her like a warm quilt wrapped around her shoulders. "I'm going home," she whispered to the house. She dreamt of returning to the stables and being caught up in a fog that carried her to the wagons where the company prepared to leave. When she awoke, she knew she could finally return.

"But have I helped this family in any way, or have I been the sole means of their ruin?" she asked aloud.

But she knew the answer. In spite of how horrible the events seemed, they were for the good of the entire King family. She'd done what she'd been meant to do, even if she had blundered her way through. Even if she had no idea exactly what she'd been meant to do. Now it was time to return.

Constance stared at the family photo on the wall. She touched the glass over Liz's face. "I will not try to leave again without saying good-bye," she said to the picture.

For all her previous haste to leave, and for the ache she had to hold her daughter as soon as possible, she slowly took in the surroundings of the home. She wanted to remember everything.

She hummed the tune to the song from the program, and her heart sung the words she now meant. *Lord, I will come . . .*

* * *

Liz trudged to her next class. She stopped for a moment, thinking she'd heard someone call her name. She looked around and saw Constance down the hall standing by the trophy case, waving her over. Liz wanted to run and hide, but her feet moved that direction anyway. For all she wanted to apologize, she could only feel shame when she looked at Constance.

"How did you get here?" Liz asked. She looked over the scrapes and cuts on Constance's face and worried about the headache Garrett had mentioned.

"I walked. It's an easy—"

"I know. It's an easy distance. Is everything okay. Are you still hurt? Garrett said your head hurt. Do you need a doctor?"

Constance's eyes softened. "I am quite well. I wanted to say something to you."

Liz waited, wanting to say something too, an apology and a plea for forgiveness, but she couldn't find the words.

"You told me last night that I will never see Zion. But you're wrong. I *am* seeing Zion. I am standing right in the middle of it. I have seen the temple and pictures of other temples scattered all over the world. I've seen the chapels where the Saints meet and have been to your classes where the youth are taught. I have seen the valley. So you need not pity me. You'd fare far better pitying yourself. For you—who were born here, who spent your entire life here, and who stands in the midst of it all— have never seen it, Liz. *You* have never seen Zion."

"So you walked to school to give me a lecture?" The words were out before Liz could call them back. "No. I didn't mean that. I'm sorry. I—"

"I understand your meaning. Do not worry." Constance shook her head. "Just listen. You have given me a gift, and I have stolen away something you love. I am sorry for that, and I would that I could make that right for you. But I can *give* you a gift as well."

Constance held her hands out wide. "*See* the world around you. Stop choosing to find fault with everything you see. I came to tell you I love you and want you to find happiness and contentment for yourself."

"If you really love me, why were you so quick to try to leave last night?" Liz brushed at a tear. "You wanted to leave bad enough that you had Garrett take you away."

"And therein rests your real anger. I'm sorry for that as well. I should have waited for you." Constance turned to go.

"Wait!" Liz said. "I'm sorry, too, about what I said last night. I shouldn't have told you about the cholera. I was just mad, and I shouldn't have said what I said about your husband and baby. Please don't be mad at me for that. I really didn't mean to hurt you. I know you could have been killed in that accident, and that would have been so much worse. I just—anyway, I'm sorry."

Constance turned back, her face warm with love and concern. "Do not be uneasy. It is *that* truth of my own death that has given me more strength than any other. All is forgiven on my side. I hoped to find something similar on yours."

Liz nodded, trying to find the words she knew she needed to say out loud.

Constance nodded as though she understood. She turned again to go.

"Wait." When Constance turned back, her eyes shining with tears, Liz said, "I forgive you. And I love you, too."

Constance reached out and hugged her for a moment. Liz exhaled, releasing everything in that breath. All the anger for her father, all the anger for her family's new poverty and the shame of her father's sin, all the hurt and ache over Sassy, and all the betrayal she felt with Constance trying to go home the night before melted out of her in the warmth of Constance's love. She wished she could eat back the words she'd uttered in anger. But through the tight embrace, she *knew* that Constance had forgiven her—knew that Constance loved her.

Constance pulled away and smiled. "You should hurry to class. Even if you run, you'll be late."

"Aren't you coming?"

"No. I'm going to go home now. It is time for me to leave."

"Okay. I'll see you later, then." Liz tried at a grin. "And go straight home—no little adventures or anything, okay?"

"No adventures. It should be a simple walk."

Liz nodded, laughed, and shook her head. "Nothing's simple with you."

"As nothing is with you. The apple never falls very far from the tree."

The bell rang, and Liz grumbled. "I'd better run now, or I'm getting detention. That'll be my third tardy!" Liz hurried to hug her grandmother again. "I love you, Constance." And then Liz bolted off in the direction of her classroom.

* * *

"Good-bye, Eliza Josephine King," Constance whispered as her granddaughter fled to class.

She hurried to make the walk back to the King household. There was not much time and yet much to accomplish.

Constance felt a degree of guilt for not telling her plans to Liz. But she also knew Liz would try to stop her. She said good-bye, even if it had been misinterpreted at the moment. When Liz realized the truth, she would understand Constance *had* said good-bye. Besides . . . Constance could not bear the pain of parting tears. She wanted to remember Liz's smiles.

She finished dressing far more quickly than she thought and walked down the stairs to Clair's study.

She left three handwritten pages on Clair's desk. Constance owed this woman of faith a proper thank-you for opening her home to a perfect stranger. Then she gathered her skirts and, with a last-minute decision, took two bananas from the fruit bowl, leaving the King home for the last time.

CHAPTER 32

LIZ SLID INTO HER DESK but noticed that her teacher seemed to be feeling a little lenient today and didn't mark her as tardy. She felt a lot better after having spoken with Constance, but her stomach hurt, though she couldn't understand why. It was like she had been told there would be a pop quiz on a book she'd never read and the score would be worth half her grade. She hoped she'd make it through her last three classes without getting sick.

Garrett waited for her outside the door when her class was over. "So is she okay, then?"

Liz stared at him. Hadn't he just asked this very thing just two hours ago? "She's fine. She seems likes she's going to be just fine. Haven't we just had this conversation?"

"Yeah, but I saw you two in the halls before last hour. I figured you'd know more now than you did then." His eyes seemed kinder and warmer than she ever remembered seeing them. "And thanks, Liz."

Liz felt her eyebrows climb her forehead. She adjusted her books on her hip. "I don't get it. Thanks for what?"

"I saw you hug her. You could see, even from a distance, that it meant everything to her that you guys were talking and stuff. She needed to know you forgave her. You should've seen her last night. All she could talk about was how she'd hurt you, how she'd ruined everything by hurting you. Thanks for . . . for getting past it and caring more about her than the horse."

Liz's lip twitched into a smile. "I'm really not some heartless cave-woman, you know." *Even if I do act like it sometimes.* "Of course I care more about her than the horse." *The horse? Did I just refer to Sassy as the horse?* She waved her hand in front of her face. "Anyway, Constance is more than just my family. She's my friend. And as soon as I get home, I'm—"

Constance's last words played through her mind. *"I'm going to go home now. It's time for me to leave . . ."*

Liz's heart beat faster. She shook her head and backed away several steps from Garrett. "I . . . Garrett, I have to go."

"What's wrong?" He took several steps to close the distance between them. The final bell rang, indicating they needed to get to last-hour classes.

"Nothing. Nothing's wrong. I just . . . I'll call you later, okay?" And she was running down the hall. *Did I just tell Garrett I'd call him later?*

She didn't bother with her final class. There wasn't enough time. Constance could be gone already! She ran to the student parking lot and threw her things in the passenger side of her dad's car. She drove home as fast as she dared, cursing at every stoplight.

Liz burst into her house. "Constance? Constance?" She ran through each room calling her name. The empty house answered with silence. When Liz got to her room, she leaped onto the bed and looked over the side. *Please let her just be napping.*

Constance wasn't there.

The sheets and blankets that had been laid out for her since the day she'd come were folded neatly and sitting in a tidy little pile.

Liz jumped off her bed and looked more closely at her room. Everything was in place except the blankets.

Everything was in place . . .

All her stuffed animals were on her bed. All the little miniatures were back on the shelves. The posters, having been ripped from the walls, were not put back, but other than that, everything looked the same. Liz stared at the folded sheets and blankets on the floor. Why did that tidy little pile seem so frightening?

She took a step toward her closet then stopped. Her heart raced, pumping fast enough she felt light-headed. In a swift moment of decision, she strode to the closet and yanked the door open. On the floor sat another tidy little pile. A pair of jeans, a red Old Navy T-shirt, and the tennis shoes she'd given Constance to wear yesterday. She stared at the pile, not comprehending what it meant sitting there benignly on her floor.

Her eyes trailed upward to the hangers. Constance's dress was gone . . .

"Oh no!" Liz gasped. Everything in her closet was hers. There was no bulky-skirted pioneer dress or strange pantaloon underclothes.

Liz bounded down the stairs two at a time and jumped the last four. She was in the car with her dad's keys out of her pocket and in the ignition in mere seconds. She sped to the stable. *How could I have been so horrible yesterday*, she thought. *How could I have been so unfeeling? How could I have not known she had come to say good-bye? Why didn't I make her stay with me in school? Why would she try to go back when she knows what's going to happen?*

She had her door open before the car stopped, slamming it into park with a lurch. Sassy's stable had never seemed farther as Liz ran. She turned the corner too sharply and smacked her elbow on the rough-cut wood. She gritted her teeth against the sting and swung the stall open.

Empty.

Liz flinched as though the emptiness of the stall were some gruesome scene. Her heart constricted, and a cry escaped her. Empty. She knew Sassy wasn't there, but how she'd hoped Constance would be.

Liz's head shot up in a moment of hope. She raced to the back of the pasture where Constance had said she'd awoken when she'd gotten there. But even at a distance, as Liz ran to the lean-to, Liz knew there was nothing there to see.

She sat on a rock next to the structure and wrapped her arms around herself. "You could've let me say good-bye!" she shouted to the wind. Liz didn't know how long she sat with the wind blowing around her. She stopped trying to pull her hair out of her eyes and let it fly around her face like brown streamers.

She didn't know when her feet started moving back to Sassy's stall. Once she was staring back inside the doorway, she realized she never wanted to return to the stables. Liz decided she should at least gather her things.

Liz moved to open her tack closet and then stopped. Paper had been slid between the curves of the handles. She ripped the paper from its perch and unfolded it, her hands clumsy from excitement.

Two earrings clung to the first sheet at the top. The emerald stones dangled against the white paper—the lost jewels of Constance Miles Brown. The family legend had been the only thing to intrigue her young mind when it came to genealogy. Now the mystery was solved, and she'd never be able to tell anyone.

My dearest Liz,

Before you condemn me for leaving to a fate you think entirely useless, please let me explain. I understand now the purpose to my life, the purpose to my suffering, and the purpose to my time with you. Had I been closer to the Lord, I'd not have needed to travel time, but I cannot pretend to regret my journey of faith in this future. I could never regret my time with you.

I am not afraid of my future or the past, as you would see it. I must return to make certain Lynnette receives the charge of my daughter. I must return to make certain I fulfill the destiny the Lord plans for me. The sooner I attain that destiny, the sooner I will be able to progress. Were I to stay, I would not progress but remain a shadow between worlds. I cannot live as a shadow, Liz, as I know you could not.

We are women of strength. Some might call us stubborn and ill-tempered, but I prefer my own point of view to anyone else's. We were meant to overcome our struggles, for ourselves—yes, of course for ourselves—but for others too. They will see our strength and, in turn, be strengthened as we always appear to others as women devoted to the Lord. With that example, we give them the strength to overcome their own weaknesses.

The world need not know we weren't always pleasant in our trials, but they must know that we did overcome them.

And since it is certain that I shall leave mortality far before you arrive, I hope to see you much sooner than later.

Remember, you are strong, and I rejoice that the same blood flows through our veins.

I had the opportunity to speak with the man you call "cowboy." His name is Sheldon Lindquist. He has a proposition that will please you. He asked me to make certain you spoke with him.

My dearest granddaughter, you have given me cause to rejoice in my posterity as I'd never imagined! How proud I am of you!

I love you.

Yours always,

Constance Miles Brown

A woman of strength . . . Liz knew that Constance was absolutely a woman of strength, but she also knew that Liz King was . . . spoiled and pampered. Liz reread the letter several times. She had to hold the letter away from her so her tears wouldn't smudge the ink.

Her hands trembled when she removed the first earring from the paper, and she had to make several tries to keep her hand steady enough to put the earring on. She'd never worn clip-ons before. The second one went on easier. She stood in the doorway of the Little Barn, blinking in the sun for a long time. Liz worked and reworked the timeline in her mind. She kept thinking that Constance still had time before she had to meet her destiny, until she realized that their time was different. Constance had already met her destiny. Cholera had taken her, and her baby had been raised by her friend. Constance was buried somewhere on the trail.

Liz had always scorned the idea of guardian angels. She knew some people told her they believed their family members were watching over them, but until this moment, she'd never hoped for anything to be truer.

"I'm going to miss you," she said to the wind. "But I'll be your woman of strength. I'll do it so I can see you again." She was surprised to find she didn't feel abandoned as she had the night before. She was surprised to feel the warmth of being loved.

Liz touched her earlobe where the stone dangled, took a deep breath, and went to speak to the cowboy.

CHAPTER 33

"HE'S AGREED TO PAY FOR all her medical care?" Liz's mom asked again. The sky was dark, and dinner had been served and washed up. The other kids were asleep or at least in bed. Liz and her mom decided on an after-dinner snack of Oreos and milk.

"Yeah, he said he'd cover all costs, even her boarding, as long as he gets the foal when he breeds her. After that she's my responsibility again. He thinks he can get fifteen thousand for the foal."

"That much?" Her mom dunked another Oreo and bit into it.

Liz shrugged. "I don't know. But after he gets the foal, and she's ours again, we may want to do the same thing. It could bring in enough money to take care of a lot of bills."

"Do you see the irony in you having to cooperate with the guy you used to call the *psycho cowboy*?" Her mom laughed. "I'll bet Constance was happy with the news."

"She was thrilled."

"I'm worried about her going home like she did. After all she's been through since she converted, I worry about her going back. I wish she would've talked to me before getting on a plane. I hope she doesn't feel like she wasn't welcome."

"She knew she could stay; she just knew she had stuff at home to do that was important. After seeing all we've had to deal with, I think she got a reminder that families are important."

"Still . . . do you think she'll stay active?"

Liz smiled and tried to blink back the tears. "Yeah, Mom. She'll stay faithful to the very end."

CHAPTER 34

CLAIR KEPT BUSY ALL WEEK. With the wedding, the accident, and Constance's bizarre exit, she had a lot to think about and even more to do. Her boss wanted her to take more hours, which she did in order to pay off one last debt; then she could cut back again on her hours. Things would be easier once it was just the house they were paying for. She'd be able to manage better then. The idea of breeding Sassy kept cropping up in her mind. If the foal could really be sold for so much, they might be able to breed Sassy several times and pay the mortgage down to a manageable amount. She might be able to quit the job and stay at home with the kids again.

Sunday morning she hurried into her husband's—*her*—study. *I need to stop calling it his,* she thought. *The house is mine. He's gone.*

She tried not to think about the fact that he was honeymooning. She had church in less than an hour, and she'd promised to take over for the Gospel Doctrine teacher today. Nerves unsettled her stomach, and the twins were messing around upstairs instead of getting ready. She could hear the thumping of their feet as they ran up and down the hall. A door slammed. She thought about yelling up to make them settle down, but her head hurt, and yelling required too much effort. Besides, it was the Sabbath, and since she'd been so useless the two previous weeks, she knew she needed to make it up to them.

She remembered she had some notes that would match the topic for the lesson in her file cabinet and riffled through the manila folders. "There you are!" She pulled out the one labeled DOCTRINE AND COVENANTS.

She set the file on her desk and turned through the pages of notes. She found the page she was looking for. "Bingo!"

She lifted the folder to put it away and noticed a small stack of papers with her name at the top. The writing was in a strong cursive hand. She picked up the little stack, forgetting the folder for a moment, and started to read.

The dates, locations, and names thrilled through her mind. "It's all here!" she cried out. "It's all here!" Information on her ancestors from England for several generations back was miraculously sitting in her hands. She hurried out of the room and all but ran up the stairs. "Lizzie! Lizzie!" she didn't knock on her daughter's bedroom door before barging in. "Where did this come from?" she said in between gulps.

Liz looked at the papers and smiled. "Constance has some connections in England, I guess. She wanted to thank you for all you did for her."

Clair hugged her daughter. "So that's what you two were up to! Pretending to be doing homework! You are so great to do this for me, honey. It means so much to me."

Clair didn't release Liz until the phone rang. "At least we know it isn't a bill collector. Everybody got paid this month." Clair chuckled at her own joke, even if Liz didn't. She answered the phone in her own room, hoping the Gospel Doctrine teacher had changed his mind and was going to be at church after all.

She took a deep breath when she realized the person on the other end of the line was not likely to bring happiness to the morning. To have to fight once again with Liz was not something she wanted. "Of course, Sister Peterson. I'll tell her you're on the phone." She held the receiver to her shoulder so she could yell down the hall. "Lizzie! Phone!"

Liz popped her head out of her doorway. "Who is it?"

Clair contemplated lying and saying she didn't know, but Liz would find out soon enough. "It's Sister Peterson."

"Oh." Liz stood there as though torn, and then she finally stepped fully into the hallway. "Okay." Liz walked up, took the phone, and said, "Hello?"

Clair had to close her mouth to mask her surprise that Liz was willing to talk to the teacher she'd been avoiding for the last month. She pretended not to be listening.

Liz nodded her head. "Sure. Yeah. I'll be happy to . . . I'll be there on time . . . No, I know. Thanks for asking again."

When she hung up, Clair tried hard not to sound nosy but couldn't resist asking, "So what did she want?"

"She wanted to know if I was planning on singing 'Families Can Be Together Forever' in sacrament meeting today."

"And?"

Liz turned around, and Clair saw the tears in her eyes. "And I told her I'd be glad to."

Epilogue

LIZ BREATHED DEEPLY OF THE damp morning air. The house loomed like a castle in front of her. *Constance was raised here?* Liz wondered. It seemed impossible that the strong girl with the tireless ability to lecture could have ever been raised in a place where tea parties and corsets were the norm.

A light gray fog settled over the estate and grasslands beyond, making it look more like a painting than it did a place to live and raise a family.

"I don't think this is a real house," her companion, Sister Schofield, said. Her blond hair was held back from her face by entirely unnecessary sunglasses.

Liz smirked at her. "It's a real house. And why do you have sunglasses when the sun isn't likely to shine for a month?"

"It keeps my hair out of my eyes," Sister Schofield said.

"So would a headband . . ."

Sister Schofield grinned. "At least when I decide to go tracting, I do it in apartment housing where we have a chance of meeting someone, not insisting on driving to the boundaries of our area where there's only one house every mile."

Liz blushed. "I just . . . have a feeling about this place and what we'll find here."

Sister Schofield laughed. "Is this going to be like that story you told me about your boyfriend when he was on his mission and ended up doing an entire day's worth of yardwork because he had a special feeling about the house?"

Liz grunted. "Don't make fun of that. That whole family got baptized." Garrett had sent her a letter describing the events of the final months of his mission to give her encouragement for the beginning months of her mission. Sister Schofield took every opportunity to tease Liz over Garrett's letters, only because Liz read them and reread them countless times.

"You better make me a bridesmaid." Sister Schofield adjusted the sunglasses on her head and grinned a knowing grin at Liz.

"We're just friends . . . *and* I'm a missionary." Liz knew the words were pointless. Everyone in the mission field had "just friends" they wrote to. Those were the missionaries who unraveled fastest when the engagement announcement letters showed up in the mail.

"Well, lead on, Sister King. Let's convert the people living in your ancestral home. You do the talking this time. It's totally your turn."

Liz nodded and wiped her hands on her black skirt before ringing the doorbell.

A small boy answered—a boy with dark brown hair and even darker eyes. He inspected them warily. "Hullo?"

Liz smiled, trying to cover her disappointment with a façade of pleasantry. Well, what did she expect? Did she really think Constance would answer the door?

In a way, she *had* almost expected it and felt let down over the fact that this little boy was here instead.

"Is your mother or father home?" Sister Schofield asked, sketching a sideways glance at Liz, who for some reason couldn't do anything but smile.

It was ridiculous. Of course Constance wasn't there. She was buried somewhere along the pioneer trail, but knowing that didn't stop Liz from wanting to search every room.

The boy scrunched his face up as he stared at the silly smile sprawled over Liz's face. "My mother is not home." His accent carried a bite of culture. Though he hadn't said much, Liz could tell the boy was raised with a good education.

"What about your father?" Sister Schofield shook her head, and Liz could tell she was getting frustrated that Liz wasn't saying anything when this was her idea.

"He's away as well." The boy moved to shut the door.

"Wait!" Liz pushed against the door to keep him from closing it. "Will they be home soon . . . it's important . . ."

"Harrison! Who's at the door?" a voice called from within.

"Girls," the boy, Harrison, said, widening the gap open again.

"What do they want?" The voice was deep, resonating with a pleasant sort of humor to it.

"I don't know," Harrison called back.

"Well let them in, then, and find out."

The door opened wider.

The two sister missionaries cast a wary glance at one another and stepped over the threshold. A young man in his early twenties with small, round glasses and dark hair that hung over his ears and into his eyes appeared from around the corner. He smiled at them. "Two *pretty* girls. Failed to mention *that* part, didn't you, Harrison?"

Harrison shrugged and wandered off down the hall and into a room that looked like a sitting room of some sort. Liz could hear noises from a television.

"So what is it I can do for you?"

Liz finally found her voice. "We're representatives of The Church of Jesus Christ of Latter-day Saints, and we came to deliver a message."

"Message? Who's sending me messages?"

"Our Heavenly Father."

"Right . . . brilliant." His smile was quick and seemed to encompass more than a little disbelief. "I thought that messages from God were delivered by people with wings, not that you don't look like angels. Quite the opposite, really." He grinned.

Liz plowed ahead for a few moments before he stopped her. "Look. I appreciate you coming here to give me this 'message,' but I don't think I'm interested." He motioned them toward the door.

Say something, Liz thought. *Say something . . .* "I know Constance Miles!" she blurted out.

He stopped, his eyebrows scrunched together, and blinked at her. "You *know* Constance Miles."

"I . . ." Liz tried to backpedal from making such a ludicrous statement—true, but ludicrous. "I've studied all about her. It almost feels like I know her. She's my great-great, well, fifth great-grandmother. I'm Eliza King. I was named after her daughter."

He studied her a moment, grinned, and nodded his head before saying, "Right. Let me show you something." He turned, leaving the two sisters with little else to do but follow him.

He led them into a spacious library with high ceilings and books shelved nearly to the ceiling. It was decorated tastefully, with large, cushy chairs and ottomans set in front of the fire, where one might enjoy hours of reading after plucking a book from one of those shelves. Above the fireplace was a portrait.

Liz gasped when she saw it. "It's . . . It's . . ."

"Amazing how much it looks like you, isn't it?" he asked.

Liz wasn't thinking that at all. She was thinking how amazing it was to see her best friend again after all these years.

"I guess this makes us cousins . . . or something. I'm Willard, Willard Miles. I come down through generations of Willard Miles men. I think they do it to keep from having to change the information on any of the paperwork. My father was Willard, but we didn't inherit the house. He's a little bitter about that, but don't tell anyone I said so. I'm here babysitting for my aunt and uncle while they holiday in France. Harrison isn't well behaved on holiday and gets left home more often than not. Course, he'd be your cousin too, then, wouldn't he? Good to have relatives. You wouldn't want to watch him for a bit while I go take a nap, now would you?"

Liz smiled. "I don't think his parents would appreciate coming home to find me here babysitting."

"Right, likely not. Pity we're related. You have gorgeous green eyes. Strike one pretty girl out." He turned to Sister Schofield. "Are you related too?"

She shook her head and blushed slightly. "No."

"Brilliant." His smile was in full force now.

Trying to steer him away from those thoughts and keep him on the matter at hand, Liz asked, "Do you know much about her?" She pointed to the portrait.

"She left the family branded as a religious zealot. Her father ordered all portraits to be removed, and so they were. When my uncle inherited the place, he decided he was tired of all the antique artifacts gathering dust and did a thorough inventory. The portrait was found in the attic along with several others."

He pointed to the wall where there were other pictures of first an infant, a toddler, and a youth. "My uncle wanted to make the house into a bed-and-breakfast with theme rooms. He calls this the Constance Library. It's listed that way in the brochures he had printed up. He hasn't done anything with the brochures, mind you. It's all some brilliant scheme he isn't likely to ever cash in on. He hasn't the first clue how to manage a business. But don't tell him I said so. Nice man, mind you. He's much nicer than my own father, who's as big a hothead as ever lived. I spend a lot of my time here."

"Do you know anything else about Constance?" Liz asked.

He shrugged and shooed a white cat off the ottoman, where he took its place. "Don't know much about her, really. When she left, she wasn't spoken of much. They found a journal of her sister, Julia, which said she had married and moved to America." He nodded appraisingly at Liz. "And so your presence would indicate."

His smile remained on his face, humored and curious too. "You have matching earrings . . ." He pointed from her to the portrait.

Liz's hand went unconsciously to one ear, where an emerald stone hung. She almost never thought about the earrings anymore. They had become a part of her. Once she'd had them altered to accommodate her pierced ears, she never took them off. "It was . . . part of my inheritance."

"Do you have the necklace too?"

"No. My mother still has it."

"The lost jewels of Constance. Family folklore for generations—well, at least my generation, since they only found Julia's diary when I was a boy. Julia mentioned the earrings and several times mentioned that she was glad Constance had them. Yep, when I was a boy, I tried searching for them on the property. I was too young to understand that they weren't lost around here, but lost because Constance went traveling with them."

"It was like that for my family too. Everyone wanted to know what happened to the earrings. They were lost on the plains as she traveled to Utah."

"So how did you come by them?"

"She ga—" Liz cut off. How could she tell someone that she got them from a dead ancestor? Oh, yes, a ludicrous story indeed. "She'd left them for her posterity."

He seemed to accept this explanation. "So . . . you said you had a message for me?" Willard motioned for them to sit, and so they did. They sat and gave a message that had once been given in the same home six generations before.

Liz could almost feel Constance grinning next to her and allowed herself to smile as well. Today, she was binding her family together and tightening the knots that kept them from unraveling. Today, she had come home.

About the Author

JULIE WRIGHT WAS BORN IN Salt Lake City, Utah. She fell in love with reading as a very small child and at the age of fifteen started writing her first novel. She currently resides in west central Utah, where she and her husband own a little country grocery store. They have three children, who keep things busy at their house. She loves reading, writing, hiking, eating, taking long walks (and even longer baths), traveling anywhere with a beach, playing with her kids, and snuggling with her husband. But her favorite thing to do is watch her husband make dinner.

She loves speaking to youth groups, women's groups, and schools. For more information regarding that, please contact her at her website: www.juliewright.com.